SPINDLE'S END

JESSICA MARTING

SHADOW PRESS

SPINDLE'S END

Spindle's End

Second Edition

ISBN 978-1-989780-19-0

Cover design by German Creative

CONTENT WARNING: This book contains parental death, narcissistic parents, terminal illness, suicide, and discussion of cancer.

CHAPTER 1

"WAKE UP!"

Sawyer groaned and rolled over, taking his pillow with him to block out his cabin lights. Lights that shouldn't be on, because it wasn't his turn to be on the bridge, or in the lab, or anywhere but his bed right now.

"Damn it, Sawyer, this is important. Get your ass out of bed." The voice was insistent and increasing in volume. He wrapped himself a little more tightly in the blankets.

"No." He'd spent the last thirty hours wide awake, fueled by too much coffee and adrenaline while he pored over ancient maps, star charts, and historical texts. He'd been hoping that this trip to the farthest reaches of space wouldn't be a total wash.

It wasn't even a real trip, he reasoned. The crew was taking the scenic route home from his archaeological team's latest dig. What Sawyer and his team hoped to find on the detour would have them returning home only a couple of days late.

She who dared interrupt his sleep pulled on his arm. "Come on, Sawyer."

He finally rolled on his back to glare at Lita Fardell, the

other archaeologist on board. In the stark lights of his cabin, her expression was a mix of excitement and irritation.

"Is the lav in the lounge backed up? Because I'm *not* dealing with that again." He threw the blanket back over his head, muffling his next words. "*Please*, Lita."

"No, Sawyer. You'll want to be awake for this."

Curiosity won out, and he lowered the blanket enough for his eyes to meet hers. "Yeah?"

"We've found a dwarf planet with readings that correspond to the *Frexic Galactica*," Lita said, but Sawyer had already sat bolt upright at the words 'dwarf planet.'

He started to get out of bed, then remembered why that was a bad idea right now. Leaping out of bed in the altogether in front of Lita would be a recipe for disaster, even if her husband didn't find out. Which he would, because he was on board the *Phantom*, too. "I'll be on the bridge in a couple of minutes," he said.

Lita looked at him quizzically. "Why not now? I thought you, of all people, would be running straight for the bridge as soon as you heard."

Might as well be honest. "I sleep naked."

She made a face and stepped away from the bed. "I didn't need to know that."

"Yeah, well, I didn't want you to know." He rearranged the covers as she backed away to the cabin door. "I'll meet you on the bridge."

"As soon as possible." A grin spread across her face. "You don't want to miss this."

The tidbit of information she'd just learned about him clearly had done nothing to quell her excitement, and now that Sawyer was fully awake, he could feel his growing, too. This could prove to be what his team had dreamed about all through their undergraduate days, what they'd been trying to find since grad school at Prime. What Sawyer had poured every spare bit of scrip he could afford into, including his purchase of the *Phantom*.

He dressed as soon as Lita left his cabin, picking out the first things he could find from the clean clothes pile on the floor. He swished around some mouthwash, ran his hand through his hair, noting that when they returned home, he should probably get a haircut, and quickly made the short trip from his cabin to the bridge.

The entire team was already assembled there, including Dian, the *Phantom*'s resident grad student and onboard medic, who still wore her pajamas. But like Sawyer, she was just as awake and excited about the possible discovery ahead of them.

"So, what makes everyone think we're near the ruins this time?" he asked.

Lita's husband, Fitch, immediately activated a holodisplay at the makeshift work table set up in the bridge area. A small dark-colored planet appeared, its surface as pitted as the *Phantom*'s hull when it ended up in an asteroid field under Lita's watch. That had been an expensive repair.

"Because the *Frexic Galactica* talked about 'a barren planet in deepest space'," Lita said.

"Which would be most planets," Sawyer said. "It isn't as though dwarf planets are uncommon, especially out here." Had he been pulled from sleep for nothing? His eyes fastened on the clock display in the corner of the ship's viewscreen: half past oh-two-hundred hours. He'd had all of two-and-a-half hours sleep since he damn near collapsed on the bridge from exhaustion.

He turned his gaze back to the holodisplay, where the projected image of the planet waited for their analysis.

"Of course dwarf planets aren't a rarity," Fitch said. He expanded the planet's size on the holodisplay until one of its craters was magnified a few hundred times. "The *Frexic Galactica* also spoke of 'treasures of the deepest pits.'"

"Again, this isn't compelling evidence. All planets have mountains and valleys. You dragged me out of bed for this?" He felt some of the initial excitement leach out of him, an almost physical sensation.

Lita slammed her palm on the table's surface, making everyone on the bridge jump. "No, we're not finished yet. You know the myth of the Immortal Spacefarer, we all do. This planet, and this valley"—she tapped the image superimposed over the holodisplay— "checks off every box of the myth." She ticked them off on her fingers. "Barren planet incapable of supporting human life. Compromised atmosphere, and don't look at me like that, Sawyer, we already did the readings. It's compromised and has been for at least a few hundred years. The story says the planet's surface is black, but that rarely happens unless it's been scorched in a war or something, so we've always assumed it meant the planet had a high carbon content, making it appear black." She gestured to the viewscreen. "Said planet is reddish-black and has a high carbon reading." She continued to check off items on her fingers, excitement again creeping into her voice. "The valley that the treasure was supposedly hidden in was lined with ice, and the valley itself surrounded by thirty ice spears of alternating size." She fixed her green eyes on Sawyer, then pointed to the holodisplay. "Take a look."

Sawyer looked at the holodisplay, taking in the deep ice-crusted pit and the ring of icy, sharp-tipped mountains surrounding it. They weren't icicles, but they looked similar.

This was the closest they'd come to finding the Immortal Spacefarer's treasure. Anticipation thrummed in his veins, and when he looked at Lita, Fitch, and Dian, he saw it in their faces, too. A smile spread across his face.

Dian finally spoke. "We've been searching for this for a long time." Her eyes never left the viewscreen.

"Let's get suited up," Sawyer said. "Lita, I'll meet you at the shuttle."

<hr>

It'd been a while since Sawyer or Lita had made time for a low-gravity sim session, something they both regretted as they carefully navigated their way down the ice-coated walls of the valley. Well, more of a pit, Sawyer thought. It was perfectly round, and he guessed it to be about six meters across, which gave Lita and him plenty of room. It made for an unwieldy descent, even wearing their late-model EVA suits and with artificial gravity holds clutched in their hands. The sensation made Sawyer feel a little nauseous, which he willed away. This find was too exciting to get sick over.

"The *Frexic Galactica* talked about the ice pit being lined with jewels," Lita said.

"If the ice pit was lined with jewels, we'd have a hell of a time getting down here, even with the gravity handholds. Besides, the legend talks about 'jewel-like' reflections. Everyone's always assumed it was just the reflections off the ice."

"Yeah, probably." Sawyer could tell that Lita wasn't going to let that small detail spoil her anticipation of what lay at the bottom of the pit. Neither would Sawyer.

And there *was* something at the bottom of the pit. Their sensors had shown a long rectangular container of a material that couldn't be identified fixed to the pit's side with an unknown fastener. Sawyer saw that as a positive. It was probable that the Immortal Spacefarer would have used materials unrecognizable to modern sensory equipment.

He and Lita continued to descend, checking-in every few

minutes with Fitch and Dian. The pit narrowed as they climbed down, making Sawyer grateful claustrophobia wasn't one of his issues. Half an hour later, they touched the solid, icy ground at the bottom of the pit. Lita and Sawyer shone their flashlights over it, quickly spotting the object the sensors had picked up. They walked over to it, bouncing as they went, thanks to the reduced gravity.

"We see you're at the bottom." Dian's voice crackled over her communicator.

"We're here. And it's a tight fit," Sawyer said. "Maybe only three meters by three meters."

"What's up with the thing down there?" Fitch's voice this time.

"It's definitely big enough to hold a treasure," Lita said.

"A jewelry box is big enough to hold a treasure, too," Sawyer said. Then addressing Fitch and Dian, he said, "It's around two meters long and less than a meter wide. With the low gravity, the two of us should be able to bring it up without too many problems."

"Let us know if you need one of us to suit up and help," Fitch said.

"Will do." Sawyer tugged at the box. It wiggled easily in his hands. "I think we'll be good, though. Whatever's holding it to the wall is already loose."

Lita gave him a hand, and together they easily pried the box from the pit's wall. Sawyer examined the fasteners embedded in the ice, noting they were early models of the gravity holds he and his crew used; they must have been at least a century old. On impulse, he popped all four off the wall and stowed them in a bag that he carried for collecting small specimens.

Even with the box held between them, the ascent up the pit's walls was far easier than going down. Sawyer and Lita loaded it into the shuttle's small cargo bay before making their way to the cockpit. Lita activated the shuttle's engines and life support system; filling the small space with light, air, and gravity. Sawyer swayed on his feet at the sensation and reached for the seals on his helmet.

Lita had already removed hers and taken a seat on the pilot's side. She caught Sawyer's raised eyebrow and shrugged. "Sometimes I like to drive," she said.

"Okay, you take the pilot's seat, and I'll open whatever we have in the cargo hold."

Her hands froze over the controls. "You rat bastard, you'd better not. Dian and Fitch would never forgive you."

"What about you?"

"You don't want to know what I'd do."

Sawyer shrugged out of the rest of his EVA suit and hung it up in a small closet at the back of the cockpit. "It's fine. I'll just take copilot and shift pilot's controls over to my side." He slid into the copilot's seat. "Can you open a line with the *Phantom*?"

He didn't care that Lita had taken the pilot's seat. She was as capable as anyone of commanding a tiny M-class shuttle. It was only a seven-minute trip back to the *Phantom*'s shuttle bay, anyway.

"Sure thing," she said and keyed in a hail on the shuttle's command console. "Fitch, honey? It's me."

The line crackled. "Everything okay?"

"Everything's fine," Sawyer said briskly. "We're coming back up."

"Good to know. Did your scanners pick up that unknown?"

He and Lita looked at each other, then down at the console. "Nothing showed up here, but we shut down the shuttle before we disembarked, to save fuel."

"We picked up an unknown vessel fourteen minutes out as soon as you landed on that rock. It's gone now, though."

Sawyer caught Lita's eye again. "No ID at all?"

"None, but I snagged a copy of its energy signature, in case you want to take a look later. The *Phantom*'s databanks weren't able to identify the model, no ID broadcasting."

"Pirates," Sawyer said, and he felt a brief wave of fear-tinged nausea wash over him. "We need to get the hell out of here and back to civilized space." The *Phantom* was only equipped with a laser cannon, and Sawyer wasn't even sure it worked. The converted freighter had been used to haul cheap dry goods before he purchased it, products that weren't usually targeted by thieves.

"I'm not sure, Sawyer," said Fitch. "The ship didn't have hot weapons, not even a laser cannon. If it weren't for its size, I would've sworn it was a pleasure craft that'd got lost."

Sawyer strapped himself into the seat next to Lita. "Did they hail?"

"No, and I didn't want to draw attention to us, so I didn't hail either."

"That's probably for the best. Okay, we'll be back in the shuttle bay in a few minutes."

"See you soon, darling," Lita sang.

They went through the standard preflight checklist. "Fuel?" Lita asked, hands dancing over her controls.

"Eighty-four percent. The efficiency upgrade was totally worth the four hundred in scrip."

"Four hundred scrip for a better shuttle fuel system, and yet you won't give anyone a raise. Thrusters?"

Sawyer had already hit the flashing thruster key before she could ask, making it change to a solid green. "Online."

"Life support at one hundred percent. Docking clamps?"

Sawyer tested them, and the grinding noise belowdecks confirmed the computer's readings. "Fully functional. Are all the doors sealed?"

"That's my job to ask." Sawyer gave an exaggerated sigh, and she said perkily, "Door seals?"

"All online, and gravity is turned on in the cargo bay, just in case there's something precious in that box."

"Of course, there's something precious in that box!" Lita said.

"Well, I'm hoping there is. Come on, Captain, let's get this bucket in the air."

CHAPTER 2

ON BOARD THE SPINDLE, *life support was failing, deck by deck. The ugly old ship was Anissa's mother's pride and joy; the place where she'd conducted so many successful experiments and made so many important discoveries, and it killed Anissa to know that she couldn't save her.*

She hadn't been able to save her mother, either. Vicora Alto was in the lab on Deck Two Aft when the Vine virus was activated in the Spindle's systems, creeping through the life support system and shutting it down. From Anissa's spot in the nav station, she could see the sensors monitoring the decks as each one shut down, taking the crewmembers with it and automatically sealing their airtight blast doors. Life support was still functional on Deck Six Forward, where Anissa stood on the bridge, but she knew it wouldn't be long before Vine strangled the system here, too.

How in the Four Hells had the Vine virus infiltrated the Spindle's systems? And how had no one noticed until it was too late?

She was the last surviving crewmember aboard the Spindle, and it was no longer worth berating herself for failing to stop the virus in time. Now, she only regretted not having an efficient way to commit suicide. She'd left her blaster in her quarters, that deck long since sealed off, and all she had to look forward to now was suffocating to death. She'd donned an EVA suit, hoping she might be able to get off the ship and ride out the danger while clinging to the ship's hull with her gravity handhelds, but the helmet remained tucked under her arm. Now, she knew she wouldn't be able to get off the bridge, never mind the ship. There was no hope of rescue nor of taking back control of the ship's computers.

She wasn't going to prolong her agony with the limited oxygen supply offered by the suit. She was going to die: sooner, or much sooner.

A beep sounded from the comm console, and she leapt to it. Hope flared in her heart. Had someone heard her distress call? "This is Anissa Alto of the Spindle,*" she said into the speaker. "Our ship's system has been infected with Vine, and I think I'm the only living person on board. Please help!" She hated the pleading note in her voice, hated that she was crying and that whoever was answering her hail could hear it, but she couldn't help it.*

A staticky crackle was her only answer. "Please!" she said. "Answer me, whoever you are!"

"Anissa?"

Her breath halted in her chest at the familiar voice. "Dr. Mollon?"

Dr. Crale Mollon was one of her mother's fellow scientists at Laresh First University, a fellow longevity biologist. He wasn't one of Anissa or Vicora's favorite people, but Anissa still wouldn't turn down help. But what could he be doing in this part of the galaxy?

She didn't care. All that mattered was that Vicora's work on the ship might be saved, and maybe Anissa herself. "Dr. Mollon, everyone on board is dead," Anissa said. "I can't get the virus to stop replicating, and I can't get the blast doors open." If she could, she might be able to make it to the shuttle bay or an airlock while wearing her EVA suit.

"I'm here." Dr. Mollon's voice was unusually calm. Anissa tried to get a computer reading on the ship he was traveling on and how far away he was, but those functions were disabled. Vine was very close to shutting down life support on the bridge.

"Dr. Mollon, I can't get a lock on you," she said. "Where are you?"

"Right above your ship," he said. As if on cue, the Spindle shimmied, and a loud scraping noise sounded above her. "I'm putting tow clamps on you now."

"Tow clamps—why would you do that?"

Dr. Mollon's voice went cold. "Why do you think?"

A chill that had nothing to do with the life support slithered over Anissa's body. It was failing on the bridge now according to her computer. In a matter of minutes, it would get cold, the gravity would shut down, and the air would stop cycling. The end was very near.

Dr. Mollon's words echoed in her mind. Why did she think he showed up?

"You're responsible for this?" Outrage colored her words, and she swiped away angry tears with a suited fist.

Fuck dying a quick death. She snapped on her helmet and activated the suit's controls as her computer screen flashed red, a final warning that life support would shut off in less than one minute.

Through her helmet, she heard a commotion outside the bridge and realized that intruders were on board. She looked around for something to use as a weapon and came up empty. The Spindle was a research vessel, not a military one.

The bridge's blast doors were forced open, and a space-suited figure stepped in, his step lighter in the failing gravity. Dr. Mollon's irritated face greeted her through his helmet.

Anissa took a few steps back as Dr. Mollon advanced on her,

and he raised his arm, an oversized blaster in his hand. But instead of firing it, he brought it down on Anissa's helmet, and her world went dark.

Fitch was the first to speak after they pried the lid from the box. "Well, fuck me."

Usually, that kind of statement would draw an equally crude rejoinder from his wife, but even Lita was silent as she, Fitch, Dian, and Sawyer stared at the woman's body in the box. Her skin was a deep golden shade, and her lips were full; and according to the tiny scanner installed on the inside of the box, she'd been in stasis for one hundred and four years. Her EVA suit's nameplate read *A. Alto, Spindle Research.*

It was a moment before anyone else spoke. "*This* is the Immortal Spacefarer's treasure?" Dian said.

"Maybe she was searching for the treasure, found it, got stuck down there, and the crew made off with it a hundred years ago," said Fitch. "It's not like it's unheard-of for treasure hunters to double-cross each other."

"And it isn't like the legend is specific about what the treasure is," Lita said. "What do we do now?"

The group exchanged glances. "Resuscitate her," Sawyer said, coming to a decision.

He could tell by the lack of reaction that everyone else was thinking the same thing, but with more reservations than he had. "Dian," he said, "You're a medic."

That earned an eye roll from her. "*Former* medic, and not a medical doctor."

"You're still qualified. Medics can revive patients in stasis," he said. "And we all know how to deactivate stasis functions, don't we? We can revive her, and Dian knows what to do after." He looked at Dian expectantly.

She sighed. "I know what to do, yes. But are you sure we shouldn't take her back to Prime and let the hospital there revive her? She's been asleep for over a hundred years."

A beep issued from the box, and all four peered at the scanner. "Apparently not," Sawyer said. "This thing is programmed to revive the patient automatically when it's opened." According to the scanner, full body functions were expected to be restored in eighty-two minutes. A hell of a long time to take to come out of stasis, but it would give them time to transport the box to the *Phantom*'s sickbay.

Fitch had already found an anti-gravity pallet and activated it, and they all helped load the box on to it. "Follow," Sawyer commanded, and the pallet zipped alongside them to the ship's cargo lift.

It was a tight fit, but they managed to squeeze into the lift with the box for the short trip two decks up to sickbay. They unloaded the box onto one of the two beds, and Dian shifted into medic mode as she set about activating the equipment necessary for resuscitation. The effect was marred somewhat by the fact she still wore her pajamas and her short hair was mussed from sleep.

Her voice was brisk. "I need to monitor her vital signs with something manufactured in the last hundred years," she said. "Fitch, Lita, get out of the way." They obediently stepped back. A med-panel dropped soundlessly from the ceiling, covering the box and sitting only a few centimeters above it. The clear plastiglas panel immediately lit up, scanning the woman for vitals. Sawyer recognized a few functions: brain waves, cardiac activity, but that was about it.

"Okay," Dian said. "I have everything under control in here. Fitch, you go back to the bridge and turn off the autopilot before we crash into an asteroid or something. Lita, you probably have a report to write about what we found on that planet."

"Sawyer does, too." Lita hated writing reports.

"Sawyer is the owner and captain of the ship, and he's had assistant medic training, so he stays here."

"I knew I should've signed up for those courses in undergrad," Lita said, but she and Fitch left the sickbay. At the doorway, she turned and said, "Call us as soon as she wakes up."

Dian's voice and expression were grim. "*If* she wakes up. Her vitals are way too weak for my liking."

Alarm flared in Sawyer at Dian's assessment. "Can't you do anything to save her?"

Her voice was detached, reminding Sawyer of every jaded medic and doctor that had learned to compartmentalize when matters of life and death were on the line. "Not when she's still in stasis. All we can do right now is observe and hope she wakes up."

Anissa flitted from darkness into light, albeit faintly. Every time she tried to force her eyes open, sleep overpowered her: a heavy, unwelcome blanket.

But this time, consciousness won, even though she knew her wakefulness would be short lived.

She saw Dr. Mollon's glowering face above her, and she tried to speak. But all she could manage was a croak. "Mmmm."

"I don't know what your mother shot you up with, but this isn't working," said Dr. Mollon. "I can't tell you how much I wish I'd saved more of her work. Her research into bio-longevity truly was remarkable."

Vicora had injected Anissa with an immune-system booster of her own design only ten days earlier, but even if Anissa could tell Dr. Mollon about that, she wouldn't.

"But I think I've worked out the kinks," he continued. "This should finally take care of the problem." He fitted a mask over her face, and everything went dark again.

Every button and panel on every piece of equipment monitoring their patient glowed or blinked green, which Sawyer knew was a good sign. His junior medic training had been minimal, and he hadn't used it since his days in undergrad. But he forced himself to sit still and not ask Dian for an update every two minutes. She might have sedated him if he'd done that, anyway. Instead, Sawyer forced himself to focus on what the sickbay computers told them about their mysterious patient: reading the glowing words on the main computer screen. *Humanoid female, approximately thirty years of age.* The computer located a subcutaneous ID chip embedded in her right wrist, origin unknown. Even if she hadn't been found at the bottom of a pit on an uninhabited planet, A. Alto—or whoever she was—was still a total enigma.

None of the crew aboard the *Phantom* had expressed any disappointment that they hadn't discovered a treasure chest or maps or anything that the *Frexic Galactica* claimed would be found on such a planet, and once again Sawyer was reminded of how much he loved his friends. The priority for everyone had been to revive the woman they'd found at the bottom of that valley, without a word of grumbling. Even better, no one had suggested contacting the university or his father just yet, but Sawyer knew they would have to deal with those issues sooner rather than later.

Dian changed into a wrinkled flight suit half an hour into their vigil, with strict instructions to Sawyer to call her if there was any change in their patient's condition, no matter how insignificant. The woman hadn't woken up yet, but judging by the green lights and Dian's calm demeanor, she might very well be out of the woods.

Now that there was a real possibility of her waking up with all her faculties intact, Sawyer had more questions than ever. Who was she? Was it really possible that she'd spent over a century interred on a barren planet?

She was a living artifact. There was so much he wanted to ask her.

"Check it out," Dian said.

His attention snapped back to the woman, still in her coffin on the bed. No one had been sure how to safely remove her from it, not knowing what kind of primitive life support system might be keeping her alive. Her face and hands, the only exposed parts, were covered with sticky patches that provided the sickbay computers with updates on her condition, as myopic as those systems were. A ship outfitted for scientific missions rarely needed top-of-the-line medical equipment.

She was stirring for the first time, her fingers twitched, and she was breathing audibly. Her eyes flickered behind closed lids, but she didn't wake up.

"What do we do now?" Sawyer asked.

"Wait and see," Dian said. "She's alive and her vitals are stronger than I thought they would be. I think she's going to be okay." She paused. "Well, physically. If she's been down there for a hundred years, she'll have some questions. I should get some tissues ready."

"What for?"

Dian was already poking through the sickbay workstation, picking up a pack of disposable tissues and snapping off its top. "Her friends and family are probably all dead."

That was something he hadn't considered, and he felt more than a twinge of shame at his lack of compassion. "Right," he mumbled.

"You weren't planning on interrogating her right away, were you? Because as the only person qualified in medical matters on board, I'm obligated to tell you to cut that shit out."

Ordinarily, Sawyer would have reminded her just who the ship's captain was and possibly of his own meager medical training, but Dian had a point. She *was* the only person even remotely qualified to handle the resuscitation of a patient in stasis, and she was a little short-tempered at the best of times. That she was functioning on minimal sleep and insufficient coffee was making her that much more irritable.

A soft moan from the box drew their attention. Their patient's eyelids fluttered. Sawyer looked at Dian, gauging her reaction to this development, but she appeared calm. "I think she's dreaming," she said. "Judging by the computer's diagnostics, she should wake up soon." Her voice rose a little. "Computer, set lights to half." The sickbay lights immediately dimmed. "It'll make things a little easier on her senses," she said to Sawyer before he could ask.

Their patient screamed, an unholy sound, setting Sawyer's teeth on edge. Her eyes opened, revealing dark irises, but they didn't fix on anything in the room. She clawed at the sides of the box, then at her EVA suit, before sitting bolt upright. "I said *stand down!*" Her voice bounced off the sickbay walls. "Get the fuck away!"

Dian pressed an epidermal sedative against the patient's hand, the only exposed skin she could get to. The delivery device hissed as the sedative entered her body.

The effect was almost immediate. Their patient slid back into the box, eyes closing again. After a moment, she was breathing deeply and peacefully again.

"What the hell was that?" Sawyer asked.

"I'm not sure," Dian replied, glancing at the monitors. "Maybe she's remembering what happened right before she ended up in that box. Maybe it's a nightmare, I don't know. But her vitals are good, and I think she'll wake up for real very soon. But we should probably make sure all the weapons lockers are secured."

"Well, yeah. That's just common sense."

"No, not just that. That ID chip the computer picked up and couldn't identify?" Dian motioned him over to the smaller computer monitor on her side of the room. "I did a quick search while she was still out, and I just got a result. It's an F-92 chip, last manufactured in 2804, ninety-seven years ago."

Vintage technology wasn't Sawyer's specialty. He nodded, waiting for Dian to go on.

"F-92 chips were issued to soldiers in the Laresh Forces," she continued.

That was certainly surprising news. The Laresh System, formerly the Laresh Empire, had been independent until 2815, when it allied with the Rodanta Quadrant. Rodanta was where Sawyer and his crew claimed citizenship. "Huh," said Sawyer.

"Yeah. So our guest was a soldier at some point."

That gave them a little more to go on. "Can you do a search for a soldier named Alto?"

Dian shot him a withering look. "Give me a little credit, Sawyer. I have a search running now, but I'm sure you've noticed we're in deep space and connections are shaky. It'll take a little longer than normal. And I meant what I said about making sure the weapons lockers are secure. If she's suffering from PTSD, and I wouldn't be surprised if she is, we could have a bad situation on our hands very quickly. We don't have a huge stash of sedatives on board, and you converted the brig into an outhouse."

"First off, this used to be a freighter, so the brig wasn't exactly high-tech anyway. A four-year-old could have managed to break out. Second, how the hell is it an outhouse? It has the only tub—a *gigantic* tub, let me remind you—on this bucket with running water. Plus, there's the sim chamber. I had that built as a favor to all of you."

"Yet Fitch and Lita are the only ones who take advantage of that gigantic tub, which is why no one else uses it."

He wondered if he was ever as irritable as Dian was on little sleep. He made a mental note to be as pleasant as possible from now on, starting with her. "Do you want some coffee?"

"I'm good. I took a stim about twenty minutes ago and it's kicked in. Want one?"

"Uh, what kind of stim?" Sawyer wasn't opposed to occasional recreational drug use, as long as it didn't occur when the crew was supposed to be working. Which meant he didn't oppose it when his crew wasn't on board the *Phantom*.

Dian picked up the underlying question in his words. "Relax, Sawyer, it's nothing illegal. Just that caffeine spray I told you about before we took off on this mission." She leaned back against the monitor station. "I still like coffee better."

The monitor chirped, and she and Sawyer quickly turned to the screen. There were four Altos listed in the Laresh military database from the relevant time period, only one of them a woman: Commander Anissa Finara Alto, born 2770, missing and presumed dead in 2801. There was no other information available, but Dian was already launching more searches. They waited, both keeping one eye on their patient.

No results yielded.

"Stupid deep space and lack of connections," Dian said. She sighed dramatically and crossed the room to where Commander Alto lay. Sawyer thought it might be important to keep her military title in mind. It just seemed more respectful.

Her breathing was deep and even, undoubtedly the result of the sedatives Dian had shot her up with. Her fingers twitched a little, and a frown marred her full lips. *She's still dreaming*, Sawyer thought. Maybe they were a little less terrifying this time around.

Her eyelids fluttered but didn't open, and he knew whatever was running through her mind couldn't be good.

CHAPTER 3

ANISSA SHIFTED, sensation returning to her body. It felt like she'd been in a hell of a fight and lost. She tried to stretch, but her arms met solid surfaces. *What in the Four Hells...?*

She was in a box.

The scene on board Dr. Mollon's ship rushed back to her, and she stilled, not wanting to set off any alarms that he might have monitoring her. She focused on her breathing instead, regulating it as she had learned to do in basic training. Maintaining control of the current situation was of utmost importance. She opened her eyes just enough to see through her lashes and saw a water-stained ceiling and dimmed exam lights above her.

So she'd been moved while she was still under sedation. Where was she now, and could she make her way to the bridge and take over command of the ship?

She knew she was on a ship; she could feel the familiar thrum and vibration of engines beneath her. The first question was *which* ship. The second question was how to free herself from the box Dr. Mollon had imprisoned her in. Tilting her head slightly, she spotted a tiny glowing screen inset in the side, numbers scrolling past.

All right, she wasn't in a coffin, then. Nor was she still locked in ground battle on Dealon during Laresh's Civil War, as she'd been dreaming before she woke up.

"Dian?"

An unfamiliar male voice interrupted her thoughts. Anissa kept her eyes closed, hoping against hope that whatever Dr. Mollon hooked her up to hadn't given away her conscious state.

"Her status says she should be fully awake."

Well, shit.

Anissa peeked through barely open eyes. A man leaned over the edge of the box and peered in. He pushed a lock of dark hair off his forehead, concern showing in his eyes. "Dian?" he said again. "I'm not crying wolf this time. I..."

Anissa launched herself out of the box as best she could, hampered by her EVA suit. Why in the Four Hells had she been put in the box still wearing that? But her military training kicked in, as automatic to her as breathing. She had the element of surprise over the dark-haired man and vaulted herself over the box's side, ignoring the protests of her stiff muscles, and swiftly sent a kick to his knees before he could register what was happening. He scrabbled for the edge of the box to steady himself but slipped to the floor, and Anissa took advantage of his position to twist his wrist in the first defensive maneuver she'd learned while in the military academy. He yelped as something in his wrist snapped, and he cradled it to his chest, eyes pinched shut in pain.

"What the hell?"

That seemed to the refrain of the day. Anissa turned to see a shocked-looking woman, much shorter than she was, her spiky, white-blond hair a halo around her face. She wore a wrinkled blue flight suit devoid of ship's patches, adding to the mystery of where Anissa now found herself.

The woman held a small canister in her hand,

undoubtedly some kind of drug. And Anissa was not about to let someone drug her again. She looked around the room—a sickbay, she noticed, although the equipment was considerably more modern than that on board the *Spindle*—and spotted a small door. She wrapped her arm around the smaller woman's neck.

"What are you doing?" the woman demanded.

Anissa dragged the woman to the door, noting that her muscles still ached. The EVA suit wasn't helping, either. She opened the door to reveal a closet, which made things easier. "Get in," she ordered the woman.

Her captive struggled against Anissa's arm, but she just squeezed a little tighter. "Fuck you," her prisoner said.

"I can still break your neck, EVA suit or no," Anissa said. "Get in the closet." Anissa let go long enough to shove her in, then slammed the door, activating the locking mechanism after struggling with it for a couple of seconds. The lock was as stiff from disuse as she was.

She turned back to the man whose wrist she'd broken, who had risen to his feet and was now looking around the sickbay, probably for something to use as a weapon. His arm with the broken wrist hung limply at his side, and his mouth was pinched with pain. "You really didn't have to do that," he said. "You don't have the whole story."

She could stay in here and chat with whomever he was, or she could find a way out and try to get to the bridge. Option two won out. She quickly crossed the room and grabbed his injured wrist. He winced, but she didn't let go. "Where am I?" she demanded.

"The *Phantom*," he said. His eyes slid shut as her grip on his wrist tightened, and he reached for her hand with his free one. She twisted his broken wrist, just a few degrees to the left, and he let out a groan.

But no screaming, which was surprising, and Anissa felt a

little respect well up in her. She'd heard wails from men after their wrists were broken in that same way, but all this guy had done was close his eyes and breathe deeply, attempting to stave off the pain.

"What kind of ship is it?"

"She's a Quinn-122." He gulped in pain, although she could tell he was trying to hide it. "Research vessel. Why?"

The name was unfamiliar to Anissa, but she didn't let on. She would still be able to figure out how to hijack it. "Come with me," she said briskly, pulling him away from the box. "We're going to the bridge."

She slammed the sickbay door open with her free hand and picked up her speed. He ran alongside her. "We found you in a valley," he said. "We're an archaeological team based out of Prime University in the Rodanta Quadrant. The woman you locked in the closet is Dian Pellar, xeno-archaeology graduate student and former medic. I'm Dr. Benedict Sawyer, but everyone calls me..."

They stopped at the end of a corridor, where a door labelled 'Lift' opened soundlessly for them. "Bridge," Anissa said to him. "Now."

"It isn't voice activated."

"I don't care. Find a way to get us to the bridge or I'll break your neck in addition to your wrist."

With his free hand, he pushed a button. "This is unnecessary, Commander," he said.

The use of her military rank surprised her, but she didn't let it show. "I haven't been a commander for a long time," she said. The lift slid into action.

"I was going to ask you about that. We know you're Anissa Alto and you were in the Laresh Forces, but that's it. We found you in that box on a planet with features that correspond to the myth of the Immortal Spacefarer, and..."

"I don't care."

"Look, I'm trying to reason with you, Commander. There's something you need to know."

"Where's Dr. Mollon?"

"Who?"

"Dr. Mollon, the man who murdered my mother's crew. Where is he?"

"I don't know who Dr. Mollon is. I'm trying to tell you that you're out of your element. It's important you listen to what I have say."

Anissa sneaked a glance at him. Beads of sweat had appeared on his forehead, undoubtedly caused by the strain of suppressing a scream after having his wrist broken and then being manhandled. "It's 2905," he said.

"Twenty-nine oh-five what?"

"The year. It's 2905. You've been in that valley for over a hundred years." The fingers on his damaged hand twitched. "Please, let's just go back to the sickbay, get Dian out of that closet and a bone regenerator on my wrist. I'm in a shitload of pain right now."

One hundred years?

He was lying. He had to be. The lift door opened, revealing a dingy corridor, its carpet devoid of color except for the occasional faded stain. Ugh.

An open door beckoned; beyond it, Anissa could see a viewscreen that revealed the familiar, welcome blackness of space. "Let's go," she said as she moved forward, hauling the man alongside her.

"Fuck!" he said.

A man and woman were standing in front of consoles and looked up when she and the man called Benedict Sawyer walked in. "The fuck?" said the man.

"Little help here?" said her prisoner.

"I need your command keys," Anissa said. "Or I'll break his neck."

"I tried to tell her," Benedict Sawyer said. "Fitch, Lita, my wrist is broken." Anissa stole a glance at his wrist, and for a second almost felt bad about what she'd done to him. It was already swelling.

She shook off that feeling. Reminding herself that he, and everyone on board this ship, was complicit in her drugging and kidnapping, and in Dr. Mollon's activities, whatever they might be.

"No shit," said the woman, then she turned to Anissa. "Look, there's been a misunderstanding. We're a research team, and we found you at the bottom of a valley. Please let Sawyer go."

They were incredibly calm for a crew about to be hijacked. Before she could offer a retort and another demand for the ship's command keys, she was jerked backward, and a cold blast of air crested over her jaw.

Light-headedness immediately overtook Anissa. She felt her grip on the man's wrist loosen and she tilted back, swaying on her feet. Her knees crumpled in her bulky EVA suit, and she slid to the bridge floor.

"You're stealthier than I thought," Fitch said, looking past Sawyer and the unconscious Commander Alto.

Dian pocketed the sedative spray. "I try." She turned to Sawyer. "Let's get you back to the sickbay and get that wrist regenerated."

"What about her?" Sawyer looked at Commander Alto.

"She'll be out for half an hour or so. Enough time to tie her up before she's awake again." Contempt was written across Dian's features as she regarded the prone woman. "See, that's why I'm not a medic anymore. This is *not* the first time something like this has happened to me." Her lips thinned, but she didn't elaborate. "Fitch, can you carry her back down to sickbay?" She turned back to Sawyer. "Please tell me there's at least one pair of sonicuffs in the weapons locker."

"There should be." Sawyer examined his wrist. It was swelling rapidly, the flesh an alarming shade of purple. Damn, but Commander Alto was strong.

"Uh, they're in our cabin," Lita said, and quickly scampered off the bridge before anyone could ask why.

"Why are the sonicuffs... damn it, I don't want to know." Sawyer did *not* need that visual. Still, a knowing grin spread across Fitch's face as he bent down to pick up Commander Alto.

When they reached the sickbay, Dian wrapped a regenerator around Sawyer's wrist while Fitch lay their guest on the unused bed. Lita was close behind, leaving the sonicuffs clipped to the bed before returning to the bridge.

"This would be easier if there was still a brig on board," Dian said.

Well, that was subtle coming from Dian.

"I told you so," she said.

There it was. "Point taken," he said.

"Want something to help with the pain?" she asked.

Sawyer shook his head. "I think the regenerator tranks are doing their job."

Fitch cuffed Commander Alto to the side of the bed. "This might be a bad time to tell you, Captain," he said. "But we passed a beacon about ten minutes ago and picked up a message from Prime." Sawyer must have pulled a face because Fitch added, "Sorry to be the bearer of bad tidings. It's marked urgent. Plus, there's the matter of the unknown ship that passed us when you were on that rock. The signature's saved in the databanks if you want to look at it later."

"Dad's messages are always marked urgent." Never, in his thirty-five years, had Sawyer ever received an urgent message from his father that contained information of actual urgency. "I'll watch it later." He kept his eyes on Commander Alto and the glowing sonicuff band around her wrist that kept her tethered to the bed. At least there wasn't any danger of her escaping this time, and he could have a rational discussion with her, starting with what year it was.

He flexed the fingers of his damaged hand, feeling the bones of his wrist already knitting themselves back together. In another hour, his wrist would be nearly healed, and within a day, any residual aches and pains from the break would be gone.

Dian checked Commander Alto's vitals while Sawyer wheeled a chair from the monitor station to the bed. "You're planning on waiting around until she wakes up?" Dian asked.

"Yeah."

"Even though she might not be receptive to being treated like a living artifact?"

Sawyer shrugged. "I'm not going to treat her like an artifact. She needs to hear that we're not out to hurt her and we have no idea how she ended up on that planet."

"And that she's been sleeping for the last hundred and four years."

"That, too." Sawyer ran his good hand over his face, exhaustion washing over him. "Does the replicator in here work?"

"Occasionally. I would expect you'd know that, given it's your ship."

Sawyer took a deep breath, controlling his urge to snap at Dian. It was early in the morning, and none of them had had much sleep, and then they'd been attacked by someone they were trying to help. He forced himself to sound as calm as he could. "Is it working now?"

Dian must have sensed the controlled aggravation in his

voice because her expression softened just a smidgen. "Let me check. Dark roast, one sugar?"

"Please."

Maybe one of Dian's stims wouldn't be such a bad idea. But a moment later she returned with a replicator-produced coffee, hot and, most importantly, drinkable. The *Phantom*'s replicators were temperamental at the best of times, so the crew usually just made their own food and drink.

"Thanks." Sawyer leaned back in his chair and waited for Commander Alto to wake up again.

Anissa stirred, but something halted her movement. Any lingering sleepiness evaporated when she looked to her left and saw her wrist held in place with a glowing blue sonicuff. "Four Hells." The epithet came out in a hiss.

"Oh good, you're awake."

She levered herself up on her right arm to glare at the man sitting next to the bed. She was back in the sickbay because, like an idiot, she'd let herself be drugged. Again.

"Are you ready to talk like a rational human being?" the man asked. He took a sip of his coffee, the smell of which set Anissa's taste buds watering.

The urge to tell him to go fuck himself were at the tip of her tongue, but she bit them back. Instead, she tugged at the sonicuff, but it didn't budge. "Are you going to let me go, Benedict?" she asked.

"It's just Sawyer, and yes, eventually, when I know you're not going to try to kill me and my crew and take over my ship. There are a few things we have to talk about first, Commander."

She narrowed her eyes at him. "I'm not a commander

anymore. I was honorably discharged from the Laresh Forces four years ago, after the civil war ended."

"Uh, yeah." He looked a little uncomfortable. "About that..."

"I need you to tell me where Dr. Mollon is, and why you're holding me," she said. There was no point in arguing with him over the sonicuff at this point; she'd simply have to gain his trust and convince him to let her go.

"I don't know who Dr. Mollon is," he said, his voice sharp. "That's what we've been trying to tell you. We found you a couple of hours ago, at the bottom of a pit on an uninhabited dwarf planet."

"Pit? Sure."

"Like I tried to tell you before, this is a research ship. We're all archaeologists, except for Fitch, and we're researching the origins of the stories in the *Frexic Galactica*. The box we found you in corresponded to details of the Immortal Spacefarer's treasure. Instead, we found you in stasis."

"Uh-huh." Anissa could buy the stasis story; that aligned with her waking up in a box that was monitoring her vital signs. But chasing purported treasures from the *Frexic Galactica*? Those stories were for children. "What did Dr. Mollon pay you?"

A frustrated edge crept into his voice. "I've never heard of the guy. And I was going to try to break this to you gently, but you don't seem to be into that. You were down there for over a hundred years. Hundred and four, if we're going to be precise."

One hundred and four years on an uninhabited planet... "That's not possible," Anissa said. "I don't believe you."

"What would it take for you to believe me, then?" He stood up and set his coffee cup on a counter before leaning back against it, and despite her anger at him, she had to admit that he was definitely easy on the eyes. His were dark-circled in a way that spoke of stress and sleepless nights, but that didn't spoil his good looks. His flight suit was wrinkled and, like the white-haired woman's, devoid of any ship's ID patches; but it still hinted at a body that was well taken care of, something Anissa respected as a former soldier. His dark hair held no trace of silver even though he looked to be in his mid-thirties. If Dr. Mollon had hired someone to abduct her, he'd certainly picked an attractive kidnapper.

Her mother. A sharp pain lanced through Anissa at the memory, and her appreciation of Sawyer's body evaporated. Vicora Alto—her mother—was undoubtedly dead.

She forced her mind to return to the question he'd just asked her. "You could release me and show me what technology looks like one hundred years in the future."

"I'm not a complete idiot."

She shrugged. "It was worth a shot."

He unsnapped a screen from the bank of monitors and brought it over to the bed. "Here," he said, holding it out to her. "This is a search record we ran on you before you woke up the first time, using the ID plate on your suit."

Written on the screen were short summaries of military records. Her own simply said *Anissa Finara Alto, missing and presumed dead 2801.* No details about her mother or the Vine virus strangling the *Spindle*'s systems, just a line about Anissa's military service and rank. But what caught her attention was the date and time at the top of the screen in tiny glowing numbers. *0604 hrs ... 344.04.2905 ...*

She recognized the dates, but that year... With shaking hands, she handed the screen back to Sawyer. "I need more proof," she said, cursing the tremor that crept into her voice.

Understanding dawned in Sawyer's dark eyes, and he picked up the screen again, running his fingers over it before handing it back to her. He'd brought up a roster of everyone on board the *Phantom*: Dian Pellar, former medic and current graduate student of the Xeno-Archaeology Department at Prime University; Dr. Lita Fardell, xeno-archaeologist, also working out of the same department at Prime; Fitch Petron-Fardell, pilot and navigator; and Dr. Benedict Sawyer, also an archaeologist. All had birthdates listed between 2870 and 2872.

The *Phantom* was a Quinn-122 model, she recalled. She'd never heard of Quinns. "Can you get me some information about the ship?" she asked. Seeing the dubious look cross his face, undoubtedly because he thought she might try to do something to the ship's systems, she added, "Where she was built. Her manufacturer."

"It'll take a couple of minutes. We're on a deep-space link."

She gestured to the sonicuff. "It's not like I'm going anywhere."

Sawyer typed something into the screen, and they waited a moment for a result. When his eyes met hers, she looked away, at the sickbay lights that were still set at half; at least the crew had been considerate enough not to hurt her eyes.

He wordlessly handed the screen back, and Anissa quickly read what was displayed there: it appeared to be a news article. Quinn Shipyards was a subsidiary of Theon Galactic Holdings and had been building basic freighters, public transport ships, and personal shuttles since its founding in 2880, twenty-five years' prior. Theon Galactic had recently hosted a charity gala in honor of the anniversary.

Her stomach bottomed out, and dawning horror left her mouth dry. She could demand more proof, but what else could Sawyer produce? She knew, from the way he and his crew had reacted to her in the sickbay and on the bridge, that they weren't trained soldiers. Dian managing to sedate her had been sheer dumb luck. Any professional outfit would have her locked up in the brig by now.

She glanced over at the box, still sitting on the other bed.

Anissa set the screen down and looked away from Sawyer. "Uncuff me," she said quietly.

"You broke my wrist not an hour ago."

"That was before I found out you're an archaeologist." She focused on the box. Coffin, she corrected herself. Whatever Dr. Mollon had shot her up with, had resulted in her being left in stasis for over a century.

"Please don't take this personally," Sawyer began.

"But I broke your wrist and locked your medic in a closet. Yeah, I get it." Sawyer didn't have to unlock the sonicuff; she'd have to cooperate with him if she ever expected to leave this bed. If what he was saying was true, he had about as much idea of what was going on as she did.

Sawyer didn't respond. Dozens of questions ran through her mind, but she couldn't bring herself ask them just yet. *What are you going to do with me?* was the first one. Stowaways, accidental or otherwise, could be legally jettisoned from a ship in the Laresh Empire. Would they do that to her?

Did the Laresh Empire even still exist?

Anissa leaned back against the bed's flat pillow. "So, what's next?" Her voice was calm, controlled. At least she could manage that.

"Are you going to try to kill my crew again?"

"I wasn't trying to kill anyone. I was going to commandeer your ship and return to Laresh Seat." The planet was the center of its government and military. "Does it still exist?"

"The Lareshis allied with the Rodanta Quadrant in 2815. The Seat still exists, but the government abides by Rodantan laws."

Anissa was shocked into silence by this piece of information. She stiffened and sat back up. "But the civil war..."

"Was between the Laresh ruling family and rebels who wanted democracy. Rodanta had nothing to do with it."

"The Rodantan military illegally intervened!" Fury, hot and bright as a star going nova, rose within Anissa at the memory of arrogant Rodantans forcing their way into a conflict on the opposite side of the galaxy.

"I'm guessing your unit wasn't on the side the Rodantans supported."

Anissa narrowed her eyes at Sawyer. "No."

He held up one hand in protest. "Hey, don't get pissy with me." She could sense the unspoken addition to his admonishment: *it happened before I was born.* "The Laresh System's civil war isn't a specialty of mine." He drained his coffee cup and gazed into it longingly. "I'm getting a refill. You want some?"

It *did* smell good, and if what Sawyer was saying was true —Four Hells, Anissa *knew* it was—she hadn't had anything to eat or drink in over one hundred years. "Can you add some brandy?" she asked.

"Let me see what we have."

Sawyer rose and left the room. He was gone long enough that Anissa wondered if he was ever going to return, and she tested the sonicuff's strength, looking for a weakness she could exploit. The bright blue energy beam didn't deliver a shock when she pulled the cord to its full half-meter length, but when she examined it more closely, its lock proved that the technology was beyond her knowledge.

This was the second time in her life she'd felt completely impotent and helpless, and the second time those feelings were the result of Dr. Mollon's machinations. As much as she hated to admit it, she was dependent on Sawyer and the *Phantom*'s crew until she could... what, exactly? File a report with Rodantan law enforcement? *Hello, officer. I'm a highly decorated former commander of the Laresh Forces, recently rescued from some backwater planet no one's ever heard of and revived by a bunch of archaeologists who believe children's stories are real. By the way, could I see Crale Mollon's death certificate in lieu of charging him with murders that occurred 104 years ago?*

Despite her internal flippancy, Anissa wanted to break down, to rant and cry about the unfairness of it all. Not just for her; the memories of her mother's murder and stolen research were more enraging than being placed in stasis for decades. Anissa was comfortable with her expendability as a soldier.

Dr. Vicora Alto and her work were irreplaceable.

But she was determined not to give in to her feelings. She was used to suppressing her emotions during tours. Maybe it would serve her best to think of this as the most difficult tour of her career.

Not all soldiers came home from a tour, after all.

Sawyer returned, bearing a cup of steaming black coffee and a half-full bottle of amber-colored liquid. "We didn't have any brandy on board," he said apologetically. "I hope Rodantan whiskey will do the job."

Anissa wasn't one to turn down a free drink, no matter its origin. "I'm sure it'll be fine." She sat up and accepted the cup. Sawyer uncapped the bottle and held it above the cup's rim, avoiding relinquishing it to her. She couldn't blame him for that. He probably thought she might hit him over the head with it.

"Say when."

Anissa let him pour a healthy measure of the whiskey into her coffee before she stopped him. "Thank you." *Bottoms up!* She drank half the cup in a few swallows and tried not to make a face at the taste.

"Do you want something to eat? Dian said you should be able to eat solid food without any problems."

That made her sound like an infant. "Dian doesn't want to tell me that herself?"

"No. She didn't take kindly to being locked in a closet. She's going to be pissed off for a very long time. No one can hold a grudge like Dian."

"Noted." She swallowed some more coffee. "So, Sawyer, what's next?"

He offered a half-hearted shrug. "I don't know."

Anissa had been afraid of that. "Are you going to take me back to the Empire or Rodanta?"

"The Empire is now called the Laresh System, and we're Rodantan citizens, so we'll go back to Rodanta. And, I have to admit that none of us has any idea what to do about you. I thought we could all talk later about what to do."

The Laresh *System*? She filed that tidbit of information to mull over later. "When you and your crew are sure I'm not going to kill anyone."

"Well, yeah."

The whiskey-laced coffee left a pleasant burn in the pit of Anissa's stomach, and loosened her tongue a little. "I'm not going to kill anyone. I wasn't even trying to kill anyone the first time."

Sawyer looked down at his wrist, still wrapped in a bone regenerator.

"In my defense, I didn't know where I was, and I responded the only way I know how. I'm sorry." The words came easier to her now. She shouldn't have let him pour that much whiskey. "Um, is the offer of food still on the table?"

"If you're okay with whatever the sickbay replicator spits out, then yes."

As long as it absorbed some of the alcohol coursing through her system, Anissa didn't care. "Surprise me."

He keyed in an order at the replicator near the bank of monitors and screens, and presented her with the plate of eggs it produced. She noticed that he handed her a fork and didn't flinch when she accepted it. Maybe he would unlock the sonicuff sooner than she expected.

"So, do you want to know what I last remember?" she asked. May as well get all of that out of the way. If she talked about what happened, she might gain Sawyer's trust, and he'd possibly let her out of the sonicuff. "I was piloting my mother's research ship, and the computer systems were infected with the Vine virus, which was probably installed before we left the university's port. Everyone on board, except for me, suffocated after life support was shut off." Tears sprang to her eyes, but she forced them away, not wanting Sawyer to see her upset. "Ever hear of Dr. Vicora Alto?"

Sawyer looked stricken, but he was able to answer, "I—no, I haven't. Commander, that's awful. I'm so—"

Anissa shook her head, as if physically brushing away his concern. She couldn't deal with that right now. "Vicora, my mother, was a brilliant geneticist. She was on the verge of discovering major advancements in bio-longevity treatments, and Dr. Crale Mollon stole it all from her. Have you heard of him?"

"No, but I'm not the person to ask. I probably shouldn't tell you this, but the only thing I'm even halfway knowledgeable about is archaeology."

Anissa set her coffee cup on a small ledge built into the bed and took a bite of her eggs. Sawyer watched her, waiting for her to respond. Finally, she said, "Dr. Mollon worked with her, on and off, at Laresh First University. Does it still exist?"

"Yes, although it's now a satellite of Prime University, where I work."

"Maybe they'll have records of his research. Is it possible to take a trip there?"

Sawyer paused, and Anissa wondered what he was thinking. "It's not that it's not possible," he said slowly, "it's that we have to get back to Rodanta soon. Our campuses have access to each other's libraries. We can look once we get there."

Anissa didn't mind that he was speaking in terms of 'we.' In fact, it would be nice to have some help as she adapted to life in the future. "Thank you."

Sawyer eyed her, a touch of wariness in his expression. Anissa swallowed another mouthful of eggs. "What is it?"

"This is going to sound weird, but ... aren't you, well, *upset* about any of this?"

Yes, she was, and as soon as she had some privacy, she would let herself fall apart. "You can take the soldier out of the Laresh Forces," she said, "but she's still a soldier." She pasted what she knew to be a brittle smile on her face. "I know how to compartmentalize. I'll grieve later."

"Okay." He looked at the sonicuff, and Anissa tried to appear casual, to not let her hopefulness show. "You're really not going to try to kill us?"

"I told you before, I wasn't trying to kill anyone."

"Fine. Maim, then. General harm," he said. "I'll unlock the cuff and show you to the spare quarters on board. Fitch and Lita share, so we have the extra space."

She nodded, and Sawyer pressed his thumb against the sonicuff's metal clasp. The blue energy beam evaporated, leaving a slight tingle across Anissa's skin. She didn't get up from the bed right away, instead finishing the eggs and coffee. It wouldn't do to look too eager; it could raise suspicions. She needed to stay on good terms with these people.

She hopped off the side of the bed when she was finished, no easy feat considering she still wore her bulky EVA suit. "Is there a hard-goods replicator on board?" she asked. She needed new clothes.

"No, I got a discount on the *Phantom* because it was mostly stripped out for parts. But we have stuff in storage lockers if you're looking for clothes, and we'll be back in Rodanta soon enough, so we can get more things."

He took her dishes and left them in the sickbay recycling unit, then led her into the corridor. Anissa wanted to ask what he thought would happen once they reached the Rodanta Quadrant and found out what Dr. Mollon had done with her mother's research, but she held back. He'd said before he wanted to have a meeting with the entire crew; there was no point in wasting her breath.

They took the stairs to the deck above, and Anissa was surprised to see the disorder in its corridor. Someone had even left a basket of laundry on the threadbare carpet. She glanced through an open door and saw a mess inside: clothes and books strewn over the deck, a pile of sheets in the doorway. She raised an eyebrow at Sawyer. "You tolerate this kind of sloth on your ship?"

"Not officially, but Fitch and Lita don't listen." They stopped at the end of the corridor and Sawyer slid open a door. "This is it. Lights, on."

Bright white light filled the small space. Anissa saw a bolted-down bed, a sleeping bag carelessly tossed on the bare mattress. An empty wardrobe, its door missing, was built into the wall beside it. Two small, round viewports revealed the starscape whizzing past the *Phantom*. Through a doorway she spotted a tiny lav, standard to any minimalist crew quarters. "This is sufficient," she said. Actually, it was better than she'd expected. "Thank you for not throwing me in the brig."

"The brig, yeah. I wouldn't do that."

She turned to face him. "Please don't tell me you don't have a brig on board. What if I wasn't a reasonable person?"

"But you are, which is why the brig issue isn't really an issue."

Unbelievable. The lack of security precautions was almost scary. "Does this door lock?"

"Yes, but it isn't bio-locked. Not that anyone is going to barge in on you." He moved away. "The only person who does that is Lita, and that's only to me. I'll find you some clothes in storage. I hope you aren't too picky. I think it's mostly men's pants."

"As long as it isn't a ball gown or swimsuit, I don't care." Or an EVA suit. Sweat trickled down Anissa's back. She was dying to get out of it and take a shower.

"Got it. I'll be back soon, Commander."

He turned and headed back down the corridor. "Sawyer," she called after him.

He stopped and turned around. "Yeah?"

"I told you already, I left the military. Just call me Anissa."

The sooner she could cobble together a new identity, the sooner she could begin her new life, and that started with finding out what happened to Dr. Mollon.

He crooked his arm in a mock salute. "Anything you say, Anissa."

CHAPTER 4

THE *PHANTOM'S* storage and weapons lockers were belowdecks, along with a cargo bay. Sawyer dug through them until he came up with some serviceable clothes that he guessed could sort of fit Anissa. She was still wearing her EVA suit, so he had no idea of her size. Undoubtedly smaller than he was—but strong, he remembered. He looked down at his wrist, now healed, with only a twinge to remind him of his first encounter with her. Even that would fade soon.

He draped a few garments over his arm and headed back to crew quarters. The intraship speakers crackled static, then Lita's voice sounded. "Sawyer? Can you come to the bridge?"

Outgoing intraship was broken in this part of the *Phantom*, so Sawyer didn't bother responding. He made the short trip to the bridge where he found the rest of the crew waiting. Dian wore an especially sour look and had changed back into her pajamas.

"Everything okay?" Sawyer asked.

"Besides the loose cannon that's taken up residence? Everything's peachy," Dian said.

"She's really sorry about that," Sawyer said.

"I'll bet."

"Look, did you call me here just to squabble?" He pinched the bridge of his nose between his fingers, feeling the start of a stress headache. "Because I'm *really* not in the mood for that. I'm taking Anissa some stuff, and then we need to sit down and talk about how she ended up on that planet and how we can help her out." What was the name of the guy who locked her in that box? "Have any of you heard of a Dr. Mollon? First name Cale or Crake or ... Crale, that's it."

He was met by three blank stares. Sawyer sighed. "We'll talk about this soon."

"Can it be after we get some sleep? It's half past six," said Dian.

At the mention of the time, Sawyer felt exhaustion tug at him again. The coffee was wearing off. "Let me talk to her first," he said. "Fitch, how much longer until we get back to the Rodantan Quadrant?"

"We'll be at the border in about twelve hours and back at the university tomorrow afternoon. We could get there faster, but I thought you'd want to save the fuel."

"Fuel, right." So they had nearly a day before Sawyer would yet again have to be accountable to his father for doing the job he'd spent so many years studying for. "Look, if you think you've come across the Immortal Spacefarer's treasure again, or anything from *any* of the stories in the *Frexic Galactica,* wake me up. I'm going to get a couple hours' sleep. Fitch, are you and Lita going to be okay to fly this bucket until, say, oh-nine-hundred hours?"

"We'll wake you up at eleven hundred," Fitch said. "It's been a rough morning. Get some rest."

Sawyer said his thanks and left the bridge. He and Dian made their way back to crew quarters in silence, and she let herself into her cabin, closing the door without saying a word. She was pissed off, he knew, and exhausted. Dian being pissed off and exhausted didn't amount to a good bedside manner, which was the main reason she'd cut short her medic career. He knew she would be in better spirits after some sleep and a couple more hours' of giving him the silent treatment.

He knocked on Anissa's door and waited. She opened it, and Sawyer did a double take. She'd taken off her EVA suit, revealing a slim-fitting gray flight suit that bore the insignia of the *Spindle*. Her dark hair was much longer than he'd initially thought; now that it wasn't tucked into the back of her suit, it hung halfway down her back in a style he wouldn't have expected on someone who was ex-military. She was actually very attractive, an observation he found a little disturbing. She had broken his wrist, after all.

He held out the clothes to her. "I brought you some stuff."

She accepted the garments offered without looking down at them. "Thanks. Um, can you help me with a couple of things?"

"Sure." She moved away from the door, and he stepped inside. "What's the problem?"

She pointed to the lav, a sheepish look on her face. "I can't turn anything on in there."

"Oh." Maybe something was malfunctioning. This was the least-used cabin on the ship. "Let me take a look." He tested out the waterless appliances. "The cleansers are still working." A thought dawned on him, and he looked over his shoulder to see Anissa standing in the doorway. "You've never used one of these before."

"Not quite like this."

"Here." He moved aside in the tiny space so she could fit. "It's mostly palm-activated." He pressed his hand against the shower's control pad.

"I figured that part out."

"Then you pick your preferences." Sawyer pressed buttons beside the palm pad, picking a short shower, warm temperature, medium pressure. The waterless cleansers glowed over his skin, pink laser lights dancing along his exposed forearm.

"Oh. That makes sense. Thanks."

"You're welcome. Anything else I can help you with?"

She shook her head. "No. I'm going to take a shower and then a nap."

"Me, too. We're going to have a meeting later this morning," Sawyer said. "We'll figure out why this happened to you. I promise."

"You're being awfully nice to someone who attacked you and your crew a couple of hours ago."

"Yeah, well, I'm already over it." Sawyer flexed his wrist. "See? All better. And Dian will forgive you eventually."

"So, I should just steer clear of her until she's stopped being angry?"

"That tactic works for everyone else, so go with it."

Anissa nodded. "I'll do that."

This close to her in the small space, Sawyer could see flecks of green and gold in her irises, more prominent to him than the circles under her eyes. Despite his exhaustion, a flicker of awareness flashed through him, briefly resurrecting long-ignored desires. He looked away before she could pick up anything untoward in his expression.

She had, as she'd pointed out, broken his wrist just a couple of hours ago.

Anissa left the lav first. "I'll leave you to it," Sawyer said. "Barring any emergencies or possible finds related to the *Frexic Galactica*, I'm not going to be on the bridge until eleven hundred hours."

"I'll set the computer to wake me up." She offered him a small smile, and Sawyer recognized that was his cue to leave.

"If you need any more help," he said, but she shook her head.

"The shower was it, and I've got it now, thanks. Get some sleep, Sawyer."

Anissa took a shower and then lay in bed in her darkened cabin, unable to sleep.

She'd been sleeping for over one hundred years. She didn't need any more right now.

Tears gathered in her eyes and she brushed at them impatiently, trying, and failing, to will them away. For the first time in her life, she was so far out of her element she didn't know what to do. The situation was frustrating, enraging... and sad, too. She'd joined her mother's crew to be the *Spindle*'s security officer and she'd failed miserably. Dr. Mollon still managed to kill Vicora and make off with her research. Anissa hoped bitterly that he'd met his end as horrifically as possible, that he never had the chance to profit off Vicora's work.

And according to the *Phantom*'s crew, there wasn't a record of Dr. Mollon anywhere that they could find, at least not yet. She needed to know what happened to him, and if she could figure out how the ship's computers worked, she could do her own research.

But she didn't know, at least not yet. Anissa had always been quick to pick up new technology, but she knew she would need some outside help living in this future.

She muffled a sob with her pillow. *The future.*

Everyone and everything she'd ever known was now gone forever, and she had no way of going back. Even the years she sacrificed as a soldier may well have been in vain. The Empire was gone and had ended up allied with Rodanta, and she had no idea what happened to the royal family she'd fought for.

All of it, her entire life's work and meaning, had been for nothing.

Anissa drifted off into a light, fitful sleep, waking up periodically. By the time eleven hundred hours rolled around, she was ready to sit down and talk strategy with the *Phantom*'s crew, the way she had with her unit during the war. She dressed in some of the clothes Sawyer had brought her and braided her hair, noting that she should probably cut it once she could get her hands on a pair of shears. She'd grown it out following her military discharge, and she'd never fully got used to it before Dr. Mollon put her under.

She found her way back to the bridge, where Fitch and Lita manned the controls. "Good morning," Lita said, her voice bright. There wasn't a hint of resentment or suspicion on her features when she faced Anissa, only an open friendliness. "There's coffee and breakfast in the office if you want some. You should probably lay claim to one of the pastries before Sawyer and Dian get up. Fitch already demolished two."

"You helped," her husband said.

Anissa forced what she hoped looked like a genuine smile onto her face and headed into the small room off the bridge. On the table was a dented metal carafe of steaming coffee that didn't smell like it came from a replicator and a plate of gooey, sugary pastries. It wasn't quite Anissa's preferred breakfast, but she took one to be polite and poured a cup of coffee.

She returned to the bridge. Fitch's voice boomed over intraship. "Wakey-wakey, Captain," he said. "You too, Dian. It's eleven hundred hours and Commander Alto's already here, bright-eyed and bushy-tailed."

Anissa hoped Sawyer's prediction that Dian would forgive her shortly was accurate. It would make the rest of this voyage so much easier.

She sat down on a bench behind the nav station, as far

away from any computers or controls as she could get. "I'm really sorry about earlier," she said.

"You didn't break *my* wrist," Fitch said.

"We're not angry," Lita said. "Sawyer said we would help you, and we will. He has contacts and privileges at Prime University that he can use. That's probably the best place to start looking for information about your mother and this Dr. Crake guy."

"Mollon," Anissa said. "Crale Mollon."

"Right."

"But what about the rest of his work?" Anissa said. "He's an archaeologist, right? There must be things he needs to get back to when we arrive in Rodanta."

"Eh, sort of," Fitch said. "He lives on this ship full time. It isn't a long story, but it's a little complicated."

"And it's not ours to tell," Lita said.

So if Sawyer lived on board the *Phantom* full time, maybe he wouldn't mind Anissa sticking around until she could get back to the Laresh System. "I see."

Any further conversation was halted when Sawyer and Dian arrived on the bridge, Dian still in pajamas and robe and Sawyer in faded black pants and a green shirt. Dian swept by Anissa. "Did you eat the last chocolate tart?" she asked.

Anissa suspected this was a test. "No." Hers was filled with fruit.

"All right. You're almost forgiven."

"That's as close to benevolent as Dian gets," Sawyer said. "Fitch, how's the course?"

"Unfortunately for you, exceedingly calm. We also passed a beacon a couple of hours ago, and I think you have mail again."

"Fuck." Sawyer cringed and ran a hand through his sleep-mussed hair.

Fitch held up his hands in mock defense. "I didn't open it, but the origin code is from Prime U. Just a heads-up. Sorry."

Anissa's curiosity about Sawyer was piqued. He was an archaeologist, employed by a university, and in her time, that sort of profession wasn't especially well paid. The *Phantom* wasn't a luxury vessel, but décor aside, it was better than decent, and decent ships weren't cheap. If she understood what Fitch was saying, Sawyer lived on board full time rather than planetside or on a station like most civilians. Sawyer seemed to be a bit of an eccentric, and she wanted to know why.

"I'll read it later," Sawyer said. He sighed, then patted his pockets. "Damn it, I forgot to bring something to write on."

Dian removed a pad and pencil from her robe pocket and handed them to him. "Right here."

"Thanks." Sawyer turned to Anissa. "So, Dr. Mollon. Let's start with him."

Anissa sipped her coffee, momentarily distracted by the fact Sawyer was using pencil and paper to take notes. Then, she focused on what he wanted, and memories of the *Spindle* came crashing back. She fought to suppress her rage at Dr. Mollon and stay professional. "He was my mother's colleague at Laresh First University, both specializing in bio-longevity. My mother was one of his protégées right after she finished her doctorate, but that was before I was born. He worked mostly in a teaching capacity and Vicora, my mother, worked in research. She was away for much of the time, even during the war."

Dian asked, "Vicora?"

"My mother's name was Dr. Vicora Alto. We didn't bother with honorifics."

"Neither do my parents," Dian said. "It's sort of pointless when we're family."

"Agreed," Anissa said, then continued. "My mother and a

small crew conducted research missions aboard the *Spindle*, and I joined as security officer and pilot after I was discharged from the military. Vicora had made a couple of breakthroughs with her bio-longevity research and published some of her findings, and Dr. Mollon, I don't know, was jealous or something. That's the only explanation I can think of for why he sabotaged our ship with Vine. I was the last person alive aboard the ship."

"Vine?" said Fitch. His brow furrowed.

"It's an invasive program," she said. "It shuts down a ship's systems one at a time, leaving life support for last. It was launched remotely in a minor computer function, like the lines of code that boiled water in replicators, or something like that, and it would replicate in other lines of code, overriding the previous functions with no way to stop it. It was designed as a slow way to kill a ship's crew. I was the only person on the bridge when Vine finished replicating, and Dr. Mollon put tow clamps on the ship and boarded it."

"Holy shit," Fitch said.

"Yeah. I was wearing my EVA suit when Vine reached the *Spindle*'s bridge, and I had hoped to kill some of Dr. Mollon or some of his crew before I died." She recalled that she'd left her weapon in her cabin, then remembered the blaster Dr. Mollon had, which she hadn't had a chance to use. "Instead he kept me alive long enough to put me to sleep for a hundred years."

"Why do you think he did that?" Sawyer asked.

"He was after my mother's research." Anissa sagged against the wall. "I don't know the exact details of it, either. Science wasn't my strong point. I was just security and, occasionally, the pilot. She and her crew were murdered by her rival, and from what everyone here has told me, there's no evidence that Dr. Mollon ever actually did it."

"We don't have access to much information yet," Dian

said. "Bio-longevity isn't nearly as sexy a field as it used to be, in part for its ethical issues, but there could be research at Prime U we can take a look at."

"It isn't?"

"Nah, the hot new field with questionable ethics is cybernetics. Turns out it's easier, safer, and cheaper to extend someone's lifespan with computer chips than by manipulating living cells and DNA. Bio-longevity is pretty much considered pseudoscience these days."

Another wave of defeat crashed through Anissa. Her mother's work was for nothing if her field of research had been relegated to the status of astrology. "Great," she said, her voice a mumble.

She'd survived whatever Dr. Mollon shot her up with and then a revival from stasis; her friends and family were dead, her home undoubtedly changed beyond recognition. If what she understood was correct, Commander Anissa Alto had been erased from history. She had nothing left except the charity she had to rely on from Benedict Sawyer and his crew.

She wanted to cry again, but her eyes were dry. So she leaned her head back against the wall and sighed.

CHAPTER 5

FITCH'S voice boomed over intraship. "We just passed the border beacon. We'll be arriving at Bliss Station in a couple of hours." He paused. "Sorry to be the bearer of bad news, Sawyer."

Sawyer groaned, but there was no one in the shuttle bay to hear him. He stood in the shuttle's tiny cockpit, avoiding everyone else on board the ship and thinking about what he should do when they returned home. He keyed in the shuttle code to connect to intraship. "Got it, and it's not your fault."

He'd watched his father's transmits from the privacy of his cabin a few hours earlier, not bothering to compose a response. There hadn't been anything new in the messages, just the usual: *You need to stop wandering around the universe looking for something that doesn't exist* and *I'm very disappointed in you, and your mother would be as well.* Once upon a time that last statement would have delivered an emotional sucker punch, but his father had said those words so often they'd lost meaning. Besides, he knew his mother wouldn't be disappointed in his life's work, no matter what path he chose.

The *Phantom* would dock at Bliss Station, her usual

haunt, and Sawyer would take the shuttle and make a stop at Prime University to file his findings with the archaeology department and have an obligatory meeting with his father. He and Lita had already put together a report of what they'd found on that planet, although neither of them had been entirely sure how to proceed with Anissa, nor if they should even submit their reports right away. *Lareshi soldier discovered in stasis, personal information appears to have been erased from history.*

As he checked the shuttle's fuel and made the final arrangements to dock the *Phantom*, he considered the reports again. Maybe it would be best if he held off on filing his findings until he'd had a chance to conduct an investigation of his own.

"Need any help?"

Sawyer jumped and turned to see Anissa watching him from the shuttle's open door. He'd been too lost in thought to hear her walk into the bay. "I think I'm good," he said, then added, "But thank you."

"You're worried I'll take it and go for a joyride?"

Actually, that was the last thing he expected. The shuttle was programmed to only accept the palm prints of authorized pilots, and she wasn't one of them. "No," he said. "To be honest, I wouldn't expect you to know how to fly it."

She stepped into the shuttle and looked around. "I could probably figure it out eventually," she said. She walked through the short cargo hold to the cockpit, sitting down in the seat Lita usually took. "What is she?" she asked.

"M-class Redfield-880."

She nodded, looking through the darkened viewscreen to the shuttle bay doors. "I remember Redfield." She leaned back in the seat and swiveled around to face Sawyer. "What's next for me?"

"I've been thinking about that, actually." He sat down in

the pilot's seat and turned it so he was facing her. The cockpit was small enough that if he didn't angle his knees away, they'd be touching. "You were a commander in the Laresh Forces," he said. "There should be *some* record of you that would be accessible to us. We've been within range of Rodantan beacons for hours, and Dian's been running searches, but there's nothing. Nothing about the ship you say you came from, nothing about this Dr. Mollon, nothing about your mother."

"I *did* come from the *Spindle*..."

He held up a hand, needing to clarify. "I believe you are who you say you are," he said. "That ID chip in your wrist is convincing enough evidence, even if we exclude the fact that we found you in stasis, in a vessel that was last manufactured over a hundred years ago. I believe your story because it makes the most sense.

"But all information about you was erased for a reason," he said. "Lita and I wrote reports of what we found for the university, but I'm not sure I'm going to file it as is. I want to do some more poking around before I do. There are a lot of things about this that don't add up."

Anissa looked visibly relieved at his pronouncement. "Thank you," she said.

"I'm not turning you loose in Rodanta or Laresh," he said. "I think you'll adapt to this time just fine, but it'll take a while. We'll be docking at Bliss Station soon, and you can stay in your cabin here."

"Do you live on Bliss? I thought you lived on the ship."

"I live on board the *Phantom* and rent a berth at the station. It's just easier for me to do that." He really didn't want to get into any discussions about why he preferred to live on his research ship rather than rent an apartment elsewhere. "I can transfer some scrip to you and you can pick up whatever you need on Bliss."

"Thank you. I really do appreciate all of this." She bit her lip, a gesture he shouldn't notice as cute but did. "Again, your wrist..."

"I told you, I'm not mad," he said. "It's completely healed. You're a soldier, I'm sure that's what they taught you to do in soldier school."

"Something like that."

He wished he had something hopeful to tell her, a promise he could keep that would help ease her way into modern life. But he didn't. He didn't even have a plan in the event he found out why Anissa and Vicora Alto's lives and achievements had been erased. "Look, no one's going to turn you loose and let you fend for yourself," he said, trying to reassure her. "At least not until you want to."

She looked a little more mollified at his words but didn't respond. Sawyer didn't blame her. She was undoubtedly still processing everything that had happened to her.

Anissa kept her eyes on the shuttle bay doors. "Can I ask you something?"

"Shoot."

"What's the deal with you and your father? I'm not trying to pry, but..."

Sawyer exhaled noisily. "It's one of those things that seems complicated, but isn't." That was a bit of an understatement. "He's the president of Prime University. I'm a university employee, working primarily in research, as you can see." He gestured toward the cockpit's controls. "He doesn't like the direction I've taken my research, and it pisses him off that I don't have to obey his commands anymore. When my mother died, she left her estate to me, which let me buy the *Phantom* and wander around space looking for artifacts that inspired folk stories and fairy tales. My dad has never forgiven my mother for not leaving anything to him even though they'd been divorced for years before she passed."

"I'm sorry."

He shrugged, ignoring the sliver of pain that surfaced whenever he thought about his mother. "It was quite a few years ago, and as I'm sure you can tell from my description of him, my father feels entitled to a lot of things he doesn't have a right to. Mom's money, my life and career, that kind of thing."

"So why work at Prime University?"

"It has the best archaeology and xeno-archaeology departments in the Quadrant, and I get a lot more leeway for taking off for extended periods than I would elsewhere. I don't think it's entirely due to Dad's position, because he loathes what I do, but I'm sure it's a factor."

Sawyer hated that. He hated to admit it to her, hated that even though what he did was sanctioned by the archaeology department and largely funded by his own money, he would never fully escape the nepotism label as long as he worked in academia. His father trimmed the department's budget every couple of years, just to remind Sawyer who was in charge, despite his not being the chair.

"That's awful."

"Some days I think about giving it all up and going into antiquities dealing." That was something he'd never told anyone, but there was a first for everything. Still, he quickly added, "Please don't tell the crew that."

"I won't. Promise."

"Thanks." He stood up and looked around the small cockpit. The shuttle was fueled and ready for the short trip to the university, which meant there wasn't anything else for him to do on here. "I'm not sure how long I'll be gone when we dock at Bliss, so I'll show you the rest of the ship now." She followed him through the chilly shuttle bay to the corridor. "Remember how you asked why there wasn't a brig on board?"

"I'm appalled there isn't, even if this *is* a research ship." She rubbed her arms in an attempt to ward off the cold.

Sawyer pressed his palm to the door's lock and waited while it cycled open.

"I had it converted to a gym. There's a soaker tub and sim chamber if you feel like working out. The sim's a cheap model but it has a lot of programs and the gravity's adjustable. It's on Deck Two Forward, right above us."

"Thanks. I'll probably take advantage of it." She relaxed as they walked through the ship's warmer corridors. "You really should have somewhere to secure hostiles, though."

"We don't get a lot of them." They stepped into the lift. "But I guess you're speaking from experience."

Speaking of hostiles...

What had Anissa been doing in the shuttle bay?

There wasn't a delicate way to bring it up. Sawyer pressed the lift button to take them to the bridge. "Why were you in the shuttle bay?" he asked, trying to keep his tone casual.

"You mean, why was I skulking around your ship?"

She was sharp. May as well be honest. "Pretty much."

"I was looking for you."

Those words shouldn't have caused a warmth to spread through his chest, but they did. However, the feeling was quickly extinguished by her next words. "It's not like I have much else to do, and I got bored staring at the walls in my cabin. But I'll check out the brig."

"There are vids and books in the cabin comps, too, if you want to download something in your cabin." He paused, remembering her difficulty with the shower. "I'll show you."

"I appreciate that."

There was a wealth of other things he should probably help her with, and not just investigating how she ended up on that planet or what happened to her mother's research. Therapy, maybe. As they walked onto the bridge, he stole a glance at her.

Her profile was regal: her jaw set, and expression

neutral. Very much a soldier, and one very much out of her element, as stoic as she appeared. "We won't go to the Rodantan authorities right away if you don't want to," he said.

She turned to face him. "I'd rather wait until we find Dr. Mollon. He's still out there, I can feel it."

Sawyer wanted to point out the impossibility of that but didn't want to crush her hopes further. It could wait, couldn't it? "So you want to conduct your own investigation?"

"Yes," she said. "He stole my mother's research. Why else would he have attacked her ship? I'm positive he's still alive."

She sounded determined. Sawyer didn't yet know her well enough to try to dissuade her.

Fitch was in his usual place at navigation when they arrived on the bridge, Lita stood next to him holding a steaming mug of tea. "We picked up another message, Captain," Fitch said. He checked a screen to his right. "Make that five. Three are for Dian, two for you."

"None for you or Lita?"

"Nah, the debt collectors decided to leave us alone for another couple of days." He reached over and squeezed Lita's thigh affectionately. "We'll be at Bliss in an hour or so, boss."

"Great." He'd take the shuttle, make the quick flight to the university, see what his father wanted, and then return to the *Phantom* for a decent night's sleep. *Piece of cake.* "I'll be right back."

He crossed the bridge to the small office, closed the door behind him, and checked his messages. Both from his father, one bearing a stamp from his Prime University address and the other his personal address. His father must be either pissed off or desperate to get in touch with his son; he was willing to bet on the former.

Sawyer sighed and started the first one. His father's face filled the screen, suit and silver hair impeccable. "Benedict," he said by way of greeting. "I haven't heard from you in some time, and neither has McKesson."

Irritation flashed through Sawyer at the mention of his and his mother's lawyer. A lawyer that Dr. Devon King had no reason to contact. So if his father was in touch with the lawyer, it meant he wanted information about Sawyer's inheritance, which meant, as usual, his father was meddling for the sake of meddling.

Sawyer deleted the message without bothering to finish it and started the second. It was time-stamped hours after the first one was sent, and this time, Devon was clearly aggravated at Sawyer's lack of response. He deleted that one, too.

The fact that Sawyer filed his flight plans with the university and Bliss Station's transit control, plans that clearly indicated that the *Phantom* would be in deep space with very few comm beacons nearby to pick up messages, didn't matter a whit to Devon King. Not for the first time, Sawyer reconsidered his decision to remain at Prime University, despite its fantastic perks. His father's meddling and pestering was usually in tolerable amounts, but he'd been ramping up his efforts lately.

He left the office and returned to the bridge. Neither Fitch nor Lita said anything, knowing what a touchy subject his father was.

Sawyer raised an eyebrow at Lita, who sat in the copilot's chair. "Really?" she said. "You want me to get up?"

"I'd appreciate that."

"Don't you have reports to write?"

"My part's already done. What about yours? I'm taking them straight to the university once we dock at Bliss. The shuttle's prepped and everything."

Lita's eyes briefly fixed on Anissa. "Including what we found this morning?" She slid out from the seat though, tea mug in hand.

"I have two reports," Sawyer said. "One that mentions Anissa, one that doesn't. I'd like to have your part of the report in case I decide that's the one I want to file."

Now it was Fitch's turn to look surprised. "You're actually considering uploading false information?"

"That's why I wanted to see everyone here." Sawyer glanced at the console in front of him, noting the course Fitch had plotted to Bliss. There were no reports of any obstructions and air traffic reports were good. "When I get back to the university, I'm going to do some digging into this Dr. Mollon Anissa told me about and try to find out why she and her mother disappeared from the history books. I think it would be safer for her, and possibly us, if we get that sorted out first."

At the blank looks from the rest of the crew. Anissa filled them in, repeating her story to them. Sawyer explained his reasoning for creating two sets of reports.

"Then there's the media aspect," Dian said.

Sawyer cringed. That angle hadn't occurred to him until she mentioned it. A media firestorm over a former Laresh Empire soldier found in stasis would last for months, if not years, and alerting others to Anissa's existence would put a damper on their investigation. And there was one more thing he'd been considering, something Anissa had brought up.

"There's the media to consider," he said. "But there's something else we need to look into, as well. What if Dr. Mollon perfected her mother's longevity serum or spray or whatever it was?" he said. "What if he continued her research?"

"Wouldn't we know about something like that?" Dian said.

"Anissa thinks he continued his bio-longevity research," Sawyer said, choosing his words carefully. He didn't want to insult Anissa or shoot down her theory immediately. "She thinks he could still be alive under an assumed name."

It was important that her ideas be explored.

"I wouldn't put it past him," Anissa said. "I told Sawyer I'm willing to go to the legal authorities, after we've tried looking for him."

Sawyer was dreading the moment she found out that finding him might be impossible.

"So factoring in the total unbelievability of finding someone in stasis on a forgotten backwater planet, the certainty of media fuckery, *and* a possible centenarian mad scientist running around, we need to keep Anissa's existence a secret," Fitch said. "Got it. None of this information leaves this ship."

"Exactly."

"So, you're saying I *don't* have write a detailed report?" Lita's voice was hopeful.

"No, you do, I'm just going to put off submitting it until we know for sure what happened to Dr. Mollon."

"Well, shit."

A muted ping sounded as the ship passed another comm beacon. Sawyer glanced down at the transmit tag; of course, it was for him from his father. He tamped down his irritation and ignored it, letting the *Phantom* return them home.

***

By mid-afternoon, the *Phantom* was anchored in a massive dry-dock berth at Bliss. Anissa had to admit that she was truly exhausted now, and Sawyer didn't look much better. Fitch, Lita, and Dian collected their things and left the ship for their homes on station, and then it was just the two of them in the empty ship.

"I'm going to the university's main campus," Sawyer said. "It's only a short trip from here. I'll make some excuses about my report, and see my father to get him off my back. Then when I get back, we'll do some research together."

Anissa had followed him to the shuttle bay, unsure of what to do with herself. He'd shown her how to download some of the vids and books available in the *Phantom*'s entertainment files, but none of them held her interest. She was torn between wanting to sleep and insisting on going with him to the university. Sawyer must have guessed her possible intention because he held up a hand before she could say anything.

"Your presence would only make this meeting with my dad much more difficult," he said. "I'm still not sure how I'm going to sneak you into the main university campus, to be honest. Stay on board for now, get some rest, work out, whatever you need to do. I'll be back in a couple of hours."

He ran a hand through his hair, the dark circles under his eyes more prominent than they were an hour ago. Anissa wasn't the only one who needed sleep.

"Stay on board," he said. He activated the shuttle doors.

"Where would I go? I don't know my way around the station, and I don't have any money."

"And I'll sort that out later. The shuttle bay doors are on automatic. You should probably leave the bay."

She nodded and walked through the cold chamber as the ship's computer sang out a warning that the doors would open in four minutes.

The interior doors cycled open, and she waited inside the control area, all of the equipment locked down. The computer counted down the minutes until the exterior doors opened as it scanned the bay for life forms. Red warning lights flashed as the doors opened to reveal the dark void of space, and a muted klaxon sounded as the shuttle was sucked out. The doors closed, and the klaxon ceased and according to the computer, life support was restored to the shuttle bay.

And Anissa had nothing to do.

She knew without checking that everything on the ship would be locked down and secured. She knew Sawyer believed her story, but doubted he fully trusted her yet, and she didn't blame him. She wouldn't trust an unknown on board, either.

Not that she knew how to fly a modern ship, anyway, but she was sure she could learn. Surely the technology wasn't that much different than it was 104 years ago.

Anissa let herself into the former brig and looked at its conversion with dismay. A soaker tub and sim chamber were nice, but they wouldn't contain hostiles. The door's lock was manual and flimsy and could easily be broken. Still, she looked at the sim chamber's specs. Plenty of training programs, with adjustable gravity. It didn't exonerate Sawyer's poor decision to convert the brig, but it mitigated it, somewhat.

She could possibly take a bath in that big tub sometime. She missed the water showers that were more common in her time although the laser cleansers made sense. It had been a new technology before she fell asleep for a century, but was already being touted as a cheaper alternative to carrying heavy loads of water and their accompanying recyclers on long voyages. She decided to make use of the sim chamber and tub once she'd had some sleep.

Sleep. Yeah, right. The last thing Anissa wanted to do was sleep again, but she knew at some point, she would have to. Since being revived, her schedule had been much more erratic than she was used to.

There was no one around to drug her this time. She reminded herself that she could sleep for a perfectly normal seven or eight hours and wake up *not* in a different time.

She boarded the lift and ordered it to take her to Deck Three where the lounge was located. The lounge was small, holding a couple of tables and long benches locked to the deck, and a pair of replicators. There were a few boxes of freeze-dried foods in the cupboards and refrigerator, and not much else. Anissa scrolled through the menu options on the replicators but didn't key in any requests.

She avoided the bridge, not wanting to arouse Sawyer's suspicions if he was somehow monitoring her whereabouts, avoiding the sickbay for the same reason. Bored, she returned to her cabin and lay on the bed, and let sleep overtake her.

May as well get this over with.

Sawyer's meeting with the chair of the Archaeology and Xeno-Archaeology Departments had been uneventful and, mercifully, brief. Dr. Janekh asked him to upload his report whenever he had time, then asked him about teaching a couple of courses the following semester. The chair didn't say so explicitly, but Sawyer knew that the teaching requests had come down from his father. Sawyer hated teaching and Devon King knew it. Sawyer said he would consider it.

Now for the hard part.

Sawyer waited in a plush seat in the foyer of his father's office. His long-serving secretary, Linette, was undoubtedly making him wait under Dr. King's orders, just to aggravate him. After twenty minutes, Linette sweetly informed him that Dr. King was ready to see him.

He let himself into his father's office without bothering to knock. "Dad," he said by way of greeting. His father sat behind his massive, ornate desk as usual, his expression pinched and irritated.

"Is something wrong with the outbound messaging on that garbage scow?" Devon's face was unnaturally smooth, a sharp contrast to his silver hair. Sawyer had no idea why his father would spring for so much work to keep his face looking young but not bother with his hair color. His father had once remarked that he and his son could pass for brothers, but Sawyer silently disagreed and prayed that he never fell victim to that level of vanity.

"No." Sawyer sat down heavily in one of the overstuffed chairs.

"Did Janekh speak to you about teaching next semester?"

"He did. I said I'd consider it."

"You *will* do it." Devon His father regarded him coolly from across the desk. "Your contract with the university stipulates occasional teaching. I'm sure you can take some time off from flying around researching fairy tales to teach freshmen Intro to Xeno-Archaeology and Material Culture Analysis."

Fuck my life. The worst courses in the department. "I said I'd consider it, and you had those teaching clauses added a year after I originally signed that contract." He rubbed his temples. He could feel a headache starting. "Look, I've been awake a long time, you deliberately kept me waiting out there, and I'd like to go home. Why don't you get to the specifics of why you're pissed off with me this time and we can go back to our lives?"

"Fundraising season will be upon us soon, and I want you to make some appearances," Devon said. "I'm putting a stop to your gallivanting, and I expect you to show up, dressed appropriately, and help me talk donors into ensuring Prime remains the best-funded university in the quadrant."

"Charity galas?" Sawyer said. "You've been trying to light a fire under my ass for *charity*? Since when have you expected me to show up to those things? You've always said I'm nothing but an embarrassment to you at society functions."

"And you have been. But people are wondering why my son with a Ph.D. isn't attending university affairs and that's turning into the bigger embarrassment. There's one being held next month to raise funds for the formation of a new department." Devon narrowed his eyes at Sawyer. "It's even being held on Bliss Station, so you won't have to travel far."

"Yeah, no. I'll teach next semester if I have to, but I'm not going to stand around in a tuxedo to make you feel like you're father of the century." Sawyer got to his feet. "Nice seeing you, Dad."

"Benedict," his father said, a warning note in his voice.

"Stop wasting my time."

"Benedict!"

Sawyer closed the office door behind him. He offered a brief wave to Linette, who ignored him.

Time to go back to the *Phantom*, and maybe reconsider his employment at Prime University after all.

CHAPTER 6

SAWYER RETURNED TO THE *PHANTOM*, checking the time as the shuttle bay doors closed. Just past eighteen hundred hours. Exhaustion kept pulling at him, but he'd still forced himself to go to a grocery store on Bliss before giving in to it. He was looking forward to eating something that wasn't either replicated or freeze-dried while they stayed on station.

He paused outside the cabin Anissa now occupied, unsure if he should risk knocking on the door and waking her up, in case she'd taken his advice and got some sleep. In the end, he settled for leaving a note stuck to her door. *I'm back. Didn't know if you were sleeping or what. Wake me up if you need anything. I bought groceries, help yourself. S.*

Three hours, he decided. He'd let himself sleep for three hours, then spend the evening doing what research he could into Anissa's background using the resources available via Bliss's connections. Then his sleep schedule wouldn't be too screwed up; he tried to keep regular Rodantan hours no matter where he was in the universe. A decent nap and he would have just enough energy to conduct some research, then go back for a proper night's sleep. He would think about the order to teach next semester at a later time. He set the cabin alarm and quickly fell into a deep slumber, not bothering to change out of his clothes.

He awoke what felt like a short time later, but to knocks on his door rather than the alarm. For those first few muzzy seconds before the sleep cleared his head, he thought it was early morning again, and Lita was about to burst into his cabin while he was naked under the sheets. Then he remembered that Lita and Fitch, and Dian were at their homes on station, and he had a virtual stranger on board.

At least the stranger knocked before barging in. And at least he was dressed this time.

He checked the clock and saw she was waking him up only fifteen minutes before the alarm was due to, so he didn't bother to feel annoyed at the interruption. He combed his hair with his fingers—he needed that haircut sooner rather than later—and crossed the room, opening the door to see a sleep-disheveled Anissa.

Sleep-disheveled Anissa was cute. Hot, even. But Sawyer pushed those thoughts out of his mind.

He'd only known her a day, and not to forget, she had broken his wrist shortly after they met.

"Sorry," she said.

"What for?"

"Waking you up."

"You woke me up to apologize for waking me up?" He tried to keep his voice light, but even allowing for his residual sleepiness, he still felt a little confused.

"No." She took a deep breath and looked away. "I had a nightmare."

Nightmares, okay. They weren't uncommon after trauma although Sawyer wasn't sure how to deal with that. "Do you want a trank or something? There are sedatives in the sickbay."

"No!" Her voice was emphatic. "No, no tranquilizers, ever again. Look, Sawyer, I'm sorry. I'm not usually like this. I used to put my boot up the asses of soldiers who fell apart."

"I'm not mad," he said gently. "You've been through a lot the last, uh…"

"Hundred years." Her expression was grim. "Believe me, I haven't forgotten."

Sawyer was unsure how to proceed. "Did you want to talk about the nightmare?"

She looked a little confused at his question, and he could almost see her thoughts swirling around her head. Of course, a Lareshi commander wouldn't speak about her feelings.

"No. It was just a replay of what happened on the *Spindle*, anyway."

A nightmare that was 'just a replay.' It must have been a horrifying experience. "I don't think either of us will be going back to sleep yet," he said. "How about we go to the common area, plug into Bliss's library databanks, and start searching? Sound good?"

"Sawyer, I'm sorry about waking you up…"

He dismissed her apology with a wave of his hand and what he hoped was a friendly smile. "Don't worry about it. My alarm's going off soon, anyway." He ordered the alarm to deactivate, then led her through the ship to the common area.

It was a bit of a mess, as it always was, but Sawyer didn't care. Someone had left a couple of books with lurid covers on the bolted-down coffee table, probably Lita. The desk built into the wall was full of pens, notebooks, spare batteries for various devices that Sawyer couldn't identify, and more books. He fished out a notebook and pencils, then activated the large comp screen inset into the wall.

Anissa left the common area and returned with two cups of coffee.

"You figured out the replicator all right?"

She set them down on the coffee table and shrugged. "Just fine. I have to say replicator coffee technology is much improved. This is actually drinkable."

Sawyer was temporarily shocked into silence. When he found his voice again, he picked up his own cup and asked, "What the hell kind of swill were you drinking in the Laresh System if *this* is drinkable?"

"Believe me, it was terrible beyond your worst nightmares." She offered him a small smile over the rim of her cup, then looked at the comp screen. "Show me how to use this thing."

He picked up a portable comp, syncing it to the screen on the wall. "Voice and key activated, take your choice. I figured it would be easier to put everything on the wall, so we could both see the search results. Plus, I'm too lazy to move the holodisplay from the bridge to here."

"Noted."

Sawyer logged in to Bliss Station's library. "I guess we'll start with Dr. Mollon," he said. He keyed in *Mollon* and waited.

Mollon, Crale. Laresh Empire (pre-Rodantan alliance), b. 2748, d. 2802. Education: Laresh First University, Keel at Rodanta Second College (both absorbed into Prime 2820). Bio-longevity research (see footnotes). Cause of death: shuttle accident, Vega System (see footnotes).

"That bastard isn't dead," Anissa said.

Sawyer keyed in a command to print off the information from the bridge office. "I'm not going to debate you on that just yet."

"He's out there somewhere," Anissa said, her voice determined and her outrage barely concealed. "He stole my mother's research, and she was so *close* to figuring out longevity."

Sawyer opened the footnotes and printed off everything related to Crale Mollon's library entry, then searched for Vicora Alto.

No results yielded.

"I'm spelling it correctly?" he asked Anissa. "V-I-C-O-R-A?"

"That's it. Try Vicora Mina Alto Plant. Plant was her ex-husband."

"Your father?"

She shook her head. "No, Keff Plant took off long before I was born. I never met him. My mother never discussed my father."

That sucked for her, despite Sawyer's feelings about his own father. He keyed in the extended name.

No results yielded.

"What about doctorates conferred?" Anissa suggested. She rattled off a list of dates and universities that Vicora Alto graduated from, and Sawyer keyed each one into Bliss's search boxes.

No results yielded.

Next, he typed in Anissa's name, and the same information he'd read earlier in the day popped up. Former soldier, honorable discharge, presumed dead at age thirty following an accident 104 years ago, but no other details nor footnotes.

"What was the name of that virus you said destroyed your mother's ship?"

"Vine."

His search for the Vine virus turned up a wealth of information, a sharp contrast to the rest of the dead ends he and Anissa had run into. Developed by Lareshi pirates and currently banned in civilized space, it was a replicating virus that shut down ship systems one at a time and immobilized engines and communications, allowing target ships to be boarded. Vine was tweaked a little for each ship and was designed to withstand any program's attempt to deactivate it. Ships manufactured in the last fifty years were installed with programs that could successfully combat Vine, and it had fallen out of favor with pirates as law enforcement increased across the galaxy. He printed everything he could.

"We have to go to Laresh," Anissa said. "There must be information available there that isn't at Bliss."

"Prime U has access to their databases," Sawyer said. "It's more likely they'll have information that isn't available on the public Bliss servers. We'll go together."

She looked pleased at the prospect of accompanying him on such a visit, as if he'd do it without her. She had a much better idea of what to look for. If he needed to, he could recruit Fitch to do some breaking and entering on protected files, but it might not come to that.

And if this research came to naught... "Anissa, there's one more thing we haven't discussed much yet."

She nodded, her expression quizzical.

"At some point soon, we *have* to take this to law enforcement," Sawyer said. "You and your mother were the victims of crime, and there's also the problem of establishing you as a citizen. You can't travel far in Rodanta or Laresh without identification. The chip in your wrist will help support your case, as will the box we found you in. But the sooner we find out what happened to your mother and Dr. Mollon, the sooner we can present that case to the authorities and get you a current ID chip and identity."

"Understood."

Her jaw was set in the line that Sawyer had begun to realize meant she was irritated or frustrated, or both. "I told you before that I'm not going to kick you off my ship and leave you to fend for yourself," he said. "I meant that. I want to build this case, so you don't end up in a brig somewhere while the media and police pester you."

"I get that. Like I told you before, I appreciate your help, but I'm still pissed off that I'm here in the first place." She set down her coffee cup. "Fucking Mollon." She stood up and paced the common area. "He erased everything. Is there any way to check the timestamps to see when those records were made or modified?"

Sawyer checked the records' histories. The Vine virus was apparently a popular topic, its history, applications, and programming often studied; but the database entries about Anissa and Dr. Mollon were dated from the time the database was uploaded to the Bliss library twenty years' prior when the station first opened.

Another dead end.

"I want to punch something," Anissa said. She glared at the wall comp screen, where the words *No results yielded* still marched across it.

"Sim chamber." Sawyer's said. "Dian installed a program that's just punching things." Subtext: *please don't wreck my wall comp.* "One of the scenes is just for punching clowns. I have a boxing ring, too."

She picked up on the pleading note in his voice. "I'm not going to destroy anything on the ship," she said. "I'm a controlled, disciplined soldier. I'll go check out that sim chamber." She took another swallow of coffee, draining the cup.

"It's unlocked. Just pick your program and gravity control. Take your time."

She stalked out of the room, and Sawyer leaned back in his seat. This was going to be harder than he originally thought.

You thought this was going to be easy? The inner voice was mocking and reminded him an awful lot of his father.

Well, no. But he didn't expect that there would be quite this many dead ends.

Anissa expected to spend another night tossing and turning but was pleasantly surprised when she didn't. She was tired, but it was different to the bone-deep emotional exhaustion she'd felt the day before. This was weariness from a difficult workout at the lowest gravity she could tolerate, hours spent in the *Phantom*'s sim chamber before she'd gone to bed. Her muscles ached pleasantly, and for the first time since Dr. Mollon unleashed Vine on board the *Spindle*, she finally felt some tiny semblance of control over her life.

She'd looked at the giant soaker tub with longing when she finally emerged from the sim chamber, panting and damp with sweat, but hadn't dared to try using it. She had no idea what water currently cost, and she didn't want to be too presumptuous regarding Sawyer's generosity.

By oh-six-hundred hours she was awake and refreshed, so she went to the lounge to look for some breakfast. Sawyer had left the printouts from their aborted research on the deck-locked table, and she sat down on one of the benches, sifting through the papers while she munched on toast and eggs. There was another sheaf of papers relating to the study of bio-longevity theory and treatments, with nary a word about the work of Dr. Vicora Alto. In fact, there were few words at all about the leading researchers in the field from Anissa's time, including Dr. Mollon. It appeared Sawyer was correct, and bio-longevity was only a step up from astrology in terms of the respect it received today. There was little point in chronicling the breakthroughs of leading scientists a century ago when no one cared about it now. The extension of humanoid life now focused mostly on cybernetics and brand-new cloned body parts for those squeamish about hardware implants.

Maybe Dr. Mollon continued his research into cybernetics or cloning. Anissa found a pencil in the mess of papers and made a few notes of her own in one of the margins. She didn't believe for a second that he'd died in an accident; she was willing to concede that he could indeed be dead, but he'd certainly lived longer than the history books were saying.

"You're up."

Sawyer appeared in the lounge doorway, hair sticking up from sleep, hand hiding a yawn. He wore a robe, which had seen better days, and the bottoms of track pants stuck out from under the hem. Anissa knew she didn't look much better in her borrowed oversized T-shirt and shorts, but he had a sort of grumpy charm about him in the morning.

"Wide awake and reading," she said, holding up the paper she'd been writing on. "What's the plan for today?"

"I have a few things to sort out on station," he said. "Minor stuff like docking fees and the ship's fuel reserves are down to her last quarter, so I need to sort that out, too. There's also a satellite university campus on station where we can do some research. You're welcome to come along, of course." Sawyer scrolled through the replicator's options, sighing at the coffee he eventually picked out. His reaction aside, it was still far superior to anything available in the Laresh Forces or on Anissa's mother's ship.

Anissa was dying to get out and see what Bliss Station looked like. A smile bloomed across her face. "That's the first time I've seen you do that," he said. "Not that I'm complaining. I'd be a lot more pissed off about what happened if I were in your shoes." He smothered another yawn behind his hand.

Anissa felt her smile fade a little at the reminder. "You're forgetting that I have the training to deal with it." Not that military academy had included a module on what to do when one found herself 104 years in the future, but she figured she could apply other lessons to her new situation. Study the enemy and his tactics. Discipline. Venting anger and frustration in a way that also provided benefits to her health.

And while she knew Sawyer and his crew weren't the enemy, she still had more studying to do. "Is there any chance I might learn how to pilot a shuttle or the ship?"

When this was over, she was still going to be stuck in this new time. She doubted she would be able to enlist in the Rodantan or Laresh military at her age, not that she wanted to. She knew how to fight and strategize, and she knew how to fly. She needed a way to support herself once she'd tracked down Dr. Mollon and exacted justice on him, or what remained of him.

Sawyer paused, mug in hand. "I'm not planning on hijacking the ship," she said. "It's just that's what I did when I was discharged. I'm going to have to work eventually."

"You're right." He set down his coffee. "I said I'd help you, and that's part of it." He leaned back, forgetting he was on a bench and not a chair, his eyes widening when he nearly fell off backward. He righted himself and leaned forward against the table.

Definitely not a morning person. Neither was Anissa, but she hid it better. *Thank you, military academy.*

"I was thinking that it might make sense to take a trip to Laresh," he said. "We'll do some more research at the university there too, just to make sure we haven't missed anything."

Anissa liked how he said *we* and the possibility of returning to the Laresh Empire. One hundred years after her presumed death aside, it was still her home, and she wanted to go back. But ... "That trip will take days," she said.

He shook his head. "There's a jumpgate a couple of hours out from Bliss that we can take. It was discovered about sixty years ago. Have you handled a converted freighter in jump before?"

"Not one this sophisticated, but I've piloted through my share of jumpgates."

Have you handled a converted freighter in jump? He was asking about her experience. Anissa took that as another positive sign. He really was willing to help her out, even though there were so many dead ends, and even after she'd broken his wrist and locked his medic in a closet.

"Well, that's a start, and I'm flattered by your perception of the *Phantom* as a sophisticated piece of machinery. Now let's get dressed and we'll take that trip to Bliss."

Sawyer arranged for the *Phantom*'s refueling while he and Anissa took care of errands on station. Bliss was a multipurpose station, its upper decks filled with apartments and residential hotels, including the one Fitch and Lita shared with their weird vintage android, Enzo, and the residential hotel where Dian and her wife lived. Bliss's lower decks were home to commercial outposts and the biggest array of dry docks in the Quadrant. Sawyer maintained a dock for his own use full time, an expense worth every last cent of scrip. It was a wise investment considering Bliss's facilities were usually full.

An expense worth every last cent, but one that still had to be paid. Bliss wasn't the most expensive station in Rodanta to rent a dock, but it wasn't cheap, either. He transferred the funds to the station at an automated kiosk on dock level, noticing Anissa's eyes widen as the total flashed across the kiosk's monitor. "You're surprised by inflation?"

"No, I'm surprised that Rodantan scrip is still an actual, acceptable form of currency."

"It's used in Laresh, too."

Anissa stared at him, shock written across her features.

"Rodantan scrip and Laresh silbors are both still used," he said. "Come on, let's go to the commercial strip and see what we can download from the library." He tugged at her elbow while she remained rooted to the spot in front of the kiosk. "Anissa?"

She shook her head and offered him a tight smile. "Sorry, let's go."

They boarded a converted freight lift, crowded with other passengers, to Bliss's commercial sector. There was a small Prime University satellite campus there, along with the public library that would, hopefully, offer more information on Dr. Mollon or, at least, bio-longevity.

He watched Anissa out of the corner of his eye while the lift trundled through the station. She looked pensive and a little irritated at the crush of people around her. On impulse, he squeezed her hand, trying to be reassuring. She jumped at the unexpected contact, then squeezed back before letting go.

The lift opened, revealing a lobby dominated by a large stone fountain that was rarely turned on. Today was no exception, and it was surrounded by a group of teenagers who lived on station, laughing and sitting in the wells where the water would usually collect. The fountain was the only decorative feature on Bliss. The rest of the station was plain and utilitarian.

"The public library and satellite campus are on the other side of the station," he said. "It's about a twenty-minute walk, unless you want to take the shuttle."

She gave him a look that clearly questioned his intelligence. "You should know that when it's a choice between getting some exercise and planting my ass on a vehicle with a hundred strangers, I'll always choose the exercise."

"Great, because I hate sharing the shuttle, too."

Most of the crowd made their way to the shuttle stand, and he and Anissa walked along the strip's corridor. It wasn't terribly crowded at this early hour; some shops hadn't yet opened, and cafes and restaurants were still mostly empty. "Why do you live on the *Phantom*?" Anissa asked.

"Slightly cheaper rent and more freedom."

"How much does it cost to rent an apartment on Bliss?"

He could see she was tallying up the costs in her head, guesstimating how much it would cost to support herself in this new era. "Depends on where you live on station. I think rents here start around nine hundred scrip biweekly." He mentally calculated the conversion to her home currency. "Uh, around seven hundred and fifty silbors."

"That's... wow. Holy shit, that sounds like a lot."

"Yeah, you can see why I live on the ship." Truth was, Sawyer *could* pay rent on a decent apartment, he just didn't want to. He could do whatever he wanted on board the *Phantom* and had a great deal more privacy. He wasn't nearly as social as Lita and Fitch and having to be polite to neighbors on a daily basis ranked high on his list of personal hells.

And now he had a roommate. He sneaked a look at her. He doubted that she would be nosy and barge into his cabin at weird hours, as his undergrad housemates or Lita were prone to. If one had to share close quarters with another, a former soldier who kept to herself was probably the closest he could get to an ideal roommate.

If she earned a pilot's license, he could hire her on. It would certainly be helpful for short-haul research missions, and he wouldn't be as dependent on Fitch, who worked on the *Phantom* around his wife's academic schedule and that of his freelance gigs. Having a copilot would make traveling through jumpspace a little safer, too.

He didn't mention that as they strode through Bliss's corridors to the public library. Sawyer pulled a couple of chairs up to one of the monitors and logged in to his account while Anissa watched. He removed a memory key from his pants pocket and plugged it in to download everything he could about bio-longevity.

"What about Dr. Mollon?" Anissa asked, reading over his shoulder.

"There isn't that much about him." Sawyer blew out a frustrated breath. "We'll definitely have to take that trip to Laresh." He ran another search on Vicora Alto and was both frustrated and unsurprised at the lack of information. Judging from Anissa's stiff posture and downturned mouth, she was, too.

"Is it even worth it to check the university archives?"

Sawyer nodded. "I think so." Of course, his father would probably send another irate transmit wanting to know why he was researching the history of bio-longevity when he was supposed to be reviewing course syllabi for his teaching next semester, but he could just delete it. Devon King's pestering and interfering were among the reasons he wanted to make the trip to Laresh, just to leave him behind for another few hours.

And who knew, maybe one of the universities in the Laresh System was looking for an archaeologist with his experience, and he could stop working for Prime, and his father, once and for all.

With volumes of information downloaded to the memory key, he and Anissa stood up, ready to leave the library and try the university next. He had a sinking feeling he was running into another dead end, and knew Anissa felt the same, but as he'd told her, it was still worth a shot.

"Maybe it would be best to just go to the authorities,"

Anissa said, but she sounded unconvinced. "I'm sure we're breaking at least a couple of laws by not reporting that I was found."

The thought had occurred to Sawyer, but he wasn't aware of any laws they could be breaking. "If anyone broke the law, it was Dr. Mollon. I'm obligated to report my findings on independent research trips to the university according to my contract, but I don't have to do so immediately. And," he said, "I don't consider you an artifact. Just putting that out there."

"And you don't want to deal with the media."

"That, too. And I doubt you want newshounds annoying the shit out of you, either."

"You're right. I don't."

She was quiet for the rest of the walk to the satellite campus. Sawyer identified himself as an employee at the main entrance's palm and retinal locks, then entered a security code that would let him admit a guest.

He hesitated when the computer asked him his guest's name. Should he use Anissa's real one or make something up?

According to the history records, she didn't even exist. He keyed in *Anissa Alto* and waited for a message from the terminal.

Please enter guest's handprint and retinal scan.

He breathed a sigh of relief. "Stand still," he said, moving aside so she could face the scanners. "It just wants to know who you are."

"My ID chip won't make alarms go off?"

"Only one way to find out." He doubted it would though.

She mimicked his earlier movements, placing her hand on one scanner and widening her eyes for the other. Sawyer knew he'd guessed correctly when neither klaxons nor security personnel heralded their arrival. She blinked at the bright flash of the retinal scanner, the locks clicked, and the door cycled open.

The satellite campus's lobby was quiet, save for a piped-in delicate piano piece Sawyer couldn't identify. He headed straight for Archives, Anissa alongside him.

What if all of this was for nothing?

He pushed aside that thought. If nothing else, he would help her start a new life in Rodanta. He would fund a professional investigation into the murders of her mother and the *Spindle*'s crew if he had to.

The archives' doors opened at their approach, and they walked in. Anissa paused, her boots frozen to the floor as she gazed around the cavernous room in shock. Sawyer waited, a smile playing across his lips.

"My gods!" she said. "This is a *satellite* campus library? What does the main campus look like?"

The Prime University archives, at all campuses, were among the very few places in the Quadrant that still stocked physical books. Thousands of them lined the shelves, taken from possibly every era in time and every known culture throughout the universe with a written alphabet. Some of them were kept in temperature-controlled cases; many more were free to be plucked from their shelves and held, read and revered.

But the archives' book collection wasn't why Sawyer was here. He doubted that anything he and Anissa would find useful could be found in one—ever-efficient Lareshi scholars had always preferred paperless recordkeeping—but the university computers still held some promise. There were some things one simply could not access from his ship, no matter what kind of authorization he held.

The archives room was already starting to fill up with students and instructors, so he and Anissa found a terminal at the opposite end of the room, away from everyone else. Once again Sawyer logged in to the system and executed searches in the university's databases.

This time, a piece on Crale Mollon appeared. He felt Anissa grip his arm as she moved closer to the screen, reading the information there. But it wasn't just birth and presumed death dates. There were journal articles he had authored about bio-longevity and its applications in patients with chronic or terminal illnesses, and other ones on gene manipulation.

"Son of a bitch," Anissa said over his shoulder. Her voice was low, tinged with anger. "Look at the publication dates."

Sawyer did so, then turned to her for clarification.

"Those were published after he launched Vine on the *Spindle*." Her voice shook. "Open the last article, Sawyer."

He did. "Can you download all of this?" she asked. "Send it to the ship?"

"Doubtful. The university's a bit touchy about intellectual property. But I can print it." He sent the journal articles and Dr. Mollon's biography to one of the archives' printers. "What is it?"

"That's my mother's research." Anissa's nails dug into Sawyer's arm, then just as quickly, she released him. "Sorry about that."

"Don't worry about it." It hadn't hurt. "Are you *sure* that's your mother's research?"

"You mean, how would a dumb soldier know anything about genetic manipulation?" Her eyes never left the screen as she read the article.

"No, and you're not a dumb soldier."

"I appreciate the sentiment, but I'm also not a scientist. Look, Vicora talked about this with me. She talked about it with the whole crew. She was the first person to theorize the manipulations of those enzymes and kinases to extend humanoid lifespans in the Laresh population. We already lived a little longer than Rodantans, and she knew it wasn't because of diet or lifestyle or anything like that." Her dark eyes shone.

"It was genes, and she was going to do exactly what Dr. Mollon has with this research."

"Well, it says that he died before he could do anything more with it."

She shook her head. "Shuttle accident, right. No, I don't think he died then. Maybe he's dead now, but his dying then would be way too convenient for everyone. I think we need to go to Laresh and do more research there. It says in his biography that he was interested in cybernetics before anyone else was. There may be some of his work in the archives there because it certainly isn't here."

Sawyer sent a few more journal articles that mentioned Mollon to the printer. At this point, it was probably redundant and a waste of money and paper printing everything, but it couldn't hurt to have everything pertaining to him in their possession. "We'll go today," he said. "As soon as the ship's refueled." A trip to the Laresh System, especially for research purposes, also meant he had an excuse to dodge communication attempts from his father. That alone, almost made the trip worth it.

Almost. His eyes fixed on Anissa, still reading the words marching across the monitor. She'd been dealt a terrible hand in life, and while he knew that nothing he could do would right what had gone wrong, he could still help her out. He could be her friend. He doubted she'd had many in her old life —she was too disciplined, too in-control. She was, and he suspected always would be, a soldier first.

And his friend second, he hoped.

Bliss Station was fully awake when they returned to the commercial strip. Sawyer's stomach grumbled, reminding him that he hadn't had much in the way of breakfast and nothing in the way of drinkable coffee, and he wondered if Anissa felt hungry too. "Want to get something to eat?"

She shrugged, her expression thoughtful. She held the folder of printouts to her chest. "I could do with another cup of coffee."

He paid for coffees and pastries at a kiosk, and they sat down on a bench facing a clothing shop, which reminded Sawyer of something else. "We'll stop in there before we go to Laresh. I told you I'd get you some clothes," he said, gesturing toward the store with his berry pastry.

She looked across the corridor to the shop, unease on her face. "You don't have to..."

"I know I don't, but I will. You need things that I don't have in the *Phantom*'s storage lockers, and we're here. Prices are reasonable on Bliss. They aren't on the border stations."

"I really don't feel comfortable with you spending that kind of money on me."

"Consider it an advance on your wages, then," he said.

She raised a dark eyebrow at him, waiting for him to explain.

"I'll hire you," he said. "Um, apprentice pilot, room and board included in your salary and a financial stipend. Would that make you feel better?"

That coaxed a smile out of her. "Like in the military and when I was on the *Spindle*, although I was also security there." Her expression grew serious. "*Please* tell me you have security measures in place and at least one weapon."

"The *Phantom* is equipped with a laser cannon and there's a stocked weapons locker on board," he said. Dian's warning about keeping the weapons out of Anissa's reach ran through his mind, but he pushed it aside. He seriously doubted Anissa was a threat to anyone on board the *Phantom*.

"Good, I was a little worried about that, what with your converting the brig into a luxury spa and all."

"Have you been talking to Dian behind my back? Because she's said almost the exact same thing."

"I'm starting to regret locking her in that closet more and more. We really got off on the wrong foot. It sounds like we have a lot in common."

Sawyer took a final swallow of his coffee and immediately wished he had more. "Next mission we take, you can tell her that."

***

She felt better about letting Sawyer pay for stuff when it was really her own money. An advance on her wages, he'd called it. She felt pleased at the prospect of being employed and of having the chance to regain her independence.

Still, Anissa disliked shopping.

The store Sawyer picked out carried something of everything, so Anissa chose a practical wardrobe: pants and shirts and a generic gray shipsuit for those times she needed to look like an employee. Some socks and underwear—Sawyer looked away, cheeks pinkening, as she draped those items over her arm—and a sturdy pair of boots. Practical and when she tested the fabric, well-made. The Rodantan Quadrant had clearly improved their goods production since she was put into stasis.

She added shampoo and soap to her pile of new things, and a pair of shears to cut her hair to a more manageable length. She gave up trying to tally the cost and how long it would take before she would start earning wages again, and let Sawyer pay for everything at the shop's automated kiosk without saying a word.

She waited until they left. "Thank you."

"For this? You're more than welcome. I told you before,

this is the least I can do. I didn't think you'd want to run around in oversized men's pants for long."

Sawyer checked in with station control when they reached dock level, receiving confirmation that the *Phantom* was refueled, and her water reserves replenished. Anissa took her new things to her cabin, folding and putting everything away, before finding him in the office off the bridge.

Lita's face filled the transmit screen in front of him, and she and Sawyer seemed deep in conversation. "Are you really sure you can hand-fly the *Phantom* to Laresh on your own?" she was asking. "If you can put off the trip until next week, Fitch and I can come with you."

"We'll be in jump for over half the trip."

"Yeah, I know, but what if there's an emergency? There's a reason copilots are recommended when you're in jump."

"I'm not going to do something stupid like force the ship out of jump before we get to the exit gate. I've taken the ship through a jumpgate alone before."

Lita looked only slightly mollified at that reminder. "Not on a trip of this length. At least let me loan you Enzo."

"No!" Sawyer looked perturbed at the idea.

Who, or what, was Enzo? Anissa crept a little closer to the office. Lita saw her and waved. "Hi, Commander."

Even though she wasn't a soldier anymore, and she'd asked Sawyer and his crew to just call her by her first name, the reminder of her old life still sent a warm, wistful feeling through her. She'd earned that rank. "Hi."

Lita looked at her expectantly. "Could you tell Sawyer that it would make more sense if he waited until next week to go to Laresh or, failing that, if he borrowed our android to act as copilot?"

Ah, Enzo was an android then. "Does Enzo talk?"

"See?" Sawyer looked at Lita triumphantly. "She doesn't like talking androids, either."

Actually, Anissa didn't mind them as long as they were useful, but she didn't get a chance to point that out before Lita spoke again.

"Fitch fixed him. He doesn't babble nearly as much as he used to, and the voice issue is taken care of. Look, I'm not trying to be difficult. It's just that even though you know what you're doing, and even though you've flown through jumpspace before, it wouldn't hurt to have backup."

"She's right," Anissa said to Sawyer. "Right now, I'm not going to be of much use to you if something goes wrong." When Sawyer opened his mouth to protest, she held up a hand, cutting him off. "We both want to know more about Dr. Mollon, and going to Laresh is our best bet at finding out what happened to him. But not at the expense of your safety."

Or his research. Both were precious to scientists as she knew well.

Sawyer exhaled noisily, and Lita smiled, knowing she'd won this fight. "I'll send Enzo to the dock in half an hour," she said.

"Do you *promise* that Fitch fixed him?"

"He's still a wicked trivia player, but yes. Fitch installed the shuttle program into him, too, so you'll have a chauffeur if you and Anissa decide to hit up the pubs while you're there."

"Unlikely," Anissa said at the same moment Sawyer said, "No."

"I'm not paying someone to pour me drinks I can pour myself," Sawyer added. His brow furrowed, and he changed the subject. "I still haven't told anyone about Anissa's existence. We're going to do some more research in Laresh, and then we'll go to the authorities. She's convinced that the guy who did this to her is still alive."

"Anything's possible," Lita said.

It pleased Anissa to know she had another ally in the xeno-archaeologist. "The timing of his shuttle accident is too convenient to be a coincidence," Anissa said. "We have all the journal articles he wrote about bio-longevity and *everything* is stolen from my mother's research." A familiar bubble of rage welled up inside her, and she had to force herself to keep her voice level. "He was working in cybernetics around the same time. If what I've read about cybernetics is true, it can extend someone's lifespan just as bio-longevity was theorized to. I want hard evidence before I accept that he's really dead."

"Shuttle accident," Sawyer said. "He would have been blown to pieces. There'd be no evidence."

"I don't believe that."

"Benedict," Lita said, a warning undercurrent to her voice. "Listen to her and listen to me. This whole situation is so bugshit insane that what Anissa's saying is totally possible. None of us expected to find a hibernating soldier when we were looking for the Immortal Spacefarer's treasure. It's been a very bizarre couple of days. Take Enzo with you, keep in touch with Dian and us, and do what you need to at the university in Laresh Seat."

"Fine." Sawyer ran a hand over his face, a gesture Anissa now recognized as one of defeat. Despite her anger at Dr. Mollon, she bit back a smile. "Tell Enzo to get to the dock. I'll file a flight plan with station control, and we'll start off for Laresh in an hour or so."

"Great! Oh, you transferred our wages, right? Rent's due next week."

Sawyer rolled his eyes. "You mean, when will I pay you? I'll transfer the funds to you before we leave."

"I appreciate that. How did your meeting with your father go, by the way?"

Irritation flitted across his face at the mention of his father. "He wants me to teach a couple of intro courses next semester. Pretty much demanded it, in fact."

"Ugh. I hate teaching, especially the intro courses. None of the students have any fucks to give."

"Your turn is probably coming up. And sooner than you'd like, since you're one of my friends."

Lita made a face in response, then brightened. "I'll find a way out of it. I always do. Look, I'll send over Enzo now." She made an exaggerated kissy face at the screen. "Fitch and I send our regards and good luck to both of you."

CHAPTER 7

THE SQUEAKY GRINDING of wheels on the bare dock floor made Sawyer cringe. Without turning around, he knew exactly what was coming toward him.

"Hello, Sawyer!" Enzo's voice had been reprogrammed to be deeper, his obnoxious high pitch, thankfully, removed. Enzo would keep talking until Sawyer acknowledged him. He didn't trust that Lita or Fitch had taken care of Enzo's endless-chattering issue.

"How goes it, Enzo?"

"It's just wonderful, Sawyer! I have new feet and new programs! Have you learned the ancient dialect of the Pelishcans?"

"Can't say that I have, Enzo. Pelishca isn't in my field of expertise."

"Would you care to learn?"

The android was still an excessive talker. "Not really."

"I've also learned two new card games. Would you care for me to teach you?"

Damn you, Lita. Damn you, Fitch. Is this your idea of a sick joke? New voice, old personality. "Damn it, we're going to be in jumpspace together."

"Sawyer? Did I miss something?"

"No. Enzo, I need you to copilot for a trip to Laresh Seat. Can you do that?"

"Of course! Piloting is one of my favorite things to do, Sawyer!"

"You'll also be teaching someone to pilot while we're in jump. Okay?"

"Of course! I enjoy teaching!"

If Enzo was already irritating the hell out of him, the android was going to drive Anissa to murder. Probably Enzo, possibly Lita and Fitch.

It was going to be a long time in jumpspace.

Anissa waited on the *Phantom* while the ship's water was replenished. In some strange way, she was looking forward to seeing Laresh Seat again, even though she knew it would have drastically altered in her absence. She wanted to see the Seat, and she needed to see Crale Mollon brought to justice.

She *knew* the sneaky bastard was still alive, could feel it in her bones.

She felt the vibration of doors closing belowdecks, and a few minutes later she heard Sawyer call out, "Anissa? You ready to go?"

"Yeah." She shut the closet door and walked out of her cabin to the bridge. A silvery, metallic-skinned android, the back of its head completely smooth, was parked in the copilot's seat. At the sound of footsteps, it turned toward her and stood up on wheeled feet, revealing its oversized T-shirt that read *GALAXY'S GREATEST SEX MACHINE!*

"You must be Commander Anissa Alto!" It half-slid, half-stepped over to her and grabbed her hand, pumping it up and down. "I'm ever so pleased to meet you! Please call me Enzo!" Its comically oversized eyes flashed a little as it scanned her face, memorizing her features. Its mouth was vaguely humanoid but moved like a puppet's, out of sync with its words.

This was Lita and Fitch's idea of a copilot? Its grip on Anissa's hand was nearly crushing. "Yes, I'm Anissa. Um, my hand."

Enzo immediately let go. "My apologies, Commander Alto! Would you care to learn a new card game while we're in jumpspace together? Or perhaps a new language?"

"I—"

"Enzo, we're good." Sawyer strode onto the bridge, irritation at the android's presence evident on his face. "We're cleared for departure in five minutes. Enzo, take a seat and we'll run through the preflight checklist."

"Of course! I was simply introducing myself to Commander Alto!"

"I thought Fitch fixed your rambling problem."

"I never had a rambling problem, Sawyer. I'm a D2800 Envoy model, sir. I am programmed to aid in a variety of activities, including, but not limited to, piloting, ship repairs, entertainment..."

"Yeah, I know. Enzo, seat, now. *Please.*"

"Yes, Sawyer."

He and Enzo sat down, and Sawyer powered up the *Phantom*'s engines. Anissa waited by the comm console and listened as Sawyer spoke to station control, waiting for clearance to depart.

"Did Enzo have a disobedience problem before that hasn't been corrected yet, too?" Anissa asked.

"Not really," Sawyer said.

The android piped up, unperturbed as usual. "I'm always obedient."

"It's sort of a delayed reaction," Sawyer continued. "And it's annoying as all hell. Lita and Fitch did this on purpose."

"Did what?" Enzo's voice sounded almost curious. "They were quite eager to see me help you."

"And if we run into problems while we're in jump or Laresh, we'll be glad of the help," Anissa said, trying to keep the peace. She wouldn't be surprised if Enzo had some kind of emotional programming, and the android's feelings, or what passed for them, could be hurt, and she wasn't experienced enough with his model to test out that possibility. Cranky androids did not make for pleasant company.

"Enzo, you'll be helping me teach Commander Alto the ins and outs of piloting the *Phantom* on our trip," Sawyer said.

"Really?" The android sounded excited, and Anissa couldn't tell if it was due to emotional programming or a canned response to an order. "I look forward to it!"

A voice from the comm console halted any further conversation. "*Phantom*, you're cleared for departure in two minutes. Enjoy your time in Laresh."

"Acknowledged," Sawyer said. They could faintly hear the blare of a warning klaxon in the station dock, then the bay's safety lights flashed red through the viewscreen as its sensors scanned for life forms. There was an audible clunk that reverberated through the bridge as the *Phantom* detached from Bliss Station's airlock, and then the old freighter was flying.

"Enzo, please give Commander Alto your seat," Sawyer said.

A thrill shot through Anissa at the thought of being in command of a ship again, even if she was only the copilot. Enzo rose from his seat, metallic joints creaking. He moved to stand beside Sawyer.

Anissa sat down and stared at the console in front of her.

It was smooth and sleek under her hands, marred by smudged fingerprints. There was a set of manual controls between the two pilots' seats, and Sawyer saw her eyeing them. "I only hand-fly this bucket if I have to," he said. She nodded.

"I'm sending a mirror of what I'm doing over to your side," he said. She watched as the panel lit up, a star chart's winking lights outlining the *Phantom*'s course. "That big purple light is the Kenwell Jumpgate." The chart shifted, and the purple light coalesced into a thick line, smaller blue points radiating from it. "That's jumpspace, with the Laresh System at the exit. Or close to the border, anyway. The exit is technically non-affiliated space."

Anissa nodded. The star chart shifted again, and a blue dot representing the *Phantom* glided across it toward the bigger purple one. An alert popped up in the corner of the screen, then quickly disappeared as Sawyer disregarded it.

"Mail," he said when Anissa looked over at him quizzically. "We just passed the last comm beacon before we hit jump. I'll open it when we're in jump, and I'm not able to reply immediately."

It was probably from his father. She didn't press the subject.

"I can set up a training protocol for Commander Alto while we're in jumpspace," Enzo said, sounding delighted at the prospect.

"That was the plan, Enzo."

"Excellent! We can..."

"Enzo, *please*." Exasperation colored Sawyer's words, but Anissa was sure that was more likely due to the correspondence the ship picked up than the overly chatty android.

She stole a quick glance at Enzo, still standing next to the copilot's seat. He was talkative, yes, but Anissa found she didn't mind it. It was nice to have someone or something pleasant around, even if it was powered by artificial intelligence.

The control panel pinged. "Strap in," Sawyer said. "We're hitting jump in four minutes. Enzo, find something to hold on to."

"I can activate the magnetic force in my feet," Enzo said. "I will remain immobile while we enter jumpspace."

"Great, Enzo, do that, please."

Anissa raked the seat's safety harness over her shoulders and hips. "Thank you, Enzo."

"You're more than welcome, Commander."

The ship shuddered, and Anissa gripped her seat's armrests. Sawyer tapped at his console, and the ship's computer announced that the hyperspace engines were engaged and repeated a safety warning about being buckled in. Even so, the force of the *Phantom* being sucked into the jumpgate had Anissa plastered to the back of her seat; her breath ripped from her lungs by the unfamiliar sensation.

A minute later, it was over. The hyperspace engines purred faintly beneath her feet, but the violent tossing of the ship had stopped, and if she hadn't known better, Anissa might have thought the *Phantom* was stranded in space.

Ah, jumpspace. The laziest and most relaxed part of travel. There was something liberating about being cut off from the rest of the universe.

Sawyer unbuckled his harness and stood up, and Anissa did likewise. "Enzo, you keep an eye on the computer," he said. "We're going to put together a plan for when we arrive in Laresh. We'll be in the lounge. Let us know if anything goes wrong."

"But Sawyer, I'm supposed to teach Commander Alto how to fly."

"And you'll do that, but we have some other stuff to do right now."

"I see." Did the android sound disappointed? Anissa sort of felt sorry for the machine.

"Soon, Enzo," she said.

His oversized eyes flashed; his version of happiness, she guessed. "I look forward to it!"

<hr>

"We'll be in jump for the next fourteen hours," Sawyer said as they walked into the lounge.

"What's your problem with Enzo?" Anissa asked, sidestepping his comment.

"Besides him being annoying as shit? I'm surprised you haven't deactivated him yet."

"Nah, I like androids. He's certainly friendly."

Sawyer flopped onto the couch. "I thought you'd find him irritating, actually. I'm surprised."

She shrugged. "Androids can be better companions than people sometimes. I'm sure he'll be a very thorough teacher. What's his story, anyway?"

"Yeah, that's the problem. He's a modified D2800 Envoy, so he was originally programmed to make conversation with difficult people. Fitch and Lita like vintage stuff and fell in love with him at an auction we all went to a couple of years ago. I think he was owned by a couple of diplomats twenty or thirty years ago."

"So, he uses enough outdated technology that a complete retrofit isn't practical."

"Exactly. Fitch installed some programs, so he legally qualifies as a copilot, and he dumped a bunch of schematics for different ships in him, too. He can make basic exterior repairs in zero-g and plot a course. He's a very good instructor, although his favorite thing to teach seems to be card games and languages. He's useful, just really obnoxious."

"And the T-shirt?"

"Lita's idea of a joke. Or Fitch's, it could be either. D2800 Envoy models aren't *that* accommodating." He sighed. "I think the 'improvement' Lita was talking about was the language update. I don't have any use for learning an ancient Pelishcan dialect." He ran a hand through his hair, aggravation evident on his features. "Anissa, I'm sorry. I'm not mad at you or Enzo or anyone. I'm just frustrated and trying not to take it out on either of you. And I know I probably shouldn't be feeling like this given that I'm not the one that was dug out of a pit on an uninhabited planet, but..."

"But you do," Anissa finished.

"I just want to get to Laresh and see if there's any evidence pointing to Dr. Mollon," he said. "Then I want to go to the authorities and get you set up as a Rodantan citizen."

"Not until we've found Mollon."

"*If* we find Mollon."

"We will." Anissa fixed her best commander stare on him. "Now, what do we do while we're in jump?"

"Let Enzo do what he likes to do best—teach you the basics of flying a converted freighter."

"What about you?"

"Open that transmit from my father and probably start studying course syllabi for the classes I'm going to be roped into teaching."

He sounded so despondent, and Anissa was unsure how she could cheer him up, or even if he wanted her to. She wasn't going to stick around the lounge and watch him mope though. She'd only known him a couple of days, but she couldn't figure out why he tolerated his father's treatment of him, and why he just didn't leave the university for another post; current academic privileges be damned. Being that stressed out over something that could be fixed wasn't healthy.

But she didn't have to wallow along with him. Anissa got

up and went back to the bridge where Enzo sat in the pilot's seat. He immediately rose on squeaky joints when he heard her.

"Commander! So good to see you!"

"I'm ready to start my flying lessons, Enzo."

"Excellent, Commander. Which ships have you piloted before? I can modify our lessons to your prior experience."

"Enzo, my experience was on ships that were dismantled and sold for scrap decades before you were built."

His eyes blinked. "I don't understand, Commander."

Now it was Anissa's turn to sigh. Enzo would undoubtedly flood her with questions as soon as she told him what she used to pilot. "I was enlisted during the Laresh Civil War, fighting for the Empire, and then I was a pilot and security chief aboard my mother's research vessel. I've flown Glazers, Sunspot-2200s, and a clunky old Thessa 800." The last one was the *Spindle*.

Enzo stared at her, and she wished she could know how his circuits were processing her words in his metallic head.

"Commander," he said. "I've analyzed those ships, and none of them were manufactured within the last fifty years."

"Yeah, I know."

"The civil war in Laresh ended over one hundred years ago."

"I know that, too. I'm the oldest thing on this ship."

"Are you a cyborg, Commander?"

"No, I was put into stasis for a hundred years," she said. "Sawyer dug me up a few days ago."

"Well, Commander, it seems I could have much to learn from you rather than the other way around."

"And I'll tell you all about what it was like to grow up in Laresh Seat before the war, but right now, I'd just like to learn a little about piloting." She sat down in the copilot's seat.

"Of course! Let's begin. I'm afraid I only have the barest

schematics for those ships you've told me about, the most information being on the Thessa 800. It utilized a jumpdrive that served as a predecessor for the one the *Phantom* uses. But we'll begin with a simulation program, so you can learn how to start the *Phantom*'s engines."

Anissa followed the android's directions as the simulator popped up on her screen, surprised at how easily she was able to follow the ship's schematics. If only finding Dr. Mollon would be so easy.

CHAPTER 8

SAWYER PUT the printouts and notes he'd made about Anissa and Dr. Mollon in a tidy stack, not even bothering to try to make sense of the clusterfuck he currently found himself in. Instead, he picked up his datapad and reluctantly found himself scrolling through Prime's recommended syllabi for the introductory courses he may very well end up teaching next semester, should he not find another position in time. Or talk his father out of it.

He gave up on reading faster than he expected, finally putting the datapad down as well. Attempts at concentration were futile.

He checked in with Enzo on the bridge and was unsurprised to see that the *Phantom* was doing just fine in jumpspace, just as he'd told Lita and Fitch. The converted freighter handled well in jump; hell, she'd handled well in most every situation Sawyer had put her through. She was an old ship but not decrepit. After declining an offer to play a round of cards with Enzo, he decided to work out some of his frustration in the ship's sim chamber.

He changed into workout gear and made his way to the former brig to find a towel and water bottle already sitting outside the sim chamber. He pressed the chamber's alert button to let her know he was there and waited. The last thing he wanted to do was barge in while she was naked in an underwater sim or something.

Well... that wouldn't be an unpleasant sight; just wildly inappropriate and incredibly creepy on his part.

But the alert indicator didn't change color from red to green, to let him know it was okay for him to come in. He belatedly realized she might not know how to use it. *Damn.*

He activated the door controls and walked into the chamber. He was immediately assaulted with the thick, stinking heat of a jungle and he had to fight the urge to crumple to the muddy, squishy floor with the increased gravity. It was even difficult to breathe.

"Sawyer? That you?"

He gave in and slid to the floor, an unwelcome heaviness settling into his limbs. "Huunnhh," he managed to say.

"This is an amazing sim." Anissa appeared above him, in the branches of a tree draped in bright blue moss. "It reminds me of the De'hai Rainforest in Laresh Seat's southern hemisphere, but not quite so hot."

Sawyer took a deep breath of humid, dirty-tasting air. "How the hell did you get up there?"

"I've been playing with gravity controls during my workout."

"Controls, now," he said, his voice a couple decibels louder. A holodisplay immediately appeared in front of him, and he tabbed down the gravity by twenty percent before closing the control panel. Sawyer could now stand up without feeling pinned to the floor.

Anissa nimbly climbed down the tree, dropping off the lowest hanging branch, a good two meters off the ground. She landed on her feet, graceful as one of the animals that probably lived in the real-life De'hai Rainforest. "What did you do that for?"

"Because I can't breathe or stand when the gravity's that high."

Anissa shook the hem of her black sleeveless shirt, trying to cool down a little. "I like it a little more intense when I'm running through simulated jungles."

"You couldn't punch clowns with Dian's program?"

"Oh, that. I tried it." A shudder rippled through her. "I wasn't afraid of clowns before, but I am now. It sort of defeats the purpose." She paused. "Where's your shirt?"

"I'd planned on doing a boxing sim, so… still in my cabin."

"I see." Was that a look of appreciation in her dark eyes? Sawyer couldn't tell. "Don't let me get in your way."

"You're done with the Laresh jungle?"

"Pretty much. Box away."

Sawyer brought up the control holodisplay again and scrolled through the programs, settling on his current favorite: an old-fashioned underground boxing ring in the style of twentieth-century Earth, complete with cigar and whiskey-scented air and spectators who cheered his every move, even when he fell flat on his ass. Which didn't happen as much as it used to.

Anissa looked around the sim chamber, mild amusement on her face. The computer-generated spectators ignored her per their programming, focusing only on Sawyer and his simulated opponent. The figures waited for the match to begin, drinks in dirty glasses clutched in their hands. The sim was a giant of a man whose strength Sawyer kept on par with his own for safety reasons. He wasn't sure how much help Enzo could be if he ended up breaking bones in the ring.

Sawyer hoisted himself into the ring, ducking underneath the ropes. "Mind if I stick around?" Anissa asked.

"Not at all."

"On a scale of one to ten, how likely is it that you're going to have your ass handed to you right now?"

His opponent swayed on his feet, waiting for the order to start fighting. "I win about half the time," Sawyer said. He flexed his hands. "The program's set for medium strength, ten-minute rounds. It's a decent workout if you want to try it sometime."

"No gloves?"

Sawyer gave her a withering look. She sat down in an empty seat beside the ring and stretched out her legs, waiting for an answer and possibly to see Sawyer have his ass handed to him. "This is an *underground* ring," he said, gesturing around the dimly lit space. "Bare hands only." Its safety features were also activated, and the opponent was programmed not to direct any punches at the user's head, but he didn't mention that.

"So, an illegal boxing match." She sat up a little straighter. "Let's say I have forty silbors riding on you, Sawyer. Don't make me regret it."

He shot her a quick smile and started the program.

The spectators sprang to life, and a referee walked into the ring, whistle at the ready. Sawyer swatted at the character and he disappeared, and then he and his opponent faced each other.

Sawyer threw the first strike, and the opponent quickly followed with his own. Then he forgot all about Dr. Mollon and what waited—or didn't—for them at Laresh Seat, and just focused on staying on his feet.

A referee materialized when Sawyer pinned down his opponent, declaring him the winner of that round. He saw Anissa clapping along with the rest of the sim's spectators, and she shouted over the din, "Another one? I have another forty on that."

Sawyer paused the program for a moment and brought up

the control holodisplay. He increased his opponent's strength by five percent and closed the controls. "I didn't peg you as having a gambling habit."

She shrugged. "Soldiers need something to do during downtime. I'll probably be taking up Enzo on his offer of a card game at some point."

Ah, good old Enzo and his never-ending quest to find a fellow cardsharp.

Sawyer won the second round with his opponent, but it tougher to do so. He hit the mat more than once this time and knew that Anissa's gasps weren't feigned. Still, when the referee announced Sawyer as the winner again, he winked at his lone living spectator, savoring the pleasant ache in his muscles. "Is your bookie going to pay up?"

"Only if you win the third round. Double or nothing. I'll split the winnings with you."

"Watch me."

The third round was the most difficult, made more so by the fact Sawyer wasn't used to being watched. His opponent pinned him to the mat twice, and both times Sawyer only just managed to launch himself to his feet before the referee declared the computer the winner. By the time Sawyer won the round, every muscle in his body screamed for him to stop, and he was ready to fall asleep in the ring.

The crowd roared at his victory, not caring that he slithered out of the ring and into a seat next to Anissa. "Let's go have a celebratory steak dinner with your winnings," he said.

"*Our* winnings."

"Fine. I like mine rare and accompanied with a shot of Laresh whiskey, neat."

"So you're a decent boxer and have good taste in whiskey, then."

"Yeah." He finally caught his breath and rubbed his

shoulder where the opponent had landed a particularly hard punch during the final round. "But I'll have to settle for a sandwich in the lounge, and whatever open bottle of wine Lita left behind." He brought up the control panel again and ended the sim. The underground boxing ring disappeared, replaced with the smooth-paneled walls of the chamber.

The door opened for them and they walked into the converted brig. Sawyer saw Anissa give the soaker tub a longing look, and he gestured to it. "Try it out."

"Are you sure?"

"Go ahead. It's one of the reasons I had the water stores replenished when we were at Bliss. Just have the water recycled when you're done."

"But don't you want to use it?"

He shook his head. "Another time."

Anissa was already at the tub, filling it with water. Sawyer took that as a cue to exit, giving her some privacy. "I won't be long," she said. "Save some of that wine for me."

"Will do."

Shoulder aching, he left the brig.

Anissa enjoyed a decadent soak in the tub, unable to remember the last time she'd enjoyed such a luxury. The *Spindle*, her last home before she was put into stasis, hadn't had any such amenities.

A wry smile crossed her face at the memory of Sawyer wiping the floor with his opponent in the boxing sim. She would never have guessed that the quiet archaeologist had a violent streak in him, nor would she have guessed that he looked that great without a shirt on. *That* had been the most surprising part of their time in the sim chamber, and her face heated at the thought.

She *really* shouldn't be thinking of her rescuer, and employer, in such a way, even though she didn't feel as guilty about it as she probably should. His irritability aside—and she could look past that, as he'd had a lot to worry about, even before she showed up—he had proved to be a good friend to her these last few days; pouring all his energy and time in to an investigation that she knew he didn't think would produce anything useful. He was taking her to the Laresh Empire, just to help her. Sawyer was even tolerating the presence of a talkative android who drove him crazy, just for her.

That devotion, and that he looked good while half-dressed, involuntarily piqued Anissa's interest. She'd dealt with shell-shocked survivors during the war, saw how some of them became infatuated with soldiers who'd rescued them, and she knew that was probably the case here. Her hormones were responding inappropriately to someone that was not only the first single man she'd encountered in over a century, but also one that helped revive her from stasis.

This will pass, she told herself. *It's just a passing fancy, and it'll end soon.*

She hoped she was right about that, or things had the potential to get very awkward very quickly.

She reluctantly climbed out of the tub when the water grew cold and sent it to the ship's recyclers. She toweled off and dressed in a loose T-shirt and pants she'd picked out at Bliss Station and made her way to the galley for dinner.

When Anissa walked in, Sawyer was already there; sandwich in hand and a plastic mug on the table. Sawyer pointed to an open bottle of white wine sitting next to his mug on the table. "Help yourself."

She picked out a soup packet from the cupboard and popped it in the food processor, then looked around the galley cabinets for a glass.

"Sawyer?"

"Yeah?"

"What happened to the wineglasses?"

"Oh, you noticed that. We have bad luck with glasses on the *Phantom*. They always end up broken. Mugs are easier."

"Oh." Anissa picked out a pink coffee mug and poured some wine into it. She was about as far from a sommelier as one could get, and to her unpracticed palette, it tasted decent enough.

She sat down opposite Sawyer and stirred her soup. "Everything okay?"

"I should be asking you that."

"I'm feeling good about what we'll find once we're in the Empire. The System," she quickly corrected herself.

"And if you don't find what you hope to?"

Her spoon hovered over the bowl. "Didn't we already talk about this?"

"You're so sure we'll find something that'll tell us more about Mollon."

The flatness in his voice alarmed her at first, but that quickly shifted to anger. "Because I need to check," she said, forcing her voice to remain calm. "I have to make sure. I need this, Sawyer. I don't expect you to understand why."

He ran a hand through his hair. "I don't, and I'm sorry about that."

"Then can we just keep things going as they are?" Anissa hated the pleading tone in her voice but didn't bother to hide it. She knew he was frustrated at the lack of progress in their investigation. His wanting to report finding her and help her move on with her life were gestures of someone who cared, and she appreciated that, but she needed to find out what happened to Dr. Mollon first.

And she was sure as shit the man was still alive somewhere. That shuttle accident was far too convenient.

Sawyer sighed. "Yeah. We'll go to the Seat, do so more

research, and then head back to Rodantan space. We'll get your citizenship sorted out and help you start over." He paused. "I never asked if you wanted to stay in the Rodantan Quadrant or resettle in Laresh."

Was returning to Laresh even a real option? "It doesn't matter," she said softly. "Rodantan space is probably the best place for me to be. I don't have any ties to the Empire anymore."

She'd already cried about that in private. She wasn't going to do it again, especially not in front of Sawyer. There were some things a soldier just didn't do in front of others.

But there was an understanding look on Sawyer's face at her words. Anissa changed the subject a little, not wanting to talk about her mother or the rest of the crew on board the *Spindle*. "I would expect that an archaeologist, especially one who's tracking down the Immortal Spacefarer's treasure, would like a mystery."

"*Trying* to track down."

"You've never told me why you're so obsessed with the *Frexic Galactica*."

"Would you believe me if I told you my mother read it to me when I was a child?"

She nodded. "Of course. Mine did, too. I think every kid in civilized space has a copy."

"This whole operation started when I was working on my master's," he said. "I've known Lita since we were kids, and she introduced me to Fitch when they started dating, and then Dian and her wife, although Tash rarely joins us on missions. She's an obstetrician at the hospital on Bliss and doesn't travel much."

Anissa nodded again, urging him to continue.

"Seriously, it started off as drunk talk," he said. "University pub, bunch of shots, seemed like a good idea. At first, we occasionally rented a couple of smaller ships to conduct digs.

Then I had the means to buy a ship thanks to the inheritance my mother left me, and after I finished my doctorate and was hired at the university, I bought this scow and had her retrofitted for deep-space science missions."

"So you were drinking your troubles away and talking about tracking down the origins of children's stories."

"It beats teaching."

"And have you found anything yet?"

"Yes, but very little related to the *Frexic Galactica*, let alone the Immortal Spacefarer's treasure. And honestly, I'm not sure we'll ever find it. If we find the planet that served as the basis for that story, I'd be happy enough."

"So you don't really think there's a priceless treasure chest just waiting to be discovered?" she asked.

"I haven't decided yet. But I like digging shit up, which is why I became an archaeologist."

"And what happens if you actually *find* the Immortal Spacefarer's treasure?" Anissa pressed.

Sawyer blinked, clearly surprised. "Whatever the university decides to do with it, and then I guess ... move on to something else."

Life without a clear purpose. The very notion drove Anissa nuts.

Enzo's voice over intraship interrupted any further conversation. "Dr. Sawyer, Commander Alto, I have just received notice from the computer that the *Phantom* will be exiting jumpspace in nine hours, should either of you wish to get some sleep before we arrive in Laresh."

Sawyer stood up and drained his mug of wine. "I'm going to do that." He rotated his shoulder, a reminder of his fight in the sim chamber.

Anissa finished her wine, too. "Sleep tight."

When she returned to her cabin and slipped into bed, she replayed their conversation in her mind, trying to decide how she felt about him. At first, his lack of direction in life had been aggravating, but the way he explained it—well, there *was* a point to it. Sawyer liked to wander, and he'd found a way to do to that while still utilizing his education.

The infatuation, the physical attraction, was still there, annoying and persistent. But, she thought as she drifted off, it would soon fade.

At least she hoped it would.

CHAPTER 9

ENZO AND ANISSA handled the jumpspace exit under Sawyer's watch, and as Sawyer expected, the *Phantom* returned to normal space as she usually did: knocked around a little, but otherwise fine. From the jumpgate exit, the ship had another, shorter, journey to Laresh Seat and the university there. The ship passed its first comm beacon since entering jumpspace back in Rodanta, and a flood of transmits kept communications pinging longer than Sawyer would have liked.

He glanced at the senders and was pleased to see only two were from his father. The rest were requests from Lita and Dian for updates, messages from the Seat's transit control approving their flight plan, and a generic one from the Laresh System welcoming them to their space and reminding visitors to abide by System laws and customs. He spent the travel time replying to the mail, even his father's.

Sawyer wasn't going to win when it came to teaching the introductory courses, he knew that now. It would be best to just give in and in doing so, perhaps spare Lita from the same fate, at least a little while longer, and stay on her good side.

It was only thirty or so hours a week for one semester.

Surely, he could manage that. He sent a short, clipped message to his father, agreeing to teach the courses and go to that stupid university fundraiser when he returned to Rodantan space; he wasn't sure which was worse: the fundraiser or the teaching. He'd have to rent a tuxedo and make small talk with dead-eyed strangers for the fundraiser, but first year students didn't have any fucks to give when it came to compulsory introductory courses.

Thirty hours a week teaching bored students, preparing tests and exams to be failed, and marking their subpar, half-assed papers. *Ugh.*

He stayed and watched Enzo and Anissa converse with the university's transit control. Anissa, under Enzo's guidance, directed the *Phantom* to her assigned berth. They'd have to take a short shuttle trip to the university, but Sawyer saw that as an opportunity to continue teaching Anissa to fly.

Despite his doubts about finding more information about Dr. Mollon and Anissa's mother, he couldn't help but feel a bubble of hope on Anissa's part. Her enthusiasm was contagious, even to an irritable, disillusioned bastard like Sawyer. He had to admit, Laresh Seat was the best place to look. The former Empire was crazy about recordkeeping, far more than the too-efficient Rodantans. Laresh First had absorbed Delta-V University, where Dr. Alto and Dr. Mollon once taught; there had to be something other than footnotes there.

If nothing else, Sawyer wanted to justify having Enzo on board. Although, he had to admit that the android wasn't quite as irritating as he used to be. Fitch had taken Sawyer's advice to heart and programmed much of the talkativeness out of him. He did wonder whose idea his T-shirt was. It could go either way with Lita and Fitch.

And Enzo was a good teacher. Or maybe Anissa was a good student. He wasn't sure which yet.

While they waited for the go-ahead from transit control to land the *Phantom*, Sawyer logged in to the university network using his Prime credentials and requested access to Laresh First's archives. The swift reply was an affirmative, and he knew Anissa would be pleased about that. But he still worried about her reaction to the changes that had occurred in Laresh Seat while she was in stasis.

Even though he had no idea what Laresh Seat or the university looked like during her time.

But then, she was shaping up to be far more resilient than he'd originally given her credit for. She would know already that her home wasn't there anymore, but he still felt a curious urge to shield her from the worst of everything that was about to happen. It would really hit her soon that everything she'd known was gone.

Anissa looked up from her controls and turned in her seat, and Sawyer realized he'd been staring at her, at her heavy, dark hair neatly tied back in a braid sitting neatly down her back. Even sitting in the copilot's seat on a battered converted science vessel, she still looked like a soldier: he saw it in the rigidity of her spine, her professional demeanor when responding to Enzo's questions.

Was that a blush tinting her cheeks? She quickly turned back to the controls, and Sawyer looked away.

Transit control granted them permission to dock, and Sawyer collected his notes, ready for more research in the university archives.

They left Enzo on board the *Phantom*, with instructions to recharge for a while, then Sawyer and Anissa took the shuttle to Laresh First University's grounds. Anissa sat in the copilot's seat, watching Sawyer navigate the small craft, occasionally looking out the viewport at the shuttle landing pad below them. She was quiet, and he guessed she was thinking about what waited for them at the university.

He received clearance to land and guided the shuttle to its assigned spot. Once it was on the ground, he shut off the engines and faced Anissa, unsure of how to put his thoughts into words.

She must have picked up on his trepidation because she looked him straight in the eye. "You're worried about me."

He nodded, a little relieved that she'd guessed what he was thinking.

"I promise I won't get angry if we don't find what we're looking for." She unsnapped her safety harness and stood up in the small cockpit. Sawyer picked up his backpack, loaded with notes and his datapad, and slung it over his shoulder.

"I wasn't worried about that." He followed her down the short corridor to the exit ramp and activated the door. "You're an adult, and anyway, I wouldn't blame you if you were angry and sad about this."

"I know you don't think we'll find anything," Anissa said, "but I still have to check."

"I get that. That's why I brought you here. I'm an archaeologist, Anissa. I like mysteries." He quickly corrected himself, realizing how that could be construed. "Not that I see this as just a regular dig, though. I just mean..."

"I think I know what you mean." She shot a quick smile over her shoulder at him. "Sawyer, I'll be fine."

They walked down the ramp into the tropical, balmy air. Laresh Seat was currently enjoying their summer. Thick clouds obscured the Seat's small twin suns, which was normal for the planet. It was always at least a little overcast.

Laresh First University was a sprawling, modern building that had incorporated older structures from the System's military academy over the years. Neither of them said anything when they walked into the university's archives, but he could tell by the set of her shoulders, the stiffness in her back, that she was anxious.

He hoped, desperately, that his predictions were wrong, and that they would find something about Vicora Alto or Crale Mollon today.

Sawyer stopped at a kiosk and booked time in a private room where they could discuss their findings without disturbing other students or faculty or drawing attention to themselves. Once there, he connected his datatab to the archives network and pulled out his sheaf of notes.

Anissa took in the small, windowless space and sat down at the large table opposite him. "I can't believe you still take notes that way."

Sawyer shrugged and then logged in to the network on his datatab. "I never have to worry about system failures with paper notes. I can always find what I need in a few seconds. Plus, there's more privacy. No one can hack into my handwritten notes."

She picked up a notebook and leafed through it. "You have nice handwriting."

"I get a lot of practice."

Sawyer ran the same searches as he had at Prime's satellite library, then waited. He had to resist the urge to drum his fingers on the tabletop and judging from the expression on Anissa's face, she was on the edge of her seat.

His datapad pinged: a positive search result. They both nearly leapt across the table to see the datapad screen.

Bio-Longevity: An Enzyme Theory. Author: Dr. Vicora Alto.

Anissa yelped in happy surprise. "Four Hells, Sawyer, download it!"

"On it." Sawyer paid the access fee—damn the Laresh

System, charging academics for century-old papers—and checked the other search results.

"Well, I'll be damned," he said.

A broad smile spread across Anissa's face as she looked at the screen. "I told you so."

Several papers from Dr. Alto and Dr. Mollon populated the search results, and Sawyer downloaded them all. He keyed in one more search: *Vicora Alto obituary.*

He and Anissa waited, breathlessly, until a short piece from an old newsfeed popped up.

First University geneticist and bio-longevity specialist Dr. Vicora Alto is missing and presumed dead following the systems failure of her research vessel, the Spindle. *The ship's crew perished along with Dr. Alto, including her daughter, former military commander, Anissa Alto. The remains of the* Spindle *were found adrift in space on the Empire-Rodantan border, two weeks after it was reported missing by Dr. Alto's colleague Dr. Crale Mollon, who is also employed by First. Dr. Alto was a pioneer in genetic manipulation for humanoid longevity purposes. She will be greatly missed by the university.*

"Is there anything about what happened to the ship?" Anissa asked.

Sawyer paused before keying in another search. There was no point in sugarcoating what the news piece said. "Yeah, but just that it was found on the border and no one knows how it got there. Systems were dead, and there was a hole in the *Spindle*'s portside hull, no survivors. No flight plan uploaded, either." Anissa was the only crew member whose body was unaccounted for.

Anissa was quiet for a few seconds. When she spoke, her voice was quiet and sad. "I guess my mother's body was on board the *Spindle*."

Vicora Alto's name was at the top of the list of recovered bodies. "Yeah."

She looked away and blinked.

"Anissa, I'm so sorry."

She closed her eyes, and a tear slid down her cheek. The sight tore at Sawyer, but he remained frozen to his seat, unsure if she wanted any comfort right now. "I knew," she said, her voice level. "But I really hoped I was wrong, and she was hibernating in a cave somewhere, too. Is there anything about where she was interred?"

Sawyer searched again. When the results came back, his eyes widened, and his stomach turned over. Anissa immediately picked up that something was wrong. "What is it?"

The situation just got sadder with every new piece of information. "She and the rest of the crew were cremated," he said. "They were interred on Kostish." Even he knew what Kostish was, despite growing up in Rodantan space: a massive cemetery on an uninhabited moon, Laresh's equivalent of a potter's field. Remains were left there, unmarked and unburied, a massive pile of urns and coffins. It had been abandoned years ago.

She was silent for a moment, absorbing this information. "She and the crew were murdered," Anissa said, "and left to rot on a moon. There's not even have a grave or marker to visit."

"Anissa..."

She shook her head and stood up. "I need some time alone."

He stood up as well. "Where will you go?"

"I can find my way back to the shuttle," she said. "I'm not completely helpless. I just need to be alone for a while."

He opened his mouth to say something, but she stopped him before he could speak.

"I'll be back at the shuttle at eighteen hundred hours," she said.

"What if I need to get in touch with you? We don't have comm badges, and you don't have a handheld."

"Sawyer." Her voice had an edge to it he'd never heard before, and he had to resist the urge to shrink back. He saw a glimpse of the power she once wielded over troops. "I need this. Please respect it."

She was about a hundred years out of her element, but she was still a soldier. Sawyer swallowed, and then nodded. "Got it. Eighteen hundred hours at the shuttle, okay?"

Anissa stalked through the university's glass-walled corridors, not making eye contact with of the students or faculty as she passed. She didn't know where she was going, only that she needed to clear her head.

The Laresh Empire military training academy used to be in this part of the grounds, she remembered. Another pang of despair, different from the grief she felt for her mother, but no less painful, gripped her heart.

Sawyer was right. Returning to Laresh was as difficult for her as he'd thought it would be.

She kept on walking, avoiding areas that required retinal or chip scans to enter, which she noticed was most of them. She knew she could easily find her way back to the shuttle landing pad; her sense of direction had always been excellent, and it wasn't like the campus was poorly designed.

Her mother had ended up in a public graveyard. Nothing to commemorate her life or work. Anissa didn't bother asking Sawyer to search for any such commemorations, knowing if her mortal remains had been tossed on an uninhabited moon like a sack of garbage, then her mother hadn't warranted enough respect for a plaque.

Belatedly, she realized that she'd forgotten to ask Sawyer to search for more information on Dr. Mollon. Part of her wanted to turn around and return to their private room in the archives to ask, but a larger part told her she needed to be alone in her grief right now.

Her mother really was dead. Dr. Mollon had made sure of that.

Then why the hell was Anissa spared? Why, of everyone on board the *Spindle*, had she been spared?

Anissa had served with soldiers suffering survivor's guilt during the civil war. She'd listened to them relate horrifying stories, full of carnage, told by people who couldn't understand how anyone could treat their fellow man in such a way. Soldiers who were the sole survivors in their squads, who didn't know why they were unlucky enough to have lived when their comrades had to die. Soldiers who knew they weren't anything special and that their only real contribution to the Empire would be their military service. She'd never understood how they felt until now.

Unlike so many of her fellow soldiers, Anissa had never truly harbored a hatred for the Rodantan Quadrant after their military intervention in the civil war. She hadn't even really cared about the royal family, choosing to fight for them simply because she didn't believe the promises the rebels spouted of a better life under democracy. She hadn't cared for the Rodantan government, but individual Rodantans—they were fine. Including Sawyer, who'd pulled her out of that hole.

Especially Sawyer, whom she'd just stomped away from while he was trying to help her.

Anissa now felt like the biggest asshole in Laresh Seat, but she didn't know what else to do. Should she go back to the archives? What if he'd already left and gone to one of the areas that required a current ID chip for admittance?

She was supposed to return to the shuttle at eighteen hundred hours. She spotted a vidscreen showing a news broadcast on the wall, a few students gathered around it. It had a time display running across the screen. She had two hours before she needed to be back at the shuttle launch pad.

Two hours and nowhere to go, since this was no longer her home and her ID chip wouldn't let her in anywhere.

Not that she'd ever been a university student, just one of the military academy's cadets.

She kept on walking, finally arriving at a set of double doors that led to a courtyard. A familiar stone outbuilding beckoned across the neatly manicured lawns: she recognized it as the military academy student barracks. The doors opened silently, and she stepped into the warm air.

A smile spread across her face. She knew where she was.

The archives building had once housed the main academy. The courtyard she stood in had been used for physical training exercises, and the sim chambers where they learned to fly combat craft was located one kilometer away. That was likely gone by now if the rest of the place had been turned into university archives, but... the barracks.

Something familiar. The only thing from her past she'd seen besides the EVA suit she'd been interred in.

She hurried across the courtyard to the building. Its door slid open at her approach, and the smell of stale beer immediately assaulted her senses.

It took a few seconds for her eyes to adjust to the dim lighting. Once they had, she saw that where there had once been rows of bunk beds, stacked three high and bolted to the floors, now stood rows of tables. A bar had been built along the wall, stools lined its front and glass bottles winked at her from behind it.

The barracks was now a student pub.

Anissa felt like she might puke. She walked on shaky legs to the bar and sat down, sure that if she didn't, she might collapse. And that would introduce a whole new set of problems for her.

"What can I get you?" A bartender set down a glass he'd been polishing and waited. Anissa reached down and touched her pocket. She had some Rodantan scrip there. "Uh, do you take scrip?"

"Yeah, but our exchange is terrible, just so you know."

She pulled it out and counted it. "What can I get for twenty-four scrip?"

His eyebrows rose in surprise, but she didn't know if it was because of her question or at her total ignorance of the cost of bar drinks. "Twenty-four scrip can get you three premium Laresh beers or twelve shots of Quilkin whiskey." Anissa had never heard of the liquor before. "Between the two," he continued, "I'd go for the beer, personally."

"I'll have a little of both, please. Um, one beer and two shots."

He opened a green bottle of beer and set it in front of her, followed by two shot glasses of the whiskey. Anissa knocked one of the shots back and grimaced.

"Bad day?" the bartender asked.

Why was he still talking to her? She looked around the bar; it was late afternoon, of course it wouldn't be full yet. Students were still in class. "You could say that." She set the glass down with a little more force than necessary, then sipped her beer.

It tasted very much like the ale she used to enjoy with her unit on shore leave. Tears welled up in her eyes, and she brushed them away impatiently. She took another swallow, careful not to choke on the lump in her throat.

"You want to talk about it?" the bartender asked.

She shook her head. "No. Thanks for the offer, though."

"If you change your mind or want something else, just holler."

She nodded and looked down into her beer bottle, then knocked back the other shot.

There were only so many places on the university grounds that Anissa could get into without any current identification, and Sawyer went down the short list. Despite her promise to return to the shuttle by eighteen hundred hours—six o'clock for Sawyer, who was always a little scrambled by military time—he couldn't help but worry about her.

She'd suffered a tremendous blow today.

He looked around the university grounds, noting the lecture halls were open only to current students and faculty. He spied the campus pub across a courtyard through the huge windows gracing the building. *What the hell, it's worth a shot.* He smiled at his own bad unintentional pun as the glass double doors opened for him and he strode across the immaculately kept lawn.

The pub was quiet, with some students eating dinner and studying. He spied a familiar dark braid and flight suit on a stool at the bar, and his heart sank.

He touched Anissa's shoulder, and she jumped. "What in the Four Hells?"

Her voice was loose despite the words, and the small row of empty shot glasses lined up on the bar in front of her confirmed his suspicions. He sat down next to her and motioned for the bartender.

"What can I get you?"

"Two glasses of water and my friend's bill, please."

"I got this," Anissa said. "Four shots and one beer costs sixteen scrip."

"You're being robbed." He glared at the bartender as he set

two glasses of ice water in front of them. "I'll be paying in silbors."

"Good idea, sir."

"And she's cut off."

"Also a good idea."

Anissa's eyes were red-rimmed, but she wasn't crying. "I want to go home," she said, her voice a hoarse whisper. "But it isn't there anymore."

"I know."

"This used to be the barracks," she said, gesturing around the pub. "I slept on the middle bunk when I was a new recruit."

Sawyer nodded, not wanting to interrupt her.

"My mother's really gone, Benedict."

He ignored her use of his first name. "And I'm so sorry about that."

"What happened to yours?"

"Inoperable tumor ten years ago." His parents had been divorced for twenty years by then. He didn't usually talk about Paola Sawyer, and he wasn't about to start now.

Anissa didn't press him for any more details. "I'm sorry, too."

"Want to head back to the shuttle?"

She drained the last of her beer and slammed the bottle down on the bar. It made enough noise that a couple of students at a nearby table looked up. "One more shot?"

"I don't think that's a good idea."

"You don't think you can carry me back to the shuttle?"

"I'm sure I can, but I don't think you're the kind of woman who likes to be carried."

"I'm sure you can, too. If the boxing's any indication, and I'm sure it is, you don't fit the stereotype of an archaeologist. And you're right, I don't like to be carried."

"I didn't know there was such a thing as a stereotype of an

archaeologist, and it's time to go." He motioned for the bartender and placed his credit chip on the counter.

"You didn't have to do that. I have twenty-four scrip."

"And you would have been ripped off here. Sorry," he said, looking at the bartender who had paid the bill with the chip.

"Don't worry about it. She *would* have been ripped off here."

Anissa took a sip of her water and stood up. "I guess we should go, then."

She was surprisingly steady on her feet for someone who was a couple of sheets to the wind. Still, she gripped Sawyer's arm when they walked across the courtyard to the archives building. "I can't even visit her," she said.

"I know, and that makes this even more awful."

"Did you find anything more about Dr. Mollon?"

"Just that he studied bio-longevity and switched his focus to cybernetics right before he was killed in that shuttle accident."

"He wasn't fucking killed in that accident. I don't believe that for a minute."

He sighed. "I know." Maybe she would be more receptive to speaking to the Rodantan authorities about her ordeal now they knew what they did. Sooner rather than later, Anissa needed to move on and start her new life. Walking past all the places in the building that required identification for admittance only reinforced this.

She kept her head down until they reached the shuttle. When they were strapped into their seats, she turned to him with sad eyes. "Guess I'm not learning to fly this thing right now."

"No, that would not be a good idea." He keyed in a request to transit control to depart to Laresh Seat's main station where the *Phantom* waited.

"I'm sorry, Sawyer."

"What for?"

"Making an ass of myself."

"You didn't. If you want to see someone make an ass of herself, give Lita a bottle of red wine and wait half an hour."

Permission to depart was granted, and Sawyer activated the shuttle's engines. At least it was only a short trip; he didn't think Anissa was in any state to be running through preflight checklists.

He was certain that they'd found out all they could in Laresh System about Anissa's mother and Dr. Mollon, but he'd already decided to stay overnight until Anissa was also sure. He stole a glance at her. She stared straight ahead through the viewport, eyes still red-rimmed. Drunk, but not monstrously so.

Sawyer waited until they were back on board the *Phantom* before speaking again. "Do you think you might be sick at all?"

"If I didn't puke when we broke atmosphere, I think I'll be fine now."

"Good point." Still, he would poke around the sickbay and find the anti-nausea tablets he knew were in there somewhere.

The sound of wheeled feet moving across the floor made him wince, and he hoped Enzo wouldn't ask them about card games. "Dr. Sawyer! Commander Alto! Welcome back!"

"You're supposed to be in downtime," Sawyer said.

"The program finished twenty minutes ago. How was your journey to the archives?"

"My mother really is dead," said Anissa.

"My apologies," said Enzo automatically, and Sawyer cringed again. The android was programmed to respond to bad news with a degree of sympathy, and it sounded false. He would have preferred that the android say nothing.

Anissa turned her gaze to Sawyer. "I see that emotional

programming hasn't improved much over the last century," she said, echoing his thoughts.

"It hasn't. Why don't you go take a nap, and I'll bring you something for your hangover?"

"Trying to knock me out before we go back to Rodanta?"

"No," he said. "I'll request to dock here until tomorrow and we'll leave then." He would try conducting more research while she slept off the effects of her adventure in the student pub.

She nodded. "All right."

"Commander, may I escort you to your cabin?" asked Enzo.

Gods, that android was weird, even with the new programming. Sawyer couldn't understand Fitch and Lita's delight with him.

But whatever charm Enzo held over his friends was also effective on Anissa because she offered the android a smile. "Why the hell not?" She looped her hand around Enzo's metallic arm, and the pair of them walked away from the shuttle bay.

Sawyer shook his head. *Androids;* then, *Lareshi commanders.*

He made good on his promise to give her something for her impending hangover. Quilkin whiskey was not generally the beverage of choice for someone who didn't have a death wish. He stopped by sick bay and found the anti-nausea tablets he knew were there, then headed for her cabin.

He knocked on her door and waited. Anissa opened it a few seconds later. "I don't see why you dislike Enzo so much. He's very nice," she said by way of greeting.

"His being nice isn't the issue." He held out the pack of tablets, but she didn't accept them. "I brought these for when you start regretting that whiskey in a few hours."

"I had the scrip to cover my drinks."

"I know, I wanted you to save it."

"Well, thanks." She looked down. "Sorry I fell apart on you back at the university."

"I'd hardly call that falling apart."

She shook her head. "You don't understand."

"I'm not even going to pretend that I can, Anissa."

"I don't mean it like that. I never fall apart, I never have. I made it through the civil war and carried on like nothing happened, and..." Tears filled her eyes and she bit her lip. She closed her eyes, clearly fighting to control her emotions.

"I know," he said simply.

There was nothing he could do at this moment, or ever, that would begin to heal the pain she was experiencing right now. He almost regretted coming to Laresh System if it meant seeing her cry.

"You're a good friend, Benedict," she said. "Can I call you that?"

"Sure, but—wow, you really tied one on at the pub."

That drew a smile from her, and with it, a corresponding warmth spread through him. "I didn't know what else to do."

"Getting day drunk is as good a plan as any."

"Yeah. Well, I didn't do *that* before, either." She looked down at the pack of tablets in Sawyer's hand. "Should I take one of those now?"

"Yeah, take one before you pass out and it'll take the edge off. You'll still feel like shit in a few hours. Sorry."

She took the tablets from him. "Thank you."

"You're welcome."

Her arms wrapped around his shoulders, and she pulled him into a hug. Sawyer was too surprised to respond at first, doubly so when her mouth found the sensitive spot under his ear and licked it.

This was... not good. Not when she was drunk, and she'd

just found out that her mother was dead. "Anissa," he said, urgency in his voice.

She pressed her lips against his, and for half a second all he could focus on was her, the whiskey's bite still on her mouth, and her body pressed up against his. His own responded, bringing him back to reality: who she was and the state she was in, and he pulled away.

She looked absolutely shocked, then mortified. Sawyer knew exactly how she was feeling in that moment because he felt it too.

"I'm sorry," she said.

"Don't worry about it." He backed away. "Maybe it's time for you to get some sleep." Or work out her frustrations in a training sim, whatever it took for her to be the Anissa he knew.

"Yeah."

"I'm going to the bridge to request permission from transit control to stay the night," he said. He knew he was babbling, but he needed something to fill the awkward space between them. "Jumpspace doesn't work well with hangovers."

"Or drunks."

"That, too." He ran a hand through his hair. "Let's pretend this didn't happen, all right?"

She nodded, and he thought she might almost have shocked herself sober. "Okay."

CHAPTER 10

ANISSA OPENED her bleary eyes and forced herself to sit up in bed, the motion provoking a head rush.

Water. She needed water. And something for her headache.

She spotted the pack of anti-nausea tablets on the nightstand, and the memory of the day before came rushing back.

She'd tried to kiss Sawyer.

Oh, Four Hells, I'm a fucking idiot.

A wave of humiliation washed over her, compounded by the headache and an equally potent rush of nausea. She forced herself to take deep breaths, then, tablet packet in hand, fetched a glass of water from the replicator. She swallowed two and hoped they would kick in soon.

She checked the time and was surprised to see it was only half past four. What time had she gone to bed—oh, Four Hells, what time had she passed out? Early evening, she guessed. She'd remembered spending the afternoon at the university pub that used to be the military academy barracks.

She still couldn't believe that. It was so disrespectful to the Laresh Forces. It should've been a museum or something she thought as she stumbled into the shower. Her indignant ruminations were cut short as she remembered the shower's laser cleansers, and she stepped out. A post-hangover shower should involve water.

It was four-thirty in the morning. Sawyer was bound to be sleeping. She wrapped a towel around herself and collected the soap and shampoo she'd bought on Bliss Station, along with a change of clothes, and opened her cabin door. Even though she knew Sawyer would be deep in sleep—at least, she hoped he was—she still stole a glance either side of the corridor before venturing out to the converted brig.

Once there, she locked the door and drew a bath in the oversized tub. The anti-nausea medication Sawyer left for her had already started kicking in by the time she sank into the hot water, which meant her only distraction from analyzing her mortifying behavior of the day before was gone.

She'd tried to kiss Sawyer. She held her breath and dunked her head underwater. But when she came back up, the embarrassment hadn't washed away.

She'd have to apologize, there was no way around that. If she didn't, the incident would hang over their heads, possibly forever, and she wanted to be able to look him in the eye again someday. That day probably wouldn't be today or tomorrow, but someday.

Anissa had never been much of a drinker, even during her days in the academy, when acting like a jackass was usually part of the package. It was one of the reasons she'd risen to the rank of commander when she was still in her twenties during the civil war. She always prided herself on her discipline, but then she was faced with a crisis yesterday and had to go and make an idiot of herself.

The worst part of it was that she increasingly viewed Sawyer with less than strictly platonic feelings. She rubbed shampoo into her hair and scrubbed at it. *I need a haircut.*

She was all about making stupid decisions at present, so she may as well cut it after her bath.

Along with discipline, she also prided herself on her discretion, and she'd intended to take her feelings about Sawyer to the grave with her. And even if her feelings for him weren't a reaction to his rescuing her—a possibility, she had to admit—she knew a relationship between a work-addicted archaeologist who didn't want to stay in one spot too long and a former soldier from a dead society was unlikely to work in the long term.

You fucking idiot.

The epithet ran over and over in Anissa's head as she tried to scrub away the previous night's embarrassment.

She didn't even know if Sawyer preferred women. And she didn't do short-term flings anymore. She'd really messed this up.

By the time she let the tub drain and ordered the computers to recycle the water, she was no closer to a solution to her problem. She toweled off, dressed, and went back to her cabin. There was still the matter of that haircut. She found the shears she'd bought at Bliss Station and set to work.

Vicora used to cut her hair, a common ritual among Lareshis when Anissa was growing up. She wondered if it was still common practice for family members to cut each other's hair, or if salons had grown in popularity since the Empire's alliance with Rodanta. Another wave of grief crashed over her as she snipped away.

Vicora really was gone, and there wasn't even a grave marker or memorial she could visit to honor her memory.

When she was done, Anissa's hair had been shaped into a simple bob, and she guessed twenty centimeters of thick dark hair was now piled up in the bathroom's trash can. Not quite as short as she used to wear it in the military, but certainly easier to deal with.

Would Sawyer like it?

Damn it, don't think about that, she chided herself. She shook out her remaining hair and left the cabin in search of some breakfast before Sawyer woke up. She vaguely recalled him talking about wanting to return to Rodantan space this morning, and she wanted to be as alert as possible when they departed the Empire. Alert, professional, and ready to take the *Phantom* through jumpspace with Enzo's help.

After apologizing to Sawyer, of course.

She was settled in the lounge with a breakfast of eggs and toast, coffee at hand, when Sawyer walked in wearing a bathrobe, his hair tousled. He yawned, and it took a few seconds for him to notice Anissa.

Not a morning person.

Seeing him again reignited her mortification and judging from the way his eyes widened when they rested on her, he felt it, too. "What did you do to your hair?" he asked

She touched it self-consciously. "I just wanted something more manageable."

"You didn't want to wait until we got back to Bliss Station? There are a few salons there."

"In my day, our parents cut it for us." She attempted to inject some levity into her tone, but it fell flat, and she realized any further attempts to do so would also until she addressed what was bothering them both.

No time like the present. "I'm sorry about yesterday." Her words came out in a rush. "For everything."

He keyed in a request for coffee at the replicator. "Don't worry about it."

"I can't do that."

He yawned again. "We all do stupid shit when we're drunk."

"I don't."

"Well, it turns out that you do, because you did yesterday.

Welcome to the club." He sat down heavily on the deck-locked couch.

"I don't usually do that."

"That's why I said, 'We all do stupid shit when we're drunk, don't worry about it.'" He sipped his coffee. "I'm trying to diffuse the awkwardness of it all."

"I appreciate that." She did, even though it didn't make the situation any less embarrassing.

"When we get back to the *Phantom,* if it's okay with you, let's pretend none of yesterday's events happened, and we'll carry on as we have."

She nodded. "Seems like a good idea." Well, that went better than she'd expected. She changed the subject. "Where's Enzo?"

"Probably in android dreamland on the bridge. I ordered him to have as much downtime as possible yesterday, but he doesn't always listen. If he was awake, he'd be pestering us by now."

"What's your deal with Enzo, anyway?"

"Besides me finding him annoying as hell? Not much. Although Fitch took care of a lot of his more irritating issues." He sighed. "He's a good pilot, anyway. And a good instructor. That android model was designed to be."

"Can I take the ship through jump today?"

Sawyer paused, coffee cup in hand. "With Enzo as copilot," he said carefully.

"Of course."

"And me next to you the entire time. I guess you'll have to learn how to handle jumpgates, eventually."

"Also, of course."

He rubbed his hand over his eyes. "Okay. Be ready on the bridge in twenty minutes. I just have to get dressed, upload a flight plan back to Rodanta, and pay the docking fees before we leave."

"You can take the docking fees out of my pay."

He shook his head. "Don't worry about it. Part of the cost of doing business."

"All right." She wouldn't argue him on that point. "I'll meet you on the bridge in twenty."

Despite the embarrassment and a few lingering twinges in her head reminding her of the day before, excitement still coursed through Anissa when she sat at the *Phantom*'s controls. It felt good to be piloting again.

Sawyer uploaded his flight plan to Laresh Seat's transit control and paid the ship's docking fees, before she and Enzo did a pre-flight systems check. There were more things on that list than there had been a century ago, but Anissa didn't care. It wasn't a bad idea to check every component of a life support system, even if it took an extra few minutes.

The quiet rumble of the engines under the deck was almost soothing, she thought. It was a short distance to the jumpgate, and she and Enzo handled it without a hitch. Still, Sawyer hung around the bridge, undoubtedly worried about what could go wrong on his ship, either here or in jump. She didn't blame him. If she were the captain of something as magnificent as the *Phantom*—and no matter what Sawyer said about his ship, it really was magnificent—she would be antsy about someone new at the helm, too.

She couldn't keep a very undignified squeak of excitement from escaping her when she and Enzo successfully guided the ship into jumpspace. Once the ship had stopped shaking, she unsnapped her safety harness and stood up, unable to keep the smile off her face.

"I did it," she said triumphantly.

"And very well, Commander," said Enzo.

"Ship's still in one piece," Sawyer said. "I appreciate that."

Had she the ability, she would have sashayed off the bridge to the lounge, but she didn't. There was a spring in her step that she didn't try to hide, though.

Taking the *Phantom* into jump was a small thing, but it meant a lot to her, especially after finding out what she had yesterday, and the possibility she had to consider that she was wrong about Dr. Mollon.

"I see your hangover isn't bothering you," said a voice behind her.

"Not really. Those meds helped a lot. Thank you again." She sat down on the couch and picked through the sheaf of notes she and Sawyer had made about Vicora and Dr. Mollon.

Her good mood immediately evaporated. "I'm wondering if I may have to reconsider my position on Dr. Mollon."

He took a seat next to her. "That isn't necessarily a bad thing."

"I don't want to stop looking for him just yet," she said. "I still think there's a better possibility of him being alive than dead. His death in a shuttle accident after he destroyed the *Spindle* is still too convenient for my liking." She took a deep breath. "But it's still possible he really is dead, and finding out about my mother yesterday..." She blinked and looked away, not wanting to see the pity reflected in Sawyer's eyes.

"I get it," he said softly.

"I thought she might be in the same situation I was," she said. "That maybe she was in stasis in a box on some backwater planet in the middle of nowhere. I really hoped for that." She looked down at her hands, at the tiny white scars on her fingers from some long-ago battle during the civil war. She didn't remember how she got them. She'd been in more than a couple of firefights then. "I need to be better prepared in case Mollon turns out to be dead. And I guess I need someone to help me out when the media gets wind of this."

"You already have that. Me, Lita, Fitch, Dian. You have friends in Rodanta who'll support you."

"That means a lot to me." She leaned back against the couch cushions. She could feel a headache building that had nothing to do with her hangover.

"Do you want to talk about your old life at all?"

Bless him. He sounded so sincere and so awkward. He wasn't used to people pouring out their emotions to him, but then again, Anissa wasn't used to crying on others' shoulders. It would be a novelty for both.

She shrugged. "There isn't much to tell. I was friendly with the crew on board the *Spindle*, and my mother and I were very close. She was my best friend. We had a few political differences during the war, since she had far more sympathies for the rebels' cause, but we were both supporters of the Empire in the end. Devil you know and all that."

"Did you have any rebel sympathies, too?"

"Not enough to fight on their side. Although I guess that point is moot, since the royal family isn't recognized anymore." She paused as something she had forgotten to ask surfaced. "Uh, they haven't executed anyone from the Laresh royal family at some point, have they?"

"Nah. There are a couple of descendants still around with a shitload of old money, but they're private citizens. And the Rodantan and Lareshi alliance occurred peacefully."

"That's a relief. At least my time in battle wasn't completely in vain." She knew she sounded flippant but didn't care. "But I still miss everyone."

"Were you married?"

She started a little at the question. "No." Before she could stop herself, she asked, "You?" The idea of marriage had never held her interest, not that she'd ever met anyone she was interested in marrying.

You're an asshole, Anissa. You can't decide whether you want to grieve your dead mother or find out if there's a minuscule chance in the Four Hells that Sawyer is somehow interested in you. Which he is not, especially since you made such a spectacular fool of yourself last night.

"Married? No. Most women wouldn't tolerate living on board a converted freighter full time."

That answered another question she'd been pondering. "Except for Lita and Dian, I guess."

"Lita's like my sister, and she doesn't live on a ship. She and Fitch refuse to. And Dian doesn't like being in space for longer than a few days at a time. She's someone who will actually be happy working at the university and teaching when she finishes her doctorate."

"She was a medic before, right?"

"Not a great one, as I'm sure you noticed."

"So, she wasn't just pissed off about me locking her in that closet?"

"No. Her bedside manner is lacking, to say the least. But she met her wife working in an emergency department, and Tash was the one to convince her to leave medicine and work with dead things instead, like she always wanted."

She knew Sawyer was talking about his crew in an effort to distract her a little, and she appreciated it. She knew the last thing either of them wanted was for her to fall apart again.

But he surprised her with a change in subject. "So Lareshis cut their own hair?"

"They did one hundred and four years ago. My mother and I always did that for each other."

There was that headache again.

Right now, the last thing she wanted to do was talk about Vicora with anyone. She stood up. "I should get back to the bridge."

"We're in jump for another few hours. You're going to play a card game with Enzo?"

"Why not? I play a mean game of Stars and Kings."

———

Sawyer sent a short transmit to his crew when the *Phantom* exited the jumpgate, asking them to meet him on board when the ship returned to Bliss Station. He didn't go into details, just in case his message was intercepted.

Why would it be? They haven't been before.

Maybe being around Anissa was making him paranoid.

She'd been acting a little cagey since this morning, although he could hardly blame her for that. What had happened last night was at the forefront of his mind, and as much as he wanted to, he couldn't erase the feeling of her body pressed against his.

She'd been drunk and grieving. In another time, if she hadn't been either of those things...

But she *had* been drunk, and she *was* grieving, and she was a century out of her time. He couldn't let himself forget that.

The *Phantom* docked at Bliss Station under Enzo and Anissa's guidance while Sawyer spoke with transit control. She was learning quickly; if and when this died down and she could start her life over, she would be a damned decent pilot.

As soon as the ship locked into her usual dock, Lita and Dian requested admittance.

Sawyer unlocked the entrance ramp, and they walked up. "How'd it go?" Lita asked by way of greeting.

Anissa was still on the bridge, chatting with Enzo. "It went," Sawyer said. "Not as well as she hoped."

"Did you find that doctor?" Lita asked, keeping her voice low.

"No, but the university archives in Laresh had a lot more information about Mollon and Dr. Alto than was available in Rodanta. We know for sure that Dr. Alto died."

Lita and Dian both looked stricken. "Oh, no," Dian said. "How's she doing?"

"I'm not sure." He didn't want to share what had happened after that. He'd leave it up to Anissa to decide how much she wanted his friends—*their* friends, he amended—to know about her jaunt to the pub and what happened afterward.

"Dr. Alto was found dead in her ship after Anissa disappeared," he said. "She was interred on an abandoned moon with other unclaimed remains. Anissa's gutted."

Dian's expression turned thoughtful. "Were there any other survivors or missing persons unaccounted for from the ship?"

"No. Anissa was the only person listed as missing and presumed dead. The *Spindle* had a hole in her hull when she was found near the Rodantan border."

"Why do you think Anissa was the only one spared?"

That thought hadn't occurred to Sawyer. "I don't have a clue." He felt like an idiot for not thinking of that sooner.

"It's just that it's weird that she would be the only person on board to be kidnapped, drugged, and dropped off on a planet in the middle of nowhere. There must be a reason Mollon targeted her."

"We'll have to ask if she has any ideas," Sawyer said, but before he could elaborate, the sound of footsteps and squeaky wheeled feet interrupted them.

"Enzo!" said Lita. "How was your trip? Come here, give me a hug."

Enzo wrapped his metallic arms around Lita. "Very good, Dr. Fardell. How did you and Fitch manage without me?"

"It was difficult, but we did it. Did you annoy Dr. Sawyer at all?"

"I don't think so," replied the android, appearing

unperturbed by the suggestion. "Although I believe Commander Alto is quite fond of me."

"He's been teaching me to fly," said Anissa.

"What happened to your hair?" Lita asked.

"I don't like to keep it long."

"Sawyer didn't do that, did he?"

"No."

"He doesn't have that level of style or skill," said Dian.

"I'm standing right here, you know?" But he knew his protest would fall on deaf ears.

"It looks nice," Lita said.

"Thank you."

An awkward silence fell over the group. Finally, Anissa said, "I guess we should go to the lounge and talk about what we found in Laresh. And then I guess figure out how we're going to weather the investigation and media shitstorm that Sawyer keeps saying is going to happen."

There was that awkward silence again.

"I'm sorry about your mother," Lita finally said.

"If there's anything we can do, please tell us," added Dian in a rare show of empathy.

Sawyer closed the ship, and they made their way to the lounge. Dian was the first to speak. "Anissa, do you have any idea why you were the only survivor on that ship?"

She shook her head. "None at all."

"Did your mother ever experiment on you?"

Her eyes widened, and Sawyer knew his were doing the same. "*Experiment* on me? No. Human experimentation has been illegal in Laresh for years." She paused. "It still is, right?"

"There are exceptions made for medical reasons, but otherwise, yes," said Sawyer. "On both sides of the border. Is it possible, though, that she might have manipulated your genes or enzymes or whatever?"

Anissa was quiet for a moment, emotions flitting across

her face. Sawyer wished he could tell what she was thinking. "Anything's possible. She took blood samples from both of us over the years, but I can't recall her ever injecting me with anything except immune system enhancers." She took a deep breath and exhaled in frustration. "I just don't know. But it's a good theory."

"Is there any way Tash could run some tests?" Sawyer asked Dian. "She's a doctor."

"She's an obstetrician, not a researcher." Typical snarky, blunt answer from Dian. But she continued, "Let me ask around. And we might be able to do some analysis on Anissa's blood or genes or whatever at the university. We all have friends outside our departments, right?" She looked around the lounge, waiting for an answer.

Sawyer and Lita looked at each other, then the deck.

"Seriously?" Dian said. "Am I the only person on this ship who has friends and acquaintances outside my academic sphere?"

"Well, you have the medical background," Lita said. "We've been living and breathing dead shit since we were teenagers. You're still friendly with medics and medical researchers, right?"

Dian shot her a look that clearly questioned her intelligence. "I wouldn't use the term *friendly*, but I've stayed in touch with a few of them, yes."

Sawyer had always admired Dian's level of self-awareness.

"We should run some tests then," Lita said. "If Anissa agrees."

"It can't do any harm," Anissa said, her voice weary. "Honestly, anything we can do to delay having the media crawl up my ass for the rest of my life sounds good. Who wants to start leeching my blood?"

"No one's leeching blood," Sawyer said. "We'll ask around Tash's contacts and the university and see what we can do. I think we all agree that the more reasons we can come up with for why Dr. Mollon kidnapped you, the easier an investigation will go. Right?" He looked around the lounge expectantly.

Instead of an answer, the ship's door chime sounded. "That'll be either Fitch or Tash," said Lita. "Maybe both."

"How much does Tash know?" Sawyer asked Dian. Tash was discreet, but none of them had ever dealt with something like this before.

Dian was blunt, as usual. "Everything. Testing Anissa's DNA was her idea." At Sawyer's look, she said indignantly, "What? We don't keep secrets from each other. She's a *doctor*. A major part of her job is keeping secrets."

She had a point, and Tash was bound to find out sooner or later, anyway.

Sawyer checked the idents of whoever was waiting at the *Phantom*'s ramp and wasn't surprised to see it was Fitch and Tash. He unlocked the door for them and waited. Soon after, their footsteps sounded through the ship's corridors.

"You left work early?" Lita said.

Fitch nodded. "That I did. Sawyer." He nodded at him, then at Anissa. "Commander Alto."

"This lovely creature you see before you is my wife," said Dian, a rare warmth in her voice when she looked at Tash. "Dr. Tash Passan. She's a *real* doctor."

Lita and Sawyer shot Dian irritated looks, but Dian didn't seem to care. Tash sat down beside Dian and squeezed her hand.

"So, let's talk about this DNA testing," Anissa said. "How do we go about that?"

"Straight to the point," Tash said approvingly. "It actually won't be that hard. I can take a couple of samples from you and sequence them at the hospital. We check for potential birth defects and genetic diseases that way. It won't take long."

"So no one has to bastardize an age-sequencing machine at the university?" Lita said.

"No one would be bastardizing those machines anyway," Sawyer said. "They aren't designed to analyze humanoid DNA. None of us can afford to replace one if something goes wrong, and let's be realistic, something will go wrong if we do it."

Lita opened her mouth as if to argue, paused a moment, then closed it. She nodded in agreement.

"I'll have to take Anissa to the hospital to run the tests," Tash said.

"Won't that raise suspicion?" Sawyer asked. "She doesn't have a current ID chip, let alone a Rodantan one."

"That won't be a problem," Tash said. "Doctors have a certain amount of privilege to get around the station. Privilege that I will, of course, be abusing." She looked around at everyone seated in the lounge. "I really hope it's worth risking my job there. After you find what you're looking for, you need to report this." Her voice took on a pleading note. "Please."

"We will," Sawyer said. "As soon as we know if Anissa's mother tweaked her genes or something."

Tash nodded. "Good. I'll take her to the hospital in the next day or two, if you're staying at Bliss."

"I don't have any plans until everyone else is available to search for the Immortal Spacefarer's treasure again." As he said the words, Sawyer realized he hadn't thought about the legend until now. He'd been so absorbed in trying to help Anissa that his life's work had completely fallen by the wayside. That wasn't like him, and everyone there knew it.

There was also the teaching conundrum to consider at some stage, but he pushed that out of his mind for now.

"Dr. Sawyer?" Enzo's voice sounded through the ship's corridor. "An incoming transmit with the university stamp has arrived. It's marked urgent."

Son of a bitch. "I doubt it's urgent, Enzo," said Sawyer.

"The sender is demanding a read receipt," the android said. "There is a verbal overlay attached that is quite insistent it be acknowledged immediately."

Sawyer's father had always been aggressive in his communication, but to his credit, he rarely appended an overlay. "Damn it," he said, and stood up. "I'll be right back." He could open the transmit here, but if it was going to be as obnoxious as he suspected it would be, he would rather do it in private.

He followed the android to the small office off the bridge. True to Enzo's word, his father's voice bellowed out, "Open the damn message, Benedict!" as soon as he came within view of the comp. "Thank you, Enzo," Sawyer said, weariness already seeping through him. Enzo nodded and returned to the bridge, sitting down at the pilot's seat and staring at the viewscreen. For a second, Sawyer wondered what the android could be thinking about.

He unlocked the message, and Devon King's face filled the screen.

"I'm not bothering with any niceties," his father said. "In one month, I expect you to be at the annual Prime fundraising gala, appropriately attired and willing to sweet talk more people into sponsorship. I want this message acknowledged as soon as you receive it." Dr. King tented his fingertips and leaned forward, in what he probably thought was an intimidating gesture. "And as we discussed at our last meeting, you will also teach those courses next semester, or I will personally see to it that yours and Dr. Fardell's contracts are terminated, Dian Pellar's research grants and stipend are defunded, and none of you work at any university on this side of the border again. That's a promise, Benedict."

The transmit ended with Prime University's logo winking off, and the screen went black.

Sawyer was too stunned to move for a few seconds. But his shock gave way to fury, and he had to talk himself out of punching something, the way Anissa wanted to when she was angry.

It was one thing to threaten his career, but Lita's and Dian's? Unacceptable, and in Dian's case at least, unethical. She was a stellar student, and she'd earned those grants and that living stipend. Grants that were awarded on academic performance and merit, not to be whisked away by the university president because she worked with his disobedient son.

He was going to have to go to that fundraising gala, and next semester he was going to have to put the *Phantom* in extended dry dock and teach a few hundred students horribly boring introductory courses. He knew every move he made would be scrutinized by his father, and it would be miserable.

He would play Devon King's games for another few months, leave Prime on the best terms he could, and start his career over at another university. He didn't have a choice in the matter anymore.

Sawyer ran his hands through his hair and breathed deeply before hitting the Reply tab on the comp. He kept his voice as level as possible, trying, and probably failing, to keep his rage out of it. "Dad," he said, "please send along some more details about this gala, and any notes from previous professors for those courses so I can get a head start on the material." He tried to inject a little levity into his tone. "The textbooks are as dry as dust, and I could use the help. Thanks." He stabbed the End Communication tab and leaned back heavily in the chair.

Fuck.

He could really use a sim chamber session to punch some of Dian's clowns. Better yet, clowns with his father's face on them.

"Sawyer?"

He wasn't surprised to see Anissa standing in the office doorway, concern on her face. She was the only person who would come looking for him when he was pissed off; Lita, Fitch, and Dian tended to give him a wide berth when he was angry. He didn't take his emotions out on others, but Lita told him once during grad school that when he was angry, it radiated from him in waves. "No one," she'd said, "wants to be around a pissed-off person when they're usually as quiet and laid-back as you are." Sawyer suspected they were waiting for him to finally snap, but they would be waiting for a long time. He would quit his job at the university before it came to that.

But Anissa didn't seem to care. She'd been a military commander. She was probably used to calming angry people.

"Yeah?" He leaned back, let his eyes meet hers.

"I want to ask if everything's all right, but I know it isn't."

"And you'd be correct. Just the usual bullshit with my father." Not quite the usual bullshit, as he didn't ordinarily let his father interfere with his life to this degree. He tried to crack a joke. "Now you can see why I took my mother's surname."

He could tell from the arch of Anissa's eyebrow that she knew there was more going on. "It's moved beyond interfering with my career," he said. "He's now threatening Lita's and Dian's, too." He hadn't meant to tell her that, and he quickly added, "Let me tell them myself, when I've stopped being so angry and I can discuss it rationally."

"I wasn't going to say anything, and I don't think you'll stop being angry over this. You'll just have to figure out a better way to counterattack."

She was right; Sawyer had to admit. He rose to his feet and changed the subject. "So you've agreed to have your DNA sequenced?"

"Yes." She looked down, avoiding his eyes. "It's not a bad idea. I don't have much else to go on."

Sawyer tried to keep his voice as gentle as possible. "Then we'll go to the authorities, right?"

"You want me out of your life that badly?"

"Of course not, and you know it. I want you to start your life over. A clean slate." He wanted to keep her in his life as much as he could, which flummoxed him. He didn't have many friends outside his immediate circle. Maybe his reaction to her meant he needed to expand it beyond academia.

A small sigh escaped her. "I know."

He looked back at the comp, waiting for an angry reply from his father, but nothing indicated an incoming message. "Enzo?"

"Yes, Dr. Sawyer?"

"Let me know if I get any more mail, okay?"

"Of course. Commander Alto, may I interest you in another flight lesson?"

"No thanks, Enzo."

"Perhaps a card game?"

"Another time."

As they walked back to the lounge, Anissa said, "I like cards, but not nearly as much as he does."

Sawyer shrugged. "It's part of his programming. Old-school Envoy models were built to provide distractions and entertainment. Fitch and Lita absolutely adore him and didn't want to take all of those quirks out of him."

"You can't keep my android, Sawyer," said Lita from the lounge.

He and Anissa took their seats in the lounge. "I don't want to," Sawyer said.

"I'll be taking him back to our apartment with us. The bathroom and kitchen need cleaning."

"Wait a minute," Sawyer said. "Enzo *cleans* now? Why wasn't I informed?"

"So *now* you want to keep him?"

"If it means I don't have to scrub anything or hire housekeepers while I'm on station, then yes."

"The cleaning program isn't that great," Fitch said. "He gets bored about half an hour into a job and wants to play cards again."

"Yeah, you really need to fix that bug."

"I like it," Anissa said. "He's been very friendly and helpful, and he plays a mean game of Stars and Kings."

"And I don't want to program that out of his personality," Fitch said. "His personality is the main reason we wanted him in the first place."

"Guys?" There was a familiar irritated edge to Dian's voice. "Tash has to get back to work at some point."

The tiny bit of mirth that had welled up in Sawyer evaporated. He pushed his anger at his father out of his mind and focused on what was most important. Anissa's expression was weary, her eyes sad. Sawyer thought she might be on the verge of giving up on finding Dr. Mollon and justice for her mother and beginning to realize it was time to start her life over a century out of her own time.

That thought depressed the hell out of him.

"I have some busy work to do at the hospital tomorrow night," Tash said. "It might be easiest if I do my tests then. Commander, would that work for you?"

Anissa nodded. "Thank you."

"I'll come and pick you up," Tash said. "I can give you a physical, too. Dian did what she could when they found you, given what she had to work with."

"But you need to know what might have happened to me while I was in stasis," Anissa finished for her.

"It's for your peace of mind, too."

Sawyer thought he might be the only one on board who could detect the shift in Anissa's mood. There was a slump to her shoulders that hadn't been there before, a desperation he could almost physically feel.

But now wasn't the time to ask her about it, and he wasn't sure if she even wanted to talk about the latest discoveries about her past anyway. His eye caught hers, and he tried to convey his own sense of caring to her. He couldn't tell if she picked up on it.

You're not alone in this, he thought. *Whatever happens, I'll be there.*

CHAPTER 11

DIAN ARRIVED at the *Phantom*'s airlock to escort Anissa to Bliss Station's hospital the next evening. Anissa was quiet and more than a little nervous as they walked through the station, but no one paid them any mind, let alone stopped them and demanded to see her identification. Still, she didn't breathe more easily until they met Tash in her office and the door hissed closed behind them.

Tash pushed her comp screen aside and stood up. "Commander, how are you?"

"I'm fine, and it's just Anissa now." She couldn't keep her gaze from darting around the office. "Are you sure this is okay?"

Tash's response was blunt. "Probably not, but the risk is greater for me, not you."

"I don't want you to get into any trouble."

"I offered," Tash said. "As soon as Dian told me about you. It makes sense that there could be genetic reasons why this bio-longevity specialist thought you were worth sparing. But first I want to complete a physical. Is that okay with you?"

Anissa nodded. "I feel fine, though."

"I'm sure there were several times you said that during the civil war and were lying about it."

"Good point."

Tash led them out of the office to the hospital corridor, nearly deserted at this time of night. They passed a woman wearing a hospital gown, cuddling a baby to her chest as she walked along the tiled floor, but no one said anything. A door at the end of the corridor opened soundlessly at Tash's arrival, and the doctor locked it behind them.

"You aren't worried about security feeds?" Dian asked.

"Not really. It's not unusual for me to be in an exam room, after all. But we'll have to make this quick." Tash removed a medistat from a cabinet against the wall.

"Am I getting undressed?" Anissa asked.

Tash's composure slipped a little. "Of course not."

"Honey, it's been over a hundred years since her last physical," Dian said in a rare show of sensitivity. "And probably longer than that since she had one that wasn't done in a galley bastardized into a sickbay during a battle. Am I right?"

"I had a checkup before the *Spindle* was attacked, but you're not far off. Lareshi doctors liked to check skin and hair, as well. That's why I asked."

"I'll be taking a few skin cells from you today, too." Tash activated the medistat. "Open your eyes. This'll only take a second."

Anissa did so, expecting a bright light to blind her, but all that happened was the device issued a small click. Tash checked her other eye, then her ears. Anissa stood still as the doctor waved another, smaller, wand a few centimeters over her body.

"That as good as I can do with what I have to work with," Tash said. She sounded a little dejected. Anissa understood where she was coming from, since she hated to half-ass anything as well. "I'm going to take some samples from the inside of your cheek next."

"Open your mouth and close your eyes," Dian said, her voice a singsong. "And you will get..."

"No surprises," Tash said. To Anissa, she said, "You should've seen her when she was still a medic."

"You're being too kind. When we met, you said I had the worst bedside manner ever."

"And that opinion still stands. Anissa wasn't the first patient who wanted to lock you in a closet, but she was the only one who actually did it."

Tash and Dian exchanged another affectionate glance, and a pang of loneliness trickled through Anissa at the sight. She couldn't remember the last time anyone looked at her like that.

Then she remembered making a drunken ass of herself with Sawyer and had to keep herself from cringing.

Tash scraped a few cells from the inside of her cheek, dropping the tiny spatula into a slim tube. "Now what?" Anissa asked.

"Now I run this through the genetic sequencing unit and see what comes up," Tash said. She turned to the desk-mounted comp in the corner of the exam room, using her fingerprints to activate the machine. She pressed a few keys on the medistat unit and pushed the tube holding Anissa's skin cells into a port on the comp's front.

All three waited as the machine analyzed Anissa's DNA. Anissa noticed she was holding her breath as the comp pinged. They looked at the comp screen, but all Anissa recognized was the twisting DNA strands that signified her genetic makeup. Nothing else made sense.

"Well, I'll be damned," Tash said.

"Sometimes I get things right," Dian said.

Anissa's heart was pounding so hard she thought they might actually be able to hear it. "Don't leave me in suspense.

Those colors and symbols mean nothing to me." There was a wobble in her voice despite her flip words.

"There's an anomaly in your DNA," Tash said. "It's weird."

"That isn't exactly reassuring," said Anissa.

"You have telomeres that have clearly been tweaked," Tash continued. Anissa had a vague idea of what a telomere was, and she nodded. Hearing the familiar term did nothing to assuage her fright at what her DNA analysis revealed. "Your telomere length has been altered, probably when you were a baby."

"And you're sure of that?" Could her mother really have experimented on her?

"Yes, and telomere length is linked to lifespan," Tash said.

It took a few seconds for Tash's words to sink in. "So you're telling me that my DNA was fucked around with to see how long I could live?"

"Yes and no," Tash said. "The way your telomeres look right now—that doesn't occur in nature, ever. This isn't a fluke of your being Lareshi. This just doesn't happen in humanoids. I have no idea if this was your mother's doing and I won't speculate on who did it, and I couldn't tell you based on the evidence I have here now how it was done. But it was."

"So am I a bio-longevity success story?" Was that why she was spared and left on that backwater planet?

"No," Tash said. "Although I'm not saying that with certainty. I'd have to do more tests. Simply extending the length of telomeres isn't enough to automatically extend someone's lifespan. There are other factors to that, and I don't see any other genetic manipulation that would contribute to that. But the telomere length could be one of the reasons you were able to be revived from stasis."

"The Empire built their products to last," Anissa said. The

quip rolled off her tongue, but she knew Tash and Dian would be able to pick up the wobble in her voice.

"That isn't my specialty," Tash said, her voice gentle. "Obviously I'd need more information to make a better diagnosis, but what I can tell you is this: you're a healthy woman in her early thirties whose DNA has been engineered. That engineering, as far as I can see, has had no effect on you besides a possible improvement of your chances of surviving in stasis for a hundred years." She took a deep breath. "Are you okay with going to the authorities now?"

The authorities. Anissa doubted they would be much help. It would only lead to newshounds harassing her for the rest of her life.

Her mother was dead.

Dr. Mollon was nowhere to be found, and she still didn't believe he died the way history claimed, if at all.

Anissa's DNA had been tweaked, and even though her mother's loss ripped a hole in her soul, a tide of anger rising now the weight of what Vicora had done was setting in.

Tash was still waiting for an answer. "I don't know," Anissa finally said. "I think I need some more time."

Would Sawyer eventually get sick of her moping around his ship? Would he allow her a few more precious days to mull over what had happened, to come to terms with how badly her life had gone off the rails, and to process her mother's betrayal?

"No one's going to force you to do anything," Dian said.

"But it'll be easier if I have ID and can move around the galaxy," Anissa said. "I know that."

"Maybe a therapist," Tash said, but a sharp look from Dian silenced her.

"You know Sawyer's in your corner, right?" Dian said. "I give him shit for everything but he's a good man."

In your corner. She remembered his boxing match in the *Phantom*'s sim chamber. "He gives you shit, too."

"And that's why we have such a beautiful friendship. But I've known him for years. He won't kick you out in Rodantan space if you don't want to do what he thinks is best. And let's be realistic, no one here knows what's best. This is unexplored territory for all of us. We're following your lead. If you want to lay low, learn to pilot the *Phantom* and punch clowns in the sim chamber, go for it." Dian raised an eyebrow. "I especially endorse punching clowns."

Anissa burst into tears.

Sobs wracked her body, and she accepted a tissue Tash pressed into her hand.

She didn't know what to do, and she hated that feeling. She felt as if her entire life was in free fall, and she didn't know the first thing to do to right it.

"Do you want a hug?" Dian whispered. "Though I should warn you I'm not a huggy person."

"Neither am I."

"Which is why it might work." Dian held out her arms.

What the hell. Anissa awkwardly accepted. "You don't do this much," she said, noting the stiffness of Dian's body.

"Not really. But I'm willing to bend my rules about bodily contact for a friend."

"Thank you," Anissa said. "You and Tash. I really hope no one gets in trouble over me."

"Don't worry about it," Tash said. Anissa heard the soft whisper of a machine behind the comp.

"Ready to head back to the ship?" Dian asked. Anissa nodded.

Tash reached behind the comp and held up some papers. "I printed your results for you, if you want to look at them yourself."

There would be little that Anissa could understand, but she could ask Sawyer for help. "Thank you."

Dian and Anissa walked through the hospital and back to

the station without anyone paying them any attention. "Don't be afraid to get in touch with me," Dian said once they reached the station docks. "Any time, day or night. Sawyer has my contact details. I know what a bear he can be to live with."

"He's not a bad roommate, actually."

"You're not working directly beneath him on a research mission. And you haven't accidentally stumbled in on him naked."

Anissa forgot her tears long enough to feel herself blush. She hoped Dian didn't notice. "Uh, what?"

"It was my fault. That's what I get for not knocking on the cabin door before going in to tell him about an asteroid breaking apart directly in our flight path. You'd think if someone slept naked he'd at least lock the door, or if he was going to sleep with an unlocked door, he'd at least be wearing pants. Especially when we're working rotating shifts, but what the hell do I know." She visibly shuddered. "That was a visual I didn't need."

Anissa smiled at the story to be polite. Inner turmoil aside, she *was* still attracted to the man.

"I meant it about getting in touch," Dian said. "I don't know when we're all going to be on a mission again."

Anissa didn't know if Dian knew about Dr. King's ultimatum, and she didn't want to say anything before Sawyer could. So she nodded. "Don't be a stranger aboard the *Phantom*, either."

"Never. Now get back on board and punch some clowns."

The *Phantom*'s door cycled open when Anissa pressed her hand to the palm lock, and it locked behind her with a loud click. As she placed the papers detailing her test results on the coffee table in the lounge, she saw a note waiting for her.

I'm in the sim chamber if you're looking for me. There's a not-horrible prefab dinner waiting for you in the food processor if you want it. S.

She smiled and checked the processor unit. A square package waited inside: some kind of soup. She turned on the unit and while it was cooking, looked at the printouts Tash had given her. The technical information was largely beyond her understanding, but she didn't care about that.

Her mother had experimented on her. Vicora Alto had been ambitious, but she'd had professional ethics, which included not conducting experiments on sentient beings without consent.

Hadn't she?

What else did Anissa not know about her mother?

This time her grief was tainted with uncertainty and anger. Even though Tash had said her elongated telomeres shouldn't have any effect on her, could she really know that? Tash was an obstetrician, not a geneticist. Her job, as far as Anissa knew, involved testing DNA for known genetic anomalies and delivering healthy babies, not original research. Research, Anissa knew, that was no longer being conducted in either the Rodantan Quadrant or Laresh System.

She barely tasted her soup as she mulled over this latest information. As angry and betrayed as she felt, she didn't hate Vicora. She just wanted to know why her mother had felt it prudent to experiment on a baby, and she damned Crale Mollon, again, for destroying all evidence of Vicora's existence. If Anissa could get her hands on her mother's research, she might get some answers.

Once again, someone else had made major decisions for her without her input or consent. Anissa's spoon scraped against the bottom of the soup dish a little too hard as she sucked back the last dregs.

Maybe punching clowns wasn't a bad idea. Or she could use Sawyer's boxing sim.

Maybe he would take part and she could see him without a shirt again.

You're an ass, Anissa.

A grieving ass who was nursing an inappropriate crush on her rescuer and possible future employer, but an ass nonetheless. Hadn't she berated her squad mates and subordinates during the war when they let infatuations interfere with their common sense?

But she wasn't in the military anymore, or even in her own time.

Still stewing over her dilemma, she walked through the *Phantom*'s corridors until she reached the former brig. The sim chamber's status light glowed green, telling her that Sawyer was still inside. She pressed the call button beside the door and waited.

It slid open, and she stepped inside, the door hissing closed behind her. Immediately, she lifted off the ground. A small scream escaped her as she struggled to right herself.

Sawyer floated among a twinkling starfield on the opposite side of the chamber. Shirtless again, she noted with a happy little thrill. "Sorry," he said. "I should've warned you I'd turned down the gravity controls."

"It's okay." Anissa righted herself, and her initial panic ebbed away. "I like low-gravity flotation."

"That answers my next question. Not everyone does."

"When I'm expecting it, I find it very relaxing." She swam through the air toward Sawyer.

"How was it at the hospital?"

Anissa thought for a moment, trying to form the right words to tell him. She hoped she didn't still have tear tracks down her cheeks, giving away her devastation. Finally, she said, "It was informative."

"You know you can tell me anything." His eyes met hers, and she felt like crying all over again.

But she didn't. "My mother altered my DNA," she said. "My telomeres are elongated, although Tash said that wasn't enough to extend my life expectancy."

Shock suffused Sawyer's features. "Anissa, I'm so sorry."

He, of all people, would understand parental betrayal, the anger, that occurred when the power of choice was snatched away. She looked away, at a small ringed planet the sim chamber had conjured, blinking rapidly. "Thank you."

"Do you want to talk about it?"

"No." He could read Tash's reports later if he wanted to.

"You know I'll always have time to listen to you, right?"

"Yeah. I just don't want to cry and have tears floating away in those little bubbles, you know? They'll plug up the chamber's gears."

He didn't smile at her attempt at a joke.

Anissa swallowed, not wanting to cry again, and willed any residual tears away. "I'll be all right, I promise. I need some time to absorb this, and then I'll report it to the authorities." She let herself float closer to him and reached for a tiny white star, which shimmered and popped under her touch before rematerializing a meter away.

She was sure she would be all right, *eventually*.

Right now, she didn't want to talk about her DNA or Vicora, anyway. "Have you heard any more about your teaching job?" she asked, then immediately felt like a dolt. "I didn't say anything to Dian," she quickly added.

"Thanks. I'll get around to telling them later. I hate suspending our research, but it's necessary if we want to keep our careers." He floated a couple of meters away, wincing when his body hit what had to be a wall. It was impossible to see where the starfield ended and the walls began.

"Have you thought any more about quitting?"

"Yes. Prime has the best archaeology department out there, but I'm willing to take a hit on prestige if I can continue my research."

"One more question."

"Shoot."

"What's with the low-gravity swimming-in-space theme you've got going on here?" Now it was Anissa's turn to bump into the wall. She pushed off it with her feet and propelled herself his his direction.

"Oh, that. I just felt like relaxing after beating the shit out of the computer in my last boxing match."

And she'd missed the match because she was eating soup and feeling sorry for herself in the lounge. *Damn.*

But the weightlessness had a therapeutic effect on her, too. Or maybe it was Sawyer. Probably both, she decided.

She moved with the sim chamber's current, letting it push her closer to Sawyer. Dian was wrong; floating aimlessly through artificial space was infinitely more stress-relieving than punching clowns.

She sneaked a glance at Sawyer. Or perhaps it was just the company.

"How do you keep doing this?" she asked. "All your research trips?"

"Many folk and fairy tales have some basis in fact. Trawling around space looking for the Immortal Spacefarer's treasure—whoever he may have been—was a dream of mine for years. I bought this ship so I could do that. The inheritance my mother left me was enough to cover the cost of purchasing it and its retrofitting, and I still receive residual payments from her family company. They and my academic writing are enough to scrape by."

Residuals, then. "Which company?" Anissa asked.

"Sawyer Housewares. My however-many-times great-grandfather was a cofounder. It makes replicator parts. As his only living heir, I'm entitled to three percent of Sawyer's profits for life. It's enough to cover dry docking at Bliss and the *Phantom*'s fuel and insurance."

It wasn't a bad life, Anissa thought. Quite the opposite. Sawyer managed to achieve what so few did: freedom. At least, until his father meddled.

"Want to listen to some music?" he asked.

"Sure."

He activated the chamber's control panel where he floated and then tapped the console. The strains of a familiar concerto filled the chamber, and memories of her primary school days came flooding back. She couldn't keep the smile off her face.

"It's the Laresh Imperial Orchestra," Sawyer said. "The Royal Battalion Concerto Number Four."

"I remember it. We studied all of the battalion concertos in school, although I have zero musical talent. The fourth was the empress's favorite."

He floated past her, a lazy smile across his face. "I hoped you'd like it."

That he'd deliberately picked something he thought she would like, sent warmth spreading through her, and beneath it, alarm. She should not grow dependent on him emotionally. That wasn't fair on him.

And besides, since when had she ever been emotionally dependent on anyone? That wasn't a trait she wanted to see herself pick up in her new life.

"I do like it, thank you." She looked over the starfield—deceptively large in the small chamber. She swam nearer to him and touched the stars, watching as they winked out of existence and rematerialized a meter or two away.

A dark gray shirt floated past her. "There it is," Sawyer said. "I forgot about it."

She caught before it could float away. "Are you cold?"

There was a teasing lilt to her voice that she didn't intend to let slip in, but it was there. Still, she held the shirt out to him.

He picked up on her tone and raised an eyebrow in her direction. His hand moved for his shirt, but he didn't take it from her. "No."

Around them, the Laresh Imperial Orchestra finished the fourth concerto, and another piece, also Lareshi, started. The delicate strains of a piano filled the chamber, an instrumental from an opera Anissa couldn't remember. Nor, at this moment, did she care about it. Not when Sawyer was only centimeters away from her.

His pupils dilated, nostrils flared as if he were an animal scenting its prey as his gaze fixed on her. That look emboldened her enough to say, "I could always take mine off, keep you company."

He froze, nearly floating away, but the shirt clutched between their hands kept them together. "You have no idea how much I want to take you up on that," he said.

When Anissa spoke, her voice contained such a rasp, she hardly recognized it as her own. "Then tell me to do it."

He let go of his shirt and closed the short distance between them, his mouth covering hers. Anissa eagerly kissed him back, tongue flicking across his lips, demanding access. He sucked in a surprised breath but responded, tongue meeting hers. His hands slid around her back, pulling her flush against his body. She let her hands explore his body, the planes and contours of his back and shoulders.

She broke their kiss but didn't let go of him. "My shirt," she said. "We're supposed to be even."

"Which is why I should probably take a shower first. You smell fucking incredible." His lips fastened on her neck, sucking and nipping at her rapidly beating pulse. His hands slid under her T-shirt, pulling it up over her body. They broke contact long enough for her to pull it up over her head and toss it away to float with his own, then he gathered her in his arms again.

The feel of Sawyer's warm skin against hers sent a flare of need through her, and goosebumps pebbled her skin as he fumbled with her bra. She fell back against the sim chamber's wall but scarcely noticed it, instead focusing on the comforting weight of the man against her, the hard press of his erection against her hip. He kissed a warm, wet trail down her neck and collarbone to her breast, sucking a stiffened nipple into his mouth. Back arching against the wall, a moan escaped her, and Sawyer's hand traced down her trembling skin to the seal on her flight pants.

Her own hands reached blindly for his waistband, wanting all clothes off, nothing between them. The need to have him inside her as soon as possible erased all rational thought, pushed everything out of her mind except her and Sawyer weightlessly floating through the sim chamber, exploring each other's bodies.

An alarm rang, briefly. They jumped in surprise, and Sawyer pulled away, pants undone. "*Fuck*!"

"What is it?" she asked.

"A hail from station transit control. Gods damn it. I have to answer it. Controls!" His voice was a harsh, angry bark as the sim chamber's holodisplay appeared in front of them. He tapped at the screen, and they slowly descended as the gravity increased. The starfield disappeared, replaced with the chamber's plain gray walls. Anissa's bra and their shirts drifted to the floor, and Sawyer picked up his. "I have to take this transmit," he said, slipping his shirt over his head.

Humiliation and frustration swept over Anissa as she did the same, leaving her bra where it lay on the floor. Sawyer re-fastened his pants as he walked out of the sim chamber, and Anissa followed a few paces behind, unsure of what to do.

He paused, then turned around so abruptly that she nearly crashed into him. "Run a bath," he said.

"I—what?"

He nodded at the soaker tub next to the sim chamber. "Fill it up," he said. "I'll take this hail. The station dockmaster will know I'm on board and they don't fuck around." His eyes searched her face. "Unless you've changed your mind."

She'd been worried about the same thing. "Not at all."

"Fill that tub and get in then," he said. "I'll be back soon." His hands framed her face, and he kissed her, the gesture rough and leaving her weak at the knees. She hadn't known Sawyer had this side to him. She liked it.

She wasn't sure she could speak, but when she opened her mouth, she managed to squeak out, "I'll be here."

Frustration and lust raced through Sawyer as he strode through the *Phantom*'s corridors to his office off the bridge. The station had better be on fire and evacuating if they were interrupting them, he thought. Even though he'd left Anissa behind, and he was about to have what was certain to be the least-sexy conversation in the history of speech, he was still so hard it was a struggle to walk.

Never in his life had he wanted anything so badly, and he was starting to realize that included finding the Immortal Spacefarer's treasure.

The alarm rang again before he could reach his office. "Fuck off," he growled at the noise, and sat down at his desk. He opened the transmit and the face and torso of a Bliss Station employee filled the screen. "Dr. Sawyer," he said crisply. "I'm with the dockmaster's office. How are you this evening?" A broad smile stretched across his face, the fake kind often worn by people used to getting yelled at.

Not as good as I could be, you grinning, cock-blocking bastard. "Very well, and yourself?"

"I'm doing great, Dr. Sawyer. Just great. I have a couple of questions for you regarding your guest who recently boarded the *Phantom.*"

Sawyer's blood chilled, his anger evaporating, to be replaced by fear. "I'm sorry?"

"We don't have any records of her ident. She's been spotted around station with you and someone else registered with your crew, but we don't have anything on her specifically. Station security protocol requires that everyone on board be accounted for, including anyone on board ships in dry dock." The employee's smile never left his face. "I'll be needing that information as soon as possible, Dr. Sawyer."

He thought quickly. He was an ideal tenant: he always paid his dock fees on time, often in advance, there had never been a complaint about his or his crew's behavior, and he consistently uploaded accurate flight plans to transit control. He was always polite to station staff. It was time for him to use his past good behavior to his advantage.

"She's a Lareshi citizen," he said. "From their Outer Reaches. Her ident chip isn't current, which is why it wouldn't have shown up during ID scans on station."

"All right, then. You understand that Bliss Station requires all residents, dry-dock tenants, and visitors to have up-to-date ident chips?" He sounded as if he was reading from a manual. Sawyer could only guess how often he'd had to deal with rogue guests.

"I do, and I apologize for the oversight. It will be corrected in the next couple of days, I promise." Because they would be going to the authorities, he thought, and that was going to turn Bliss Station into a media shitstorm. "Could I give you her information now, and she'll stay on board the *Phantom* until we have her ident sorted out?"

"It isn't SOP—"

"I know, and I would really appreciate you giving me and my guest a break on this," he said. "I've always played by Bliss Station's rules, and I will continue to do so." Sawyer stared levelly at the man, daring him to argue with him.

If the dockmaster's office refused to cooperate, he would have to move the *Phantom* to a short-term dock on a station that wouldn't have the amenities Bliss did. Which would mean delaying what they'd started in the sim chamber, and that would seriously piss him off and possibly lead him to permanently severing his ties with Bliss Station out of spite.

"I understand, Dr. Sawyer," he said. "Ordinarily we wouldn't do this, but as you pointed out, you've always been a good tenant, and sometimes life happens, right?" He let out a nervous chuckle at his own attempt at a joke. "I'm sure her ident will be updated in the next day or two, correct?"

"Of course. Her name is Anissa Alto." There was no need to lie about her name.

The dockworker typed on something off-screen. "Could you spell that for me?"

Sawyer did so.

"Place and date of birth?"

Shit. Sawyer couldn't remember her birth date—which was bad, considering he planned to go back to the soaker tub and show her exactly what had been bothering him for days—but he quickly made one up that matched her age of thirty. "Kova Two," he said for place, the only planet he could think of offhand in the Lareshi Outer Reaches.

"Very good. That will be all, Dr. Sawyer. I'm sorry for bothering you."

No, you aren't, you prick. "Not a problem. You're just doing your job."

"That I am, sir. Have a good night." The comp screen went dark as the dockworker signed off.

Sawyer left the bridge and hurried through the ship, back to the old brig section. Thoughts warred within him, each demanding his attention, but all were muffled by hormones. Had he fucked up answering the dockmaster's office questions about Anissa? Would it be a terrible mistake if they slept together? Would she end up hating him later?

He would regret it forever if she put a halt to what he wanted right now, but he would respect her decision.. Unfortunate, but a fact of life.

He stopped at the lounge and checked the pantry, smiling when he found an unopened bottle of red wine. Not the best vintage and it had 'Property of Lita, don't touch!' written on it in menacing black letters, but he knew Lita would understand. *If* he told her, which was still up for debate.

Don't think about Lita right now. He turned the bottle so he couldn't see the label.

He collected a pair of mugs, damning the fact that glasses simply didn't last on board his ship, and headed toward the brig.

Towels, you idiot.

Fuck, he'd forgotten about those, too. He made a quick side trip to the laundry room and draped a pair of mismatched beach towels over one shoulder. He really was making a mess of things. But somehow, he felt that Anissa wouldn't mind.

Assuming they were still on the same page. Gods, he hoped so.

He opened the brig door and found the room darkened: the lights turned down to a dull yellow glow. He heard a splash across the room, and when his eyes adjusted to the darkness, he saw Anissa's clothes in a pile by the sim chamber door. "Took you long enough," she said. "I was starting to think you'd forgotten about me."

"Never." He crossed the short distance to the tub and

tossed the towels on a bench attached to the wall. "I brought wine. And coffee mugs from which to drink the wine."

"It'll go well with the sexy prison lighting ambience."

He could see her in the tub now, hair dark and shining, golden skin and curves shimmering in the water under the dimmed lights. Even though every cell in his body screamed at him to strip off his clothes and jump in with her, he couldn't keep himself from smiling at her quip. With shaking hands, he pulled off the wine bottle's cap and poured it into the mugs, then placed them on the edge of the tub.

Anissa reached for one and took a sip. "The water's getting cold."

That was all the encouragement Sawyer needed. He stripped off his clothes, not bothering to check where they landed, and climbed into the tub, settling opposite Anissa.

Contrary to what she'd said, the water was still hot, and he sank into it, enjoying the heat and the feel of Anissa's legs against his own.

She set her drink aside and flowed across the short distance of the tub to him, pressing her mouth against his. Sawyer could taste the wine on her tongue; feel the heat of her body against him that had nothing to do with the water temperature. She rearranged herself, so she straddled his thighs, her legs bent at the knee.

"Is this just a onetime thing?" she asked.

The question threw Sawyer for a loop. Was it? Their situation was complicated, but he sincerely hoped not.

He realized she was waiting for an answer, and he had to be honest. "Only if you want it to be."

"I don't."

Thank every god in every heaven there is. "Good." His voice was hoarse and rough from desire. Her body slid along his, wet flesh taunting him. "There's more that I want to do to you, and I can't do it all in a soaker tub." His teeth nipped at her earlobe, eliciting a gasp from her.

Pebbled nipples scraped along his chest as she adjusted her body, her hand reaching between them to clasp his cock. Now it was his turn to suck in a harsh breath as she ran her fingers along his length. He was on the verge of begging her, before she took him into her body, enveloping him in her slick heat.

They paused for a few seconds, both shocked at what had just happened. Sawyer wasn't sure who moved first, but their lips met in a clash of tongues and teeth, and she rose on her knees, sliding up and down his length.

That was all the encouragement Sawyer needed. He thrust into her, scarcely paying attention to the water sloshing out of the tub to the tiles and only dimly aware of a coffee mug falling off the edge. His hand reached down into the water between their bodies, and Anissa caught it, guiding him to where she wanted him. Almost as soon as he touched her, she thrashed against his hand and buried her face in his neck. She tensed and clenched around him, teeth scoring his skin as a muffled cry was ripped from her throat.

That was enough to send Sawyer over the edge. He felt himself surge inside her, and she lifted her head to face him, lips swollen, eyes half-lidded and glazed with lust in the semi-darkness. He pulled her face to his, breath ragged as he kissed her, while his own orgasm ripped through him.

She sagged against him, and he didn't make a move to slide out of her. Instead, he enjoyed her weight against him, both of their hearts thundering against their ribs. Finally, he pressed a kiss to her temple.

Anissa lifted her head and looked over the edge of the tub. "We made a mess."

"It was worth it."

She lifted herself off him and he winced at the loss of contact. She picked up the remaining mug from the tub's edge and took a drink, then passed it to him. "You can see why I don't keep glasses on board now," he said, and took a sip.

She giggled. "You do this often, then?"

"Honestly, no. I would've thought my performance would have answered that question."

"Now you're fishing for compliments."

"I'm not," he insisted. She settled back against him, snuggled between his legs, head resting against his chest. Her wet hair tickled his skin. "It was a long dry spell." Realizing how that might be construed, he quickly added, "And I like you. A lot."

She didn't appear to take offense. "Good, because I like you a lot, too."

<hr>

Anissa woke up and looked around the unfamiliar cabin, taking a few seconds to reorient herself. She turned on her side, wrapping herself a little more tightly in the blankets, to look at a still-sleeping Sawyer.

A smile spread across her face at the sight, and with it, a corresponding, delicious ache between her legs. Last night had been... unexpected. But welcome, and incredibly satisfying. She wasn't sure if she could ever get enough of him.

The near-empty wine bottle was standing in the corner of the cabin, finished last night after they left the brig. She yawned and stretched, remembering there was still the matter of cleaning it up, since neither of them had felt like doing so last night. She may as well do it now, get a head start on the day. She slipped out of bed and pulled one of Sawyer's shirts over her shoulders.

Sawyer stirred, and his eyes blinked open. "Good morning," he said. He levered himself up, one arm on his pillow. "Where are you going?"

"To clean up the mess in the brig."

"It's just a little wine, and it'll come right off the tiles. Come back to bed. It can wait."

She didn't need any more encouragement. Anissa slid back under the warm covers, letting Sawyer collect her in his arms. Any doubts she might have harbored evaporated when he pressed a kiss to her lips.

A shrill, insistent beep halted their kiss. "Damn," Sawyer said, throwing off the covers.

"What is it?"

"That's a call on my personal transmit address. We really can't catch a break." He slipped a robe on and glanced at the glowing comp screen mounted on the wall opposite the bed. He gave a frustrated sigh. "And it's tagged from my father. Of course it is."

"Can't you ignore it?"

"I usually would, but he'll keep on calling. Plus, I don't want him destroying my friends' careers. He's angry enough to do that." He adjusted the comp screen, and Anissa realized he didn't want her in the camera's view.

She slipped out of bed. "I'll get us some breakfast."

"Anissa..."

"I know it's nothing personal. I wouldn't have wanted my mother seeing a man in my bed either, and we were close." Or at least Anissa had thought they were.

Sawyer's expression softened. "It won't always be like this, I promise."

Warmth and affection spread through her at those words. Anissa was aware that neither of them knew what they were doing—it was uncharted territory for both—but his assurance she wouldn't always be hidden away meant that Sawyer didn't see what happened last night as a once off. She was hoping it was more than that but hadn't had the opportunity to ask him. Not that she would have. She felt herself blush all over at the memory of the sim chamber and soaker tub.

She left Sawyer's cabin before he could accept the transmit from his father. She stopped first in the brig to quickly clean up, then headed to the lounge to scrounge up some breakfast. She toasted a few slices of bread and stuck some dehydrated eggs in the processor, then poured cups of coffee. Nothing fancy, but it would have to do.

Sawyer appeared in the lounge doorway before she could load everything on a tray, any trace of his sleepiness gone. "We're running a little low on fresh food," Anissa said. "I could take a quick trip to the grocery store later, if you like. Not that dehydrated eggs aren't delicious, but..."

"Dehydrated eggs aren't delicious, but that's what hot sauce is for." There was a darker undercurrent to Sawyer's words, one that put Anissa's senses on high alert. She set down plates at the table and gestured for him to sit.

"Is there something you want to tell me?" she asked

"Yeah, a couple of things."

She felt a wave of nausea roll over her, and she sat down heavily. Her stomach turned over. A million things ran through her head at his words, none of them good. "Sawyer, what's wrong?"

He sat down opposite her. "First off, I have to apologize."

"What for? Last night? Last night was..." She fumbled for words and came up short. "Well, you know."

"No, not for that. For what happened right before, when I had to take that hail in the bridge office."

She'd forgotten all about that hail. But she did remember what had happened afterward, heat flooding her body at the memory. She'd had no idea that he could be that demanding and couldn't wait to experience it again.

"The hail was from the dockmaster's office," he said. "They wanted to know who you are."

Anissa froze.

"I told them," he said. "They've noticed your movements around station, and Bliss's SOP states they have to know the identity of everyone on the station and anyone on board ships in dry dock. All they know is your name, and I told them you're from the Lareshi Outer Reaches and that you'd be updating your ID soon. They don't know who you are, not really."

She relaxed a little. "That doesn't sound too bad."

"It isn't. But it means that we have to go to the authorities, soon. You can't spend your entire life on the *Phantom* and without a current ID."

"Of course not. Did your father get in touch to yell at you again?"

"No."

"Was it about your teaching or your friends?"

"*Our* friends."

Irritation flared inside her. She tamped it down before speaking again. "Sawyer, you're avoiding my question."

"That gala he's insisting I go to?"

"Yeah, what about it?"

He turned wide, fearful eyes to her. When he spoke, his words were rushed. "Prime University wants to reopen studies into bio-longevity."

CHAPTER 12

SAWYER COULD SEE the instant the words hit Anissa. She leapt up, knocking her plate askew. "What the *fuck*?" she yelped. "Are you serious? Is your father serious?"

"Yes." He felt sick thinking of his conversation with his father. "The gala's focus is on raising funds to establish a department of bio-longevity and bio-cybernetics. The department is on schedule to open in less than a year."

"Headed by whom?"

"I'm sorry?"

"University departments have head professors, don't they? Who's going to run the bio-longevity department?"

Sawyer knew what she was thinking. "The chair's name is Farel Polchin. I made sure that Devon spelled it out for me. We'll check his credentials, and..."

Anissa interrupted him. "Expose him as Dr. Mollon. Or one of his minions. Sawyer, I *told* you Mollon was still alive!"

"We'll check," he promised. "I'll get a feed from the satellite campus's library, and we can do as much research as we want. I guarantee if my father approved his hiring, there'll be more about Farel Polchin than Crale Mollon."

"Or Vicora Alto."

Sawyer detected the note of bitterness in her voice. Her mother had inexcusably betrayed her, and the effect of this on her long-term health was unknown. He also had to admit she may also possibly be right about Mollon not dying in a shuttle accident. He wasn't convinced that Farel Polchin was just her mother's murderer surfacing after a century, but he wouldn't discount it either. It just seemed strange, otherwise, that a long-abandoned field of study was about to be resurrected in the Rodanta Quadrant's most prestigious university.

As if she could read his thoughts, Anissa asked, "How in the Four Hells did someone convince the university to dedicate a department to bio-longevity?"

"That's what I asked him," Sawyer said. He'd been roundly cursed out for it, too. "He didn't tell me why."

"I thought genetic engineering was outlawed in Rodantan space?"

"It is, with medical exceptions." It was why Tash Passan could conduct genetic testing, but she had to submit documentation to the Quadrant's medical board asserting birth defects before fetal DNA could be altered. "I don't feel right about opening it up as an academic path. It's weird, and I don't know how my father was bamboozled into doing this."

"Did you tell him that?"

"Of course not. He would've fired Lita and me immediately." He ran a hand through his hair, trying to put his thoughts into logical order. "I don't get it. Why would he and the university's board of directors approve this?"

"Blackmail?"

Sawyer considered that for a few seconds, then shook his head. "No. My father is very well-connected politically, and he could have any blackmail threats taken care of." He blew out a frustrated sigh. "I don't know, Anissa. This is all very out of character for him."

"So, we'll start that research then." Anissa stood up, breakfast forgotten.

"No." He placed a proprietary hand on her wrist before she could leave the room. "We'll finish eating first." Then, before he could stop himself, he added, "We need to replenish our energy after last night."

She felt herself blush. But she sat down again and sprinkled hot sauce on her reconstituted eggs.

"I didn't know you had that side to you," she said.

He looked at her quizzically, waiting for her to continue.

"You know, a little dominant," she said. "I liked it."

Dominant? He would have used the same word to describe her, taking charge the way she did. He'd been suffering from pent-up lust for what felt like forever, then to be so rudely interrupted by the station dockmaster's office...

And yeah, he had to admit to himself, he'd sort of liked how that felt. Maybe Anissa wasn't completely off with the 'dominant' statement.

"Do I get a repeat performance?" she asked.

A fresh surge of lust roared through him, and he pushed aside his plate. "I thought you wanted to do research." Damn it, why the hell had he said that?

"It can wait a few minutes."

"This'll take longer than a few minutes."

Her eyes were half-lidded already, and he knew that nothing could tear him from her at this instant. Maybe ever. "Don't you want to finish your breakfast?"

"I've suddenly lost my appetite for food." She was already on her feet, crossing the short distance between them, pinning him against the table.

He caught her lower lip between his teeth and gently sucked at it, drawing a gasp from her. She reached for the belt on his robe, but he stilled her hands. "Not here," he said. "My cabin." He clasped her hand in his and led her out of the lounge.

"Worried someone might drop by?"

Well, that was a concern, but Sawyer would hear anyone before they reached the lounge, if they were impolite enough to let themselves in instead of pressing the chime first. "No, the main entrance is locked. I just think you deserve a bed instead of a dinner table."

She squeezed his hand. "I don't care, as long as it's with you."

That was sweet, but not Sawyer's issue. "I'm not an animal."

Her soft giggle was her only response.

Anissa took the initiative, leading Sawyer to the bed. She peeled off the shirt and tossed it over the side and he did the same with his robe.

"Would it be inappropriate to suggest that you just not wear clothes when we're alone?" Sawyer asked. His hand traced the outline of her lips, as if memorizing her features.

"Only if you can promise that no one will walk in on us, including Enzo."

"Enzo's probably seen millions of things that would blind living beings. His programming keeps him too polite to say anything about it."

"Would you also be naked in this hypothetical situation?"

"Why not? Let's make archaeology even more interesting. Oh, *fuck*!" Anissa wrapped her hand around his shaft and slowly pumped her hand up and down. His cock throbbed and thickened under her touch.

"Want me to stop?" she asked.

"No, never."

Anissa dipped her head down, tracing her tongue over his chest and abdomen until she could put her mouth where her hand had been. His hips bucked in response, his fingers threading her hair, as she took him deeper.

But then he stopped her and pulled her up along his body, lips claiming hers in a fierce kiss as he flipped her beneath him in one smooth movement. Elbows braced on either side of her head; he guided himself inside her. He didn't take his eyes off Anissa's face as he thrust inside her, and by all the gods in all the universes, she wasn't going to last long.

"Touch yourself." His voice was a harsh, hoarse whisper in her ear. "I want to see it."

She couldn't say no to this man. He'd ruined her for anyone else; she knew that already. She obediently slid her hand down her body, Sawyer's eyes leaving her face long enough to watch. When she touched her fingers to her aching clit, the heat that had been stoking inside her mushroomed into a fireball. Her cry was muffled by Sawyer's mouth on her own as he moved faster inside her, stiffening as his own climax overtook him.

She wrapped her arms around his shoulders. He rolled onto his side, taking her with him, gaze fixed on hers. She could feel the rapid beat of his pulse all over as he tenderly tucked a few strands of hair behind her ear.

"I think," he said, "that's the best possible way to start the day."

She let herself enjoy his heat for another few moments, not wanting to leave the bed. But there was still a lot of work to be done before she and Sawyer could relax and see where this... relationship, Anissa happily supposed, took them.

He must have noticed the almost imperceptible shift of her body as she considered what was ahead of them. "I guess that means we have to get to work."

"Don't look at me like that," she said as he withdrew from her body. "I don't think either of us wants to leave this bed."

"I'd be willing to leave the bed to go back to the sim chamber or tub."

Four Hells, Anissa would never be able to run a program again in that sim chamber without remembering what had happened in there. "We'll do that again," she promised.

"I'll hold you to that." He crawled out of bed. "It isn't terribly romantic since it uses laser cleansers, but you could join me in the shower."

"Don't be so sure about the romance thing," Anissa said, following him to the washroom.

Twenty minutes later, clean and dressed, they returned to the lounge. The replicator kicked out some drinkable coffee, and Sawyer sent quick transmits to Lita and Dian, asking them to come to the *Phantom* when they had time. Then, they started their research in earnest.

Compared to the scant information available on Vicora Alto and Crale Mollon, there was a mine of data about Farel Polchin. They discovered that he'd been born in the former Section Five colony, a remote territory that had been absorbed with the Rodantan government forty-eight years' prior. He held medical and doctorate degrees in genetic engineering and had worked in hospitals and taught at smaller institutions in Section Five and along its border with Rodanta proper. His credentials, when Sawyer checked them, proved to be genuine.

"Are there any pictures?" Anissa asked as she and Sawyer raked through piles of printouts, adding to the already-large stack on the lounge coffee table. More data was displayed on the wall-mounted comp screen.

"Not yet, but we still have more information to go through. He's written quite a bit on the subject of bio-longevity, but it looks like he wasn't taken that seriously at more prestigious universities, which isn't a surprise." His eyes widened. "Holy fuck."

"What?"

"You're not going to believe this."

Anissa made a "get on with it" gesture, urging him to continue. Despite the flip movement, her insides were shaking.

Sawyer's voice was low, unexpected rage barely contained. "He has a research ship. Her name is *Spindle's End*."

Spindle's End.

It took a few seconds for the words to register.

My mother's research ship...

When they did, the only words Anissa could manage were, "Are you sure?"

"It's right here. Registered out of a depot in Section Five. Science-class vessel, five years old. It's included in the information packet sent to Prime."

Anissa turned her gaze to Sawyer's stricken face. "Do you believe me now?" she said.

"I—holy fuck, Anissa, yes, I think I do."

She stood up on shaking legs. "What's the code to the weapons locker?"

"I only have two laser rifles, and I'm not sure if they're even charged. And we are *not* going after Farel Polchin on our own."

"Do you really think the authorities are going to believe us when we tell them that an obscure researcher from Section Five—and I know all about Section Five, they meddled in the civil war, too—is actually some kind of super-villain who's managed to live forever?" She stared at him archly, and Sawyer flinched. "I wouldn't. I don't think you would, either."

"Are you suggesting we go to my father and calmly explain that the professor he hired is just that?"

"No, I'm suggesting we track him down and kill him ourselves. Now, what's the code to the weapons locker?"

Now Sawyer rose to his feet. "No."

"Fuck it, Benedict, some things fall outside the realm of the law." She paced around the lounge, feeling as caged in as a zoo animal and just as powerless. "And before you say anything else, there is no fucking possibility that all of this is a coincidence. I don't believe for a second that a bio-longevity specialist popped up out of nowhere and has a research ship with a name nearly identical to my mother's."

"Anissa..."

"He stole my mother's research!" Anissa shouted. "It wasn't enough to murder her. He had to steal her life's work! You're a scientist. How angry would you be if someone murdered you and stole all your research and then took credit for it?"

He opened his mouth as if to speak; then obviously thought better of it and closed it.

"And don't say that you'd be dead, so you wouldn't mind," Anissa added.

"I wasn't going to say that," Sawyer said, his voice quiet. "I was going to say that I'd find a way to come back from the dead and haunt the bastard for the rest of his days."

Anissa relaxed a smidgen, the urge to find the nearest weapon ebbing enough for her to think clearly. It was probably a good thing that Sawyer hadn't given her the code or location of the weapons locker. She plunked down on the couch next to Sawyer. "Why in the Four Hells is the university funding that department?" she asked, knowing Sawyer was unable to answer the question. He stayed quiet. "Even if you hadn't found me on that planet," she said, "wouldn't you be pissed off that he's funneling money into a discredited science instead of your department?"

Sawyer stood up so suddenly that Anissa nearly tipped over into the cushions. "The planet we found you on," he said.

"Yeah, what about it?"

"There was another ship nearby when we picked you up," he said. "Fitch said he saved the energy signature in the *Phantom*'s command console. Let's go look."

He hurried out of the lounge, Anissa behind him. "What are you talking about?" she asked.

"I forgot about it until now. We all did after we opened the box and found you." Once they reached the bridge, Sawyer slid into the captain's seat and signed in to the computer. Anissa hovered behind him, watching as he scrolled through lines of code. "Lita and I went down to dig you out," he said. "We took the shuttle, and before we got back to the *Phantom*, Fitch told us that the long-range sensors picked up an unidentified vessel ten or fifteen minutes out from where we were. No ID broadcasting and the ship itself registered as an unknown in the computer. We assumed it was a pirate ship."

"And then you forgot about it."

"Well, instead of finding the Immortal Spacefarer's treasure, we found a living person, so it slipped my mind." He looked up at her, unexpected warmth in his eyes. "Better than treasure, to be honest."

Despite the gravity of the situation and her rage, Anissa felt something shift inside her at those words. Sawyer wasn't about to kick her off his ship for yelling at him or getting angry. She couldn't remember the last time she'd let a man see that side of her off the battlefield. It made her feel flustered, and she wasn't used to that.

So she slipped into the copilot's seat, unsure how to answer, and leaned over to look at the pilot's console screen. "Let me send it over to you," Sawyer said. Before she could tell him that she didn't mind sharing, he mirrored his work on the copilot's console.

She might have just fucked that up by not responding, but she would worry about it later.

The lines of code scrolled along with Sawyer's movements

until a file was opened. "Here it is," he said. Anissa recognized the code that made up a ship's energy signature, along with the words underneath: *Unknown/unidentified vessel*.

"No weapons signature," Sawyer said. "Nothing that indicated the ship's manufacturer. Judging from this, it's medium-sized, but that's all the *Phantom*'s computers has on her."

Anissa touched the lines of code and watched as it coalesced into a rough outline of an unknown ship. Her heart leapt to her throat. "You need to do some serious upgrades to the *Phantom*'s files," she said.

"Why? Do you recognize it?"

"I'd need a little more information to be certain, but this looks like a modified fourth-class Lareshi destroyer," Anissa said. "The rebels used them during the civil war." Anissa stared at the rotating image. "See those tubes?" She pointed a fingernail at the image.

"Not really."

"They're there," Anissa insisted. "They stick out only a little because they were meant to fire at very close range. Fourth-class destroyers were designed to be flown by a single pilot and only carried a couple of torpedoes. They were insanely expensive to make and only good for a couple of shots, which is why the Empire never really bothered with them. As far as I know, only a limited number went into mass production."

"And you're saying this is a hundred-year-old, single occupant Lareshi rebel warship that just happened to be in the same region as us when we found you?"

"I'm saying it's too close to be a coincidence."

"Wouldn't someone recognize this ship?" Sawyer asked. "War history buffs or gearheads?"

"I wouldn't know. I've been asleep since then." Her mind worked frantically, trying to reconcile everything she'd learned so far. "Section Five helped the rebels. It's not inconceivable that they would have some old warships lying around."

"To be honest, Section Five only helped themselves," Sawyer said. "Their government only agreed to join Rodanta officially after the colony went bankrupt and the Lareshis stopped sending them aid."

"So it stands to reason that Section Five would still have warships or weapons or something. Farel Polchin's a citizen, isn't he?"

"Yeah, but even if he managed to get his hands on an antique warship, surely someone would notice it floating around space," Sawyer said. "It's probably priceless."

"Unless it had been altered to look like a science-class vessel instead of a fourth-class destroyer." Anissa tapped the screen. "This signature only shows what a ship would look like coming off the production line. It wouldn't indicate any cosmetic changes, unless the technology has greatly improved since I was in stasis."

"I don't think it has."

"Do you think we could get more technical information on the *Spindle's End*?" she asked.

Without a trace of hesitation, Sawyer said, "Yes. But we'll need some help."

FITCH AND LITA, flanked by Enzo, showed up at the *Phantom*'s airlock less than fifteen minutes after Sawyer summoned them, far faster than he'd expected. He and Anissa both scrambled to get dressed when the door chime sounded, although Sawyer suspected that his friends would figure them out anyway. They, and Dian, knew him better than anyone.

"How goes it, Captain?" asked Fitch.

"Not too shabby," Sawyer replied.

"Commander Alto!" Enzo said, canned enthusiasm in his voice. "How are you?"

"Very well, Enzo."

To Sawyer, Enzo said, "Sawyer."

Was that *disdain* in the android's voice? Had his AI finally developed an aversion to offering to teach Sawyer card games? Could he be so lucky?

Before Sawyer could voice a question to that effect, Lita spoke. "How's your lesson plan going?" she asked, not trying to hide the anger in her voice.

"I've hardly looked at it," Sawyer said. "And once we have a chance to sit down and I tell you what's going down at the university, I'm not sure we'll be stuck teaching next semester after all." That remark earned him a withering look from Anissa, and he added, "Not that we're doing this just to avoid a bunch of functionally illiterate students with no interest in archaeology."

"That's just a fringe benefit," Lita said. "Are we waiting for Dian?"

"She and Tash will be here soon. Tash had some paperwork to finish up at the hospital." Not that Dian and Tash's presence was strictly required for what Sawyer hoped to accomplish, as Fitch's skill set was necessary for that, but it was important they be included. They would find out what was going on as soon as they arrived.

Once in the lounge, Sawyer and Anissa shared with them with the news that Prime University was planning on funding a new department devoted to bio-longevity research and that they were hiring Farel Polchin to head it. "That's what this gala is for," Sawyer said. "It's to drum up money for pseudoscience."

"Pseudoscience or not, I was still experimented on," Anissa said.

He realized then that Lita and Fitch still weren't up to date with the bombshell Tash had delivered at the hospital, but Anissa spoke before he could. "My mother altered my DNA when I was a baby," she said. "Not that it will affect anything in the long term as far as we can tell, but she definitely experimented on me."

Both Lita and Fitch looked shocked at this development, and Anissa handing over the papers detailing her genetic testing did nothing to change their expressions. "Lareshis always had a slight advantage over Rodantans in terms of lifespan," Anissa said. "Even I knew that. In part it's due to genetics, helped out by our better diets and lifestyle habits."

"That's already been established. The Empire picked up a lot of Rodantan bad habits over the years after the alliance," said Lita. "I think our lifespans are neck-and-neck now." Seeing the distraught look on Anissa's face—one that tore at Sawyer as well—she added, "But that's not relevant, is it?"

"No." Anissa sat up a little straighter. "I just want to focus on Farel Polchin and the ship's signature the *Phantom* picked up the day you found me."

"Oh, shit!" Fitch said. "I totally forgot about that after everything that happened that day."

"We all did," Sawyer said. "Which brings me to my next point. Fitch, can you dig around a few databases and find out what kind of shuttle Farel Polchin has?" At Anissa's look, he explained, "Fitch has a skill set that extends beyond piloting."

"I was expelled from Prime's data engineering program," Fitch said, a touch of pride in his voice. "For hacking. The university board went easy on me and let me re-enroll in a pilot diploma program instead, which is why I'm a law-abiding citizen instead of a hacker for hire."

"Pilots live longer," Lita said.

"At least until there's a war. Anyway, Sawyer, to answer your question, I absolutely can do some questionable research. I'll need some time to set up a secure link, but it shouldn't be too difficult. Can I use the bridge office comp?"

"Of course. And thank you."

Fitch stood up. "Enzo, come with me. I can use you as a proxy."

Enzo followed Fitch out of the lounge. "Will I have to do anything?"

"No, just stand still and let me plug a couple of wires into your hands. You won't be able to play cards while I'm working."

Their voices sounded down the corridor. "Shall we practice speaking De'lah?"

"Not today, Enzo."

"You really need to make that robot less irritating," Sawyer said. "Doesn't the constant babbling wear down his batteries?"

"It's part of his charm," Lita said. "If you want a boring android, get your own."

Sawyer let the matter of Enzo drop. If the annoying android could help Fitch break into Section Five and university systems, Sawyer could tolerate him. Plus, Anissa was fond of him.

Lita's expression turned serious again. "What happens if this Farel Polchin is involved in Anissa's mother's murder?"

"Then I'll kill him," Anissa replied.

"Okay, that's one option," Lita said. "What did you have in mind that won't get you sent to a prison colony?"

Some of Anissa's steely reserve melted a little. "As much as I want to kill him, and he deserves it, we all know there's only one option."

"You would have to deal with the authorities eventually," Lita said. To Sawyer, she said, "When were you planning to tell your father about this particular bit of research?"

"Are you referring to Anissa?"

"Not in as many words, but I *was* referring to your theories about Farel Polchin."

"I don't know." Sawyer leaned back in his spot on the couch. "I don't have any plan aside from figuring things out as they happen. I guess we find out if the energy signature Fitch captured matches anything registered to Polchin, then we confront the authorities with our theories. We haven't broken any laws, technically. We didn't need a permit to dig around the planet we found Anissa on." Which was why everyone had automatically assumed pirates were nearby that morning. That area of space was rarely, if ever, patrolled. There was nothing there to protect, unless someone was trawling around space looking for the origins of children's stories.

"Are you planning on exposing everything at the gala you're being forced to attend?"

"No. For one, security will be too tight, and I have no idea if Polchin is even going to be there," Sawyer said.

"The idea is tempting," Anissa said. Sawyer raised an eyebrow at her. "I'm not usually one for exacting justice in such a public manner, but the idea has its appeal."

"Until we crash the podium while dear old Dad introduces Polchin and we get ourselves arrested before we can get a word out," Sawyer said. "Because that's how it'll go down if we do that. We need to get as much proof as we can that Polchin is tied to you, and then go the proper, legal route to exposing him."

"He makes sense," Lita said, and sighed. "As much as I hate to admit it."

The door chime sounded, and Sawyer stood up. "That'll be Dian and Tash."

When he opened the airlock to let them in, Dian was more than a little impatient. "What did I miss?" she asked.

"How is Anissa doing?" asked Tash, ever the physician.

"We have a possible, uh, person of interest," Sawyer said. "Fitch is doing some dark magic with the ship's computer right now to find out a little more about him. And Anissa's doing okay." He wasn't going to elaborate on Anissa's feelings of betrayal at finding out what her mother had done to her; it wasn't his place. Nor was he eager to announce whatever it was they had going on to his crew just yet. It was bound to come out at some point, but not now. He'd leave the decision of when to reveal that up to Anissa as well.

He hoped she wanted to. He hoped that after all of this was settled that she would want to stay with him, in a capacity beyond her piloting.

But now wasn't the time to be contemplating that. The three of them headed in the direction of the lounge, and ran into Fitch and Enzo in the corridor. "Next time," Fitch said, "give me a challenge."

"Mission successful?"

Fitch nodded. "Very. There's an old ship registered to Farel Polchin that has the same signature as the one I picked up when we found Anissa. Its registration certificate lists its manufacturer as Bartel, which went out of business about twenty-five years ago."

"Never heard of them," Sawyer said.

"They were a small, and very shady, outfit that worked in Section Five. Cheap shuttles and generic parts, and they would do any mods for the right amount of scrip. It would have been easy to make cosmetic enhancements to a single-pilot warship so it resembled one of their models with no one being any the wiser."

"But you're *sure* that this shuttle's signature matched the one saved in the computer?" Anissa asked.

"Yeah. That is *definitely* the ship that stalked us out by that rock."

Dian and Tash looked at the group expectantly. Dian's voice was brusque. "Care to fill us in?"

It took over an hour for everyone in the room to speak their piece and finally understand what was going on. By the end of it, they had opened the remaining bottle of wine Lita had left on board, and downed the contents in an attempt to minimize the impact of what had been discovered, and what still had to be investigated. The situation was, Anissa thought, much bigger than any of them had thought.

But not her. She'd expected to feel a sense of justice, if not self-righteousness in the knowledge that she was right. But instead, all she felt was relief that they believed her and that she wouldn't be taking down Dr. Mollon alone.

And she *knew* Farel Polchin was Dr. Mollon.

Just as she knew Dr. Mollon wasn't going to get out of this new century alive.

Polchin showing up seemingly out of nowhere, from an area known to keep to itself, his shuttle's energy signature matching that of the vessel that appeared at the same time as the *Phantom*'s crew arrived to retrieve Anissa—none of that was a coincidence.

The very name of his ship itself: *Spindle's End*. It was nothing more than a giant fuck-you to Vicora Alto, Dr. Mollon's cold dismissal of his crimes a century after the fact.

There was that sense of relief for her, knowing she was finally believed, but anger simmered beneath it. This was far from over.

"Do we know where Polchin is now?" Anissa asked the room.

"Somewhere in Rodantan space is my guess," Fitch said. "I don't feel confident enough to hack into the flight networks to see what plans he's uploaded." At Lita's aghast expression, he said, "What? I can't be of much help if I'm arrested. Poking around the databases for a Section Five depot is only sort of illegal. Breaking into secured Rodantan networks means a minimum six-month stint on a prison colony, and I'd lose my pilot's license."

"And you're too pretty for jail," Anissa said. "I appreciate everything you've done, Fitch. That goes for all of you." A lump formed in her throat, unexpected and unwelcome.

All eyes were on her. She gulped and hoped none of them noticed.

"I didn't have a lot of friends in the Empire," she said. "For a long time, it was just me, my mother, and her crew on the *Spindle*. I wasn't friends with my platoon, either." She tried to lighten the mood a little. "I'm sure you've noticed I'm not the friendliest person out there."

Dian raised her hand. "Before everyone starts crying and turning this into a love-in, let me say that I have a duty to maintain the title of least-friendly person on this crew." That earned a withering look from Tash. "What?" said Dian. "Everyone here is about to start bawling."

Anissa knew it was just her on the verge of tears. "I'm not," she said, although a tear leaked down her cheek. "I just wanted to say I appreciate everything you've done for me, a total stranger who should've been a treasure chest at the bottom of a freezing-cold pit."

"You're a better surprise than a treasure chest," Sawyer said.

The look in his eyes sent a bolt of heat through her, another unexpected feeling. It added another complicated layer to the myriad emotions running through her. It bolstered both her courage and anger.

She wasn't alone.

She could do this.

"The fundraising gala is being held here on Bliss in a couple of weeks," Sawyer said. "I think it's best if we go to the authorities before then."

"We'll protect you from the media shitstorm," Lita said. "I promise. Keep your head down and it won't last forever."

"Do you think there's any chance this'll stay out of the news?" Anissa asked, clinging to the faint hope that all of this could be swept under the rug.

"Not if it involves Prime University," Lita said, her voice gentle. "I'm sorry."

"It's up to you," Sawyer said. "This is your life."

This is your life. After having had her life stolen from her … Her gaze met Sawyer's. She hadn't planned for any of this to happen, but if it had to, at least it had brought Benedict

Sawyer into her life, even if she wasn't totally sure where she stood with him.

She realized they were waiting for an answer, but she didn't really have one. What she wanted was to track down Farel Polchin and kill him herself, but she knew that wasn't going to happen. Not if she wanted to restart her life outside of a prison colony.

"Give me a few days," Anissa finally said. "Then we'll all go to the authorities together."

It was nearly dinnertime before everyone left the *Phantom*, and Sawyer was at a loss what to do next. He suspected Anissa was too.

"Are you hungry?" he asked.

"Not really."

"Want some more wine?"

She unfolded herself from the couch to sit up. "What the hell. I'll have another glass."

Sawyer uncorked the last bottle he had on board and refilled their coffee mugs. Even though he acutely felt the stress Anissa was under, knowing what he felt was nothing compared to her grief, he remembered drinking wine the night before out of those same mugs and actually felt himself blush. He settled next to her and couldn't suppress a small, happy thrill from coursing through him when she cuddled into him.

"This is going to be bad," she said.

There was no point in sugarcoating the truth. "Yeah."

"Even if Polchin turns out to be Mollon and he ends up on a prison colony or dead or whatever, that won't change anything," she said.

"I know." He draped an arm around her and she leaned her head against his shoulder. "If you're concerned about the media, we'll move to another station for a bit. Or we'll go on a research expedition if you want to get away."

"The media." He heard the cringe in her voice. "That's going to be bad, too."

Sawyer dreaded it on her behalf. "It will be, yeah. But you won't be doing that alone."

"What about teaching?"

"I'm not sure I'll be teaching next semester," he said. "Assuming Polchin has something to do with your mother's murder, it will cause a major scandal at the university." He paused. "My father might lose his job."

She turned her face up to him, a smile across it. "I bet you'd love that."

"Yeah, I would."

She was quiet for a moment, thinking. Finally, she said, "Maybe my mother really did discover the secrets to longevity, if Dr. Mollon's managed to live so long."

"Maybe."

"Does your job offer still stand?"

"Of course." That job offer introduced another, more delicate, issue between them, and he could tell by her shifting position that she'd thought about it, as well. "It stands no matter what."

"Even though we're sleeping together?"

He hadn't expected that; he thought they might dance around it for a few minutes. "I like that you're direct."

"So were you last night and this morning. Was that a one-night stand?"

He couldn't form a coherent answer. "I—uh, well ..."

"I don't do one-night stands, Sawyer. Especially with my boss."

He relaxed a smidgen, but some uncertainty remained. "I don't do one-night stands, either."

"So can I assume we'll keep on sleeping together? Because I'd like that."

That was a relief. "I'd like to take you out to dinner or something, too, once you can leave the ship," he said.

"Even better."

I could fall in love with this woman. He didn't voice the thought, not wanting to scare her off or make things awkward, so he tightened his hold on her instead.

I will never let you go, and I'll never let anyone hurt you again.

CHAPTER 14

SAWYER STALKED onto the *Phantom*'s bridge, irritation across his features. "Damn it."

Anissa looked up from the training program running across the ship's navigation console. "Is something wrong?"

"My father's en route to Bliss. He wants me to meet him at the Prime satellite campus on station."

"Why?"

"Something to do with the gala. Plus, it's just another way for him to meddle in my life."

"But you can find out some more about Farel Polchin," Anissa said. "It might not be all bad."

A few days had passed since their discussion with the rest of the crew about Polchin and Mollon, and while Sawyer hadn't said as much, Anissa knew she needed to stop prolonging the inevitable and file a report. The gala Sawyer was being bullied into attending was only a couple of days away; that was undoubtedly the reason Devon King was showing up at Bliss Station.

Being confined to the Phantom was also making Anissa a little stir-crazy. "What would you say if I told you I was willing to walk to the station's authorities with you and file that report?" she asked.

Shock suffused his features for a moment. When he recovered, he said, "Already?"

"I've been putting it off way too long," she said.

"No, you haven't. I understand why you want to wait."

"I have," she insisted. "It's time to start my life over legitimately, and if we do this now, you won't have to go to that stupid gala. We have as much information as we can get about Polchin and Mollon, there's my old ID chip in my wrist, and you still have my coffin, right?"

"In the lab, along with the anti-gravity holds that kept it from floating away. But are you sure you want to do this now?"

"No," she said. "But I have to. I'm not afraid of starting my life over, not anymore. I'm worried about all the shit that'll be thrown at me while I do it."

He crossed the short distance to where she sat at the controls. She stood up and wrapped her arms around him. "I want those dinner dates," she said softly. "I want my life back. I can't spend the rest of it hiding out on your ship, pissing off the dockmaster."

"Fuck the dockmaster."

"I'd rather not." That earned a small chuckle from Sawyer. "I'd never put off anything unpleasant in old my life. Procrastination isn't a habit I want to pick up in Rodanta. Send a transmit to your father and tell him you can't meet him when he docks here."

"I wasn't going to meet him anyway. He'd find a way to invite himself to stay on board the *Phantom* and then insult her every chance he gets."

"Why is your dad so awful?"

"I've been asking myself that for thirty-five years and still don't have an answer. My mother felt the same way." He pulled away from her enough to make eye contact. "When did you want to file the report?"

"Now. Before I lose my nerve and your dad's ship arrives."

"In his transmit he said he was about forty minutes out, so we have time." Taking her hand, he led her through the ship to the lounge. "We'll bring our research. I hope it'll be enough to get my father questioned."

"Are you going to tell the others?"

"I'll send them messages and let them know what's going on. Do you want them there?"

Anissa felt terrible for what she was about to admit. "It doesn't matter either way. But I need you there."

He squeezed her hand reassuringly. "And I will be. You won't be alone while we're on Bliss. I'm not sure it's safe."

"The dockmaster's office knows my name."

He blanched a little at that reminder. "I'm still sorry about that. I wasn't thinking."

She blushed, remembering when he'd been called away. Color bloomed on his face as well. "I'm still not mad about it," she said.

"I am, but the alternative was your being arrested or something."

He sent a short transmit to the crew. They gathered their research, putting it in a satchel that Sawyer slung over his shoulder. He unlocked the *Phantom*'s exterior door and they were immediately hit with a rush of cold air, typical of station docks.

Nervousness twisted her gut, and she gripped Sawyer's hand. Her heart beat so hard in her ears she was sure anyone passing could hear it. When was the last time she'd been this nervous?

You lived through a war. You lived through your attempted murder. You can report this, you can start your life over.

This was unprecedented territory for her. Plenty of people

had made it through wars and survived murder attempts. But how many had woken up 104 years in the future? Anissa felt herself break out in a cold sweat.

When they passed the dry-dock checkpoint, she looked up at the incoming arrivals message board, listing all vessels whose flight plans included Bliss Station stopovers. Her heart skipped a few beats when one ship's name caught her eye, and she stopped dead in her tracks. "Sawyer," she said urgently. She discreetly pointed at the sign, and he looked up. His eyes widened.

Spindle's End, ETA 13:07.

"What the fuck?" Sawyer said.

"When's your father due to arrive?"

"He said he was forty minutes out before we left. It's been about half an hour since I got that transmit and we left the *Phantom*."

"Are any of those ships' names familiar to you?"

He scanned the list. "No. Most of them are commercial passenger ships, which my dad would never travel on, and what looks like a couple of personal shuttles, none of which he's traveled on before."

"How can you tell which ship is which?"

"The names of commercial passenger ships are displayed in blue, everything else is in yellow, including the *Spindle's End*. But it's the ETA that makes me think my dad's on board that ship."

"He's with Polchin," Anissa said. "Oh, Four Hells. Do we stay here and confront him or file that report now?"

The vessel's name flashed on the arrivals board. "It's requested permission to dock," Sawyer said.

"So it's nearly here," Anissa said. They had to make a decision. When she looked at Sawyer, she saw uncertainty playing across his face, too.

Neither of them knew what to do.

"Maybe we should hide out somewhere and see what Farel Polchin looks like," she suggested. "See if he looks like Dr. Mollon and if he's with your father."

It was a weak idea, and she could tell from Sawyer's expression that he thought so, too. "Then we'll go file that report?"

"Yeah. I need to know if Polchin is really Mollon."

"He could have changed his appearance."

"Maybe, but there aren't any publicly available images of either of them. I don't think that's a coincidence."

"Okay." Sawyer looked around. "They'll probably be docking in a private or semi-private berth, so we can't just hang around the commercial arrivals drop-off and hope for the best." Indecisiveness flitted across his features. "We'll go to the satellite university office. That'll probably be the first place my dad will go, and I won't have a problem checking in. Neither will you."

It was the only idea either of them could come up with. Anissa nodded.

As they hurried through Bliss's corridors, bypassing checkpoints, she tried to lighten the mood. "I'm sorry my hand's so sweaty."

"Oh, that sweaty feeling isn't you."

"I think that's the sexiest thing you've ever said to me."

He caught her eye and she couldn't help but laugh. She needed it, and judging from the smile on his face, he did, too.

They strode into the satellite campus's main entrance easily enough, and Sawyer led her through an unfamiliar glass-walled corridor lined with office doors. "The office for the archaeology department is close enough to Bliss's vice-president's," he said. "We'll be able to see them as they walk by if we stick around the waiting room." They stopped outside a door whose nameplate read MATERIAL CULTURES/XENO-MATERIAL CULTURES: ALL

DEPARTMENTS and waited while Sawyer's retinal and palm prints were read.

The door slid open soundlessly, and Anissa sat down facing the glass walls, so she could see the corridor. Sawyer took the seat across from her and craned his neck to watch the corridor. The receptionist looked up from behind her desk after seeing them check in. "Dr. Sawyer?" she said curiously. "Is there anything I can help you with? You don't have an appointment."

"I'm waiting for someone," he replied.

"May I ask the name of your guest? She's registering as an unknown in my system."

"Anissa Alto," Anissa said before Sawyer could reply. "I'm working on that unknown thing."

The receptionist looked a little a confused but entered the name into her comp. "All right. Dr. Sawyer, you *are* aware of security protocols at this campus?"

"Very much so," Sawyer said. "And Ms. Alto is not a security threat." Anissa noted that he didn't use her *Commander* title as his crew and Enzo had, undoubtedly reducing the number of questions that could be lobbed her way. The receptionist gave up on asking any more questions and returned to her work.

Occasionally an employee walked through the corridor, but no one that either of them recognized.

Dr. King or Polchin might have stopped by a hotel first, or Dr. King might have taken the time to send another bullying transmit to Sawyer. Anissa settled into her seat for a long wait. She hoped the receptionist hadn't decided to inform security of her presence. Judging from her bored expression and lack of interest in her and Sawyer, her fears were likely unfounded.

There was still Farel Polchin to think of. She quickly revised that. Her fears about the *receptionist* were unfounded.

She and Sawyer kept their attention on the corridor as the

minutes ticked by. Anissa checked the wall-mounted clock periodically, noticing that more than half an hour had flown by without any sight of Dr. King or Mollon, assuming he still resembled his old, balding self.

Half an hour... thirty-five minutes... forty-five minutes...

"There's my dad," Sawyer said, and quickly turned away to face Anissa. He slouched low in his seat, and she saw the hope written across his face that Dr. King hadn't spotted him.

She straightened her spine and looked up over the back of Sawyer's chair. Walking alongside the silver-haired Dr. King was a shorter, paunchier man with a shock of yellow- white hair. But when he raised his head a little, replying to something that Dr. King said, his face sent Anissa's blood running cold.

"Oh, Four Hells," she said under her breath. She remained in her seat.

"Anissa?" Sawyer whispered urgently.

"That's him," she said. "That motherfucker... Sawyer, they're coming in here."

"Shit." He bolted to his feet and grabbed her arm.

But they couldn't move quickly enough. The door opened easily for Dr. King and Dr. Mollon, the former spotting Sawyer immediately. "Benedict?" he said, surprise in his voice.

"Fuck," Sawyer said.

But it was Dr. Mollon's reaction that captured Anissa's attention. Shock flooded his features as he caught sight of her. Anissa clutched at Sawyer's arm. Finally, all she could muster was an accusatory, "*You.*"

All four of them engaged in a staring contest, none of them sure what to do or say.

The receptionist broke the silence. "Dr. King? How may I help you?"

Anissa and Sawyer's eyes met, and Anissa read the silent command there.

Run.

They bolted past Dr. King and Mollon, racing as fast as their feet could carry them through the corridors.

"Benedict?" Dr. King roared behind them. Then he shouted, "Security!"

"Keep going!" Sawyer said, easily keeping up with her.

They retraced their steps as they raced through the corridors, stopping at the exit checkpoint only long enough for Sawyer's eye and hand scan. As soon as the door opened, he grabbed Anissa's arm and they continued running.

She glanced over her shoulder. Dr. King and Dr. Mollon were behind them, but more alarmingly, a pair of burly security guards ran just ahead of the doctors. Sawyer and Anissa ran out to the commercial part of the station just as one of the guards yelled, "Lockdown! Gods damn it, *lockdown!*"

Anissa and Sawyer kept running, dodging and weaving around people who either looked irritated or alarmed at their movements. Bliss Station, Anissa knew, wasn't exactly a hub of chaos. "Where are we going?" she said.

"Straight ahead. There's an authority station there."

Anissa threw another look over her shoulder. She saw the university security guards moving more carefully than they were, and she and Sawyer had a decent lead on them. Still, she breathed a sigh of relief when doors emblazoned with the words BLISS STATION LEGAL AUTHORITY appeared in front of them.

They sailed through the doors, stopping at the reception desk where a pair of startled authority officers nearly dropped their coffee cups from shock. "We want to file a report," Sawyer said, his voice carrying over the foyer. "Kidnapping and attempted murder."

The officers sprang into action. "It's for me," Anissa said before either of them could ask. "My name is Anissa Alto, and

I was a commander in the Laresh Forces. I served in the civil war for the Empire."

They paused for half a second. "The Lareshi Civil War was a hundred years ago."

"It ended one hundred and eight years ago," Anissa said. She whirled around and saw the pair of university security guards crash into the foyer. "The gentleman behind those two," she said, pointing. "His real name is Crale Mollon. He stole my mother's work and murdered her and her crew one hundred and four years ago."

Dr. Mollon appeared between the pair of security guards, looking as shocked as Anissa had felt back at the university; Sawyer's father watched the whole spectacle from behind Mollon's shoulder.

Let them be surprised. Anissa wasn't afraid of Mollon anymore.

She could prove who she was. She and Sawyer could prove that she'd been dug out of that valley on that backwater planet. Dr. Mollon's ship's energy signature matched the one saved in the *Phantom*'s databanks.

"He put me into stasis," Anissa said, her voice rising. Now that her fear had given way, anger rose: hot and dangerous as an electrical fire aboard a ship in deep space. "That's where Dr. Sawyer found me with his crew."

Sawyer finally spoke. "Did you know about this, *Dad*?"

Sawyer suspected that this had to be the first legal interrogation ever held in a university lab, but there was a first time for everything, he supposed. At least he and Anissa were allowed to stay together.

The authorities had already summoned Lita, Fitch, and Dian for questioning on their own, although Sawyer only knew that they'd been called in, and nothing of what they were being asked. He had no idea how they were faring, but right now he wasn't terribly worried. All they had to do was tell the truth, and he knew they would. That was what he and Anissa had been doing for, what felt like, hours.

An apologetic white-coated doctor cut her antiquated ID chip from her wrist while Sawyer held her hand. "I'm really sorry about this," the doctor said quietly, under the stern gaze of the authority officers questioning them. He quickly sealed the small wound and smoothed a pain patch over the site. "I'll have the analysis results in a few minutes. Does that sound okay?"

"Hurry it up," the interrogating officer barked.

"Do you have the results from the box we found her in?" Sawyer asked.

That question only earned another glare from the officer. He couldn't interpret that look.

The satellite campus's Materials Department had been cleared of all academic staff pending an investigation. Sawyer had turned over everything from the trip to the planet where Anissa was found for evidence. The *Phantom* had been temporarily impounded while the station's authorities combed over it, and Sawyer cringed to think of the mess they would leave his ship in.

They hadn't detained Anissa. For that, he was grateful.

"Has my father told you anything?" he asked, not for the first time. As soon as he and Anissa announced that she'd been kidnapped over a century earlier, his father and Dr. Mollon had been whisked away for questioning, although the authorities hadn't been forthcoming with information about what they were saying. It was all part of the investigation, Sawyer supposed. But that didn't make it any less frustrating.

The officer glowered at him again.

Sawyer sighed. They'd turned over their research: the scant

information they'd found about Vicora Alto and Crale Mollon, Anissa's DNA analysis from Tash, the *Spindle's End* energy signature. The crew had been questioned for a couple of hours by different pairs of authority agents. Now, they waited in a makeshift holding cell in the satellite campus's Materials office, waiting to be released or arrested. He hoped for the former. They hadn't done anything that would warrant charges, having left out the small detail of how Fitch tracked down what model of shuttle Crale Mollon owned.

But it was still an unbelievable story, and he knew that. He only hoped that his father's answers implicated Mollon as much as Sawyer and Anissa's evidence did. There was no reason Sawyer could think of as to why Dr. King would authorize and raise funding for an entire department devoted to a long-discredited scientific field.

The officer detaining them straightened and touched the earpiece resting against his tragus. "Yeah," he said, sounding disgruntled. His expression shifted. "Seriously?"

Anissa and Sawyer exchanged glances. Hope shone on her face, and he knew it had to be reflected in his, too.

"Well, fuck me." He quickly cleared his throat. "Sorry, sorry. I'm working on the language thing. How much more paperwork does this mean?" He paused. "Uh-huh." He tapped the earpiece and turned to Sawyer and Anissa. "You're done here."

"Really?" said Anissa before Sawyer could.

"Really. You're to report to the hospital to have a new ID chip implanted, and I'll be escorting you there." He didn't look thrilled at the prospect. "Neither of you can leave the station for any reason until further notice, but you can return to your ship."

"I'm sure I'll have a lot to clean up there," Sawyer said.

"Probably. Get up. Let's go."

They dutifully followed the officer from the office. Anissa

immediately reached for his hand and he squeezed it, trying to be reassuring.

Gods damn it all, I love this woman.

He'd tell her when they were back on board the *Phantom*, when they had some privacy and could celebrate her officially starting her life over. He watched her expression carefully. It was guarded, but optimistic. There were shadows under her eyes, just as he was sure they were under his, but a small smile uplifted the corners of her mouth at the prospect of having a real identity. Freedom beckoned ever closer for her.

"Have they arrested Dr. Mollon?" Anissa asked their guard.

He shrugged. "Don't know yet. I'm sure you'll find out soon enough."

They were issued a list of instructions pending their release, including an order to stay at Bliss Station and notifying the dockmaster's office when they left the *Phantom* until further notice. Sawyer didn't care about any of that; he was willing to wait as long as it took to complete the investigation.

Even though they were accompanied by an authority officer, he didn't breathe easy until they were back at the *Phantom*'s airlock, where they found Lita and Fitch, accompanied by the ever-cheerful Enzo, and Dian and Tash. All had duffels with them, and Tash's face was streaked with tears.

"We're moving in for the time being," Lita announced, but her usual perkiness was muted.

"Hello, Commander, Sawyer," said Enzo, unperturbed as usual as he nodded his tarnished metallic head at them.

"What's happened?" Sawyer asked.

"Why are you holding hands?" Lita countered.

He ignored that. "Tash? What's wrong?"

"The hospital has suspended her," Dian said. "And I hate

to be the bearer of bad tidings, but reporters showed up to our apartments about half an hour ago, and none of us can leave the station. I'm surprised they didn't follow you to the docks."

It had already started then. Sawyer unlocked the ship's exterior door and silently thanked all the gods out there that the *Phantom*'s water and fuel reserves were stocked, as he was going to have a full house. He waited until everyone was on board and re-locked the doors, setting the ship's alarms as a precaution. Who knew what length reporters and gawkers would go to? Who knew what Crale Mollon told the authorities?

"Tash, I'm sorry," Anissa said in a small voice.

Fresh tears slid down her cheeks. "It's temporary," Dian said. "It's routine, right?" She wrapped her arm around Tash. "I keep telling you, honey, they're only doing this while Anissa's being investigated. All you did was analyze her DNA and forget to make a record of it."

"You deliberately didn't do a full analysis for that reason," Lita reminded her.

"It's SOP to suspend a doctor while an investigation's ongoing," Dian said. "You're still being paid. That means the hospital's on your side. It's not like you dropped a newborn on the delivery room floor."

Tash nodded, but judging by her expression, their words didn't seem to carry any real weight for her. Sawyer felt doubly terrible for her. "It's *temporary*," Dian said again reassuringly. "That's what the hospital said. Just a few days. You won't lose your license."

"They might fire me," Tash said.

"And we'll get through that, and you'll start over at another hospital. That's the worst-case scenario, remember? You'll still be the best obstetrician in the Rodantan Quadrant."

"Allow me to take your bags," Enzo said, holding out his

metallic arms. Lita and Fitch obediently draped their duffels over one proffered arm, and Dian and Tash followed suit.

"Third deck, Enzo," Lita said. To Sawyer, she said, "You never answered my question. Why are you two holding hands?"

"Not now," Sawyer said wearily.

"Not ever," Dian said, a visible shudder rippling through her.

"Let's decompress for a few minutes," Sawyer said. "Then we'll meet in the lounge and talk about what we know."

He knew his words made everything sound much simpler than it really was. On the one hand, he was relieved that Anissa could finally, officially start her life over. On the other, he had no idea what kind of damage had been done to everyone's careers, particularly Tash's. When push came to shove, Sawyer could live off his inherited residuals from his mother's company; it would just be a far more frugal and boring existence than he preferred. He enjoyed being an archaeologist.

He knew that Lita's and his careers would recover from this scandal, even if neither of them could work in strictly research positions any longer. Dian could continue to pursue her studies, and Fitch would still be able to fly. Sawyer was unsure if their careers could continue at Prime University, and he didn't want to anymore, not if his father was still president.

Any remaining shreds of respect or affection he once had for Devon King had evaporated into nothing. Where aggravation at his father's meddling and controlling once existed, now nothing remained but hatred.

He could die tomorrow, and I wouldn't give a shit.

While everyone tossed their things in their usual cabins, he checked the comp in the office off the bridge, pulling up media reports, and his heart sank as he scanned them.

Lareshi Civil War veteran brought back to life... Scandal

brewing at Prime University... Bliss Station home to time traveler...

He slammed down the screen, not wanting to read any further. He felt sick even though he knew and had warned everyone else that this was going to happen. There was no way to keep Anissa's existence a secret.

This was going to be a shitshow. All he could do was encourage everyone to remain quiet about it and hope that it blew over as soon as possible. Maybe in a year or two.

Living off replicator patent residuals for a while might not be a bad idea if it meant helping Anissa escape the media clusterfuck.

How bad *was* it outside the *Phantom*'s airlock?

He activated the cameras outside the ship's exterior doors and saw a couple of unfamiliar people hovering around; people who shouldn't be in his private dock. He opened a comm link with the dockmaster's office, trying to tamp down his irritation.

A young woman's face, hair pulled back in a ponytail, filled the comp screen. "*Phantom*? This is the dockmaster's office," she said, voice crisp.

"Benedict Sawyer here," Sawyer replied. "I'm letting you know that there's a security issue in my private dock. Unauthorized people are in there. The only people who should have access to it are already on board."

"Should I notify station security?"

"I'm not sure. Only if they don't leave when asked. I'm not leaving the ship for the time being. None of us are. Has the authority office notified you of our orders to remain on board until further notice?"

She looked a little puzzled and tapped at a console Sawyer couldn't see on the screen. She bit her bottom lip a little as she typed. "Okay. Your ship has been placed on temporary hold by the authorities, yes, but because you aren't under arrest..." She kept on typing. "The *Phantom* has been ordered to remain docked, and you and an Anissa Alto are to remain on board according to this report from the authority."

"Yeah, I already know that. Could you do something about the reporters outside my ship?"

"They're reporters?"

"They want to talk to her. Have you read the news yet?" The news hadn't mentioned Anissa's name as far as he could tell, and he prayed it would stay that way.

She looked a little taken aback. "Uh, well, no. Not lately."

"It's going to be a big scandal. As soon as we're given the all-clear, we're taking a trip away from Bliss until this all dies down." *If* it died down, he added mentally.

"Oh." She seemed at a loss for words, which only increased Sawyer's irritation.

He tried to make himself sound as genial as possible, needing to curry her favor. "Please have station security remove them," he said. "I pay for this dock, so I don't have to deal with other people. And going forward, please ensure that the only people who can get into it are those I've authorized." His bright tone faded, as much as he tried to keep it up. "I need to be notified first. This was a serious security breach for my friends. And I'd appreciate it if you didn't discuss anyone on board with the media."

"Right away, sir." She blinked. "On behalf of the dockmaster's office, I apologize."

"Just please fix this." He signed off.

"Sawyer?"

He started, then stood up when he saw Anissa in the office doorway. "Hey," he said. "Everything okay?" The words sounded hollow to him, and he wished he could take them back.

Judging from her bemused expression, she thought so, too. But the tiny, knowing smile on her face vanished, and she sank into him. He wrapped his arms around her, needing her close by.

"I wish I knew why your dad hired Dr. Mollon," she said into his shoulder.

That was a mystery Sawyer was determined to get to the bottom of. "We'll find out," he said. "I promise." Finding out Devon King's intentions with Dr. Mollon's research was going to be the basis of the very last conversation he ever had with his father.

"Everyone's in the lounge," she said. "They want to know what's going on."

"So do I."

"We know more than they do. And Tash is very upset."

He disentangled himself from her. "Let's go talk to them, then."

But before they could make the short trip to the lounge, she clasped his face and pressed a kiss to his mouth, a gesture that sucked the air from his lungs and made him forget for a few seconds that they were prisoners on his ship for the time being, that his father was an absolute monster, and that Dr. Mollon was still alive. All he could focus on was the feel of her mouth against his, how her body brushed up against him, and how he would love nothing more right now than to lock his office door and see how creative they could get with only the desk and chair for support.

His tongue teased her lips apart, and she eagerly responded, but she broke the kiss before he could do what his instincts were screaming to. "We need to talk to them," she said, voice hoarse. "They deserve to know what we do. And I think Lita has... other questions."

"I'm sure she does."

"Are we going to tell them?"

"Not the specifics," he said, noting that she blushed a little at that. "But it's part of the story. Let's go."

Tash looked slightly more mollified when Anissa and Sawyer arrived in the lounge, but that didn't do much to assuage Anissa's guilt. Out of everyone on board the *Phantom*, Tash had the most to lose.

"I'm not sure where to start," Sawyer said.

"How about starting with an apology for all the fucking reporters outside our homes?" Dian said.

"The reporters aren't our fault," Sawyer said, his tone unusually sharp. Dian narrowed her eyes at him, and the pair engaged in a staring contest, something Anissa had never seen either of them do before. Judging from the wary looks on Lita and Fitch's faces, they hadn't seen it either.

"Enough," said Tash. "Dian, Sawyer's right about the reporters. I'm not angry with any of you, okay? I volunteered to run those tests knowing what the consequences could be. Being removed from my office by security was the biggest shock out of everything that's happened, and you're right about my probably getting to keep my job. It's not knowing for sure that driving me crazy."

Anissa understood the last part but refrained from joining the conversation. Dian looked angry enough to eviscerate the next person who looked in her direction.

Tash continued, "Sawyer, Anissa, tell us what happened and why all of us were questioned today."

"Farel Polchin is Dr. Mollon," Anissa said. No one looked surprised to hear that.

"You saw him?"

"He brought my father to Bliss Station," Sawyer said. "We'd decided to file a criminal report, but on the way, Anissa saw the *Spindle's End* listed on the arrivals board near the docks. We decided to wait in the satellite campus's Materials office to see if Polchin was actually Dr. Mollon without them noticing, but they saw us."

"And then you ran like a couple of crazy people through Bliss," Dian said.

Now it was Anissa's turn for her ire to rise. "That man killed my mother," she snapped. "He murdered her crew and left me in a pit for a hundred years, remember?"

Dian's eyes widened, and she stopped talking.

"It wasn't crazy of us to run," Anissa said. "The alternatives were either being kidnapped again or killing Mollon myself and ending up arrested. Neither appealed to me."

"So, you found out he managed to survive," Lita said, trying to steer the conversation back to its original subject.

"And that's all we know so far," Anissa said. "They've questioned us all, and analyses run on my old ID chip, the box you found me in and the fastenings that held it in place, my DNA, all of that. Everything I've ever claimed has been backed up by science."

"And now we wait," Sawyer said. "I have no idea when I'll be able to break dock."

Fitch finally spoke up. "You haven't done anything wrong, except waiting a while before reporting finding Anissa, and even then, I don't think there's a specific law against not reporting the discovery of a coma patient on an uninhabited planet. I think for all of us, Tash included, this is going to blow over fairly easily."

"I'm not sure I'll be continuing my career at Prime," Sawyer said.

"Me neither," said Lita. Everyone looked surprised at that pronouncement, including Fitch. "What? I've been thinking about it for a few days. I don't want to work for a university that endorses bio-longevity. I have a professional reputation to maintain. We all do."

"That's assuming my father remains university president," Sawyer pointed out. "If he had any sense, he'd resign after this. And I know the reporters are horrible, but it's going to die down eventually, and they'll sink their teeth into my dad as soon as they can."

"Do you really think your father would resign over something as minor as a kidnapping and genetic-engineering scandal?" Lita said.

"No. But the board of directors will, hopefully, force it. This is going to be too much of an embarrassment to the university to keep my father on." As Sawyer said the words, Anissa saw some of the worry ease from his face, as if giving voice to his thoughts was a reassurance.

It was. She already knew that.

"So we don't how Dr. Mollon managed to live as long as he did," Lita said. "We also don't know if Dr. King knew what Mollon was up to, although I don't think it's an unreasonable hypothesis to consider."

"How else would Dr. Mollon have convinced your father to fund a bio-longevity department?" Tash said. "Sawyer's dad knew something."

That was the most plausible explanation. But how much did Dr. King know? Had Mollon ever mentioned the woman he'd left buried at the bottom of an ice-lined pit on an unnamed planet?

Something clicked into place in Anissa's mind, as easily as a couple of puzzle pieces fitting together.

"He was coming back for me," Anissa said.

All eyes swiveled in her direction.

"The day you found me," she said. "That's why you picked up his ship's energy signature. Dr. Mollon was coming back to retrieve me, to show me off as proof that bio-longevity worked, that the research he'd stolen from my mother proved what he wanted it to about genetic engineering, or something like that. He was going to show me to Dr. King to prove that it worked and then he would get his state-of-the-art lab at Prime. It doesn't matter that I was in stasis all that time. All that Mollon had to do was produce an authentic Lareshi citizen from that era, with my DNA manipulated the way it was, and Sawyer's dad would give him anything he wanted."

Silence descended over the lounge for a few seconds. Finally, Sawyer said, "That's the most reasonable explanation I've heard."

"It's the closest thing to making sense," Dian agreed. Fitch, Lita, and Tash slowly nodded.

Something else occurred to Anissa, one of Mollon's possible intentions after he'd managed to show her off to Dr. King. "I bet he was going to kill me after he'd received his funding."

Everyone else remained silent. She added, "Either that or present me to the media for proof, too. But then he'd probably have to confess to murder."

Right now, more than anything, she longed to track down Dr. Mollon and demand answers, by any means necessary. But that wasn't going to happen. She only hoped she would get a chance to talk to him even if it was only a supervised prison visit.

"Or he could have found a way to silence you without killing you," Sawyer said.

The possibilities of how that could be achieved raced through Anissa's mind. Dr. Mollon could have mind-wiped her, or used cybernetics to turn her into a living robot, doing whatever he wanted, her body entirely under his control. Four Hells, he could have just cut out her tongue if it came down to that. She didn't know which of those scenarios was the worst.

She didn't bother voicing those thoughts; what was the point? "Yeah," was all she managed.

The wall-mounted comp chimed an incoming transmit.

Sawyer looked at it, his brows knitting together. "It's from my father's personal address to mine," he said. "I don't know—should I accept it here?"

"We all know you'll tell us what he says," said Dian.

"I know, but maybe—we should all get a chance to yell at him, you know?"

"We'll get that opportunity at the university disciplinary hearing," said Lita. "This might be your only chance to tell him to his face what a piece of shit he is. Go on and take it in your office or cabin privately."

Sawyer nodded. "All right."

Anissa felt she should go with him to let him know that she was ready to stand by his side, just as he'd pledged to her, but he didn't ask to her to accompany him. She didn't trust herself not to get worked up into an incoherent rage. Judging from the look on Sawyer's face, he might have the same problem.

She gave him a look as he walked out of the lounge. *Talk to me when you're ready.*

He paused. "Anissa, do you want to come with me?"

No. But there was an imploring look on his face, one she had never seen before, and she rose from her seat. This was something couples did, right? Supported each other during difficult times? Still, she couldn't keep the trepidation out of her voice. "Okay."

He waited until they'd left the lounge to grip her hand, a gesture just as reassuring for her as it was for him. Nervousness and fear lodged themselves in the pit of her stomach, just as tangible as what she'd felt on Bliss Station during the chase.

Once in the bridge office, he closed the door behind them and pressed the blinking Accept tab. His father's face filled the screen. He looked a lot like Sawyer, but with well-maintained silver hair. Now she saw him up close, Anissa could tell he'd clearly had cosmetic work done because skin was never that smooth and flawless, even in someone much younger. Despite the man's obvious cosmetic enhancements, worry lines graced the corners of his mouth and dark half-moons marred his under-eye area. His eyes were reddened as if he'd been crying.

This was the appearance of a man used to living on a pedestal, whose fall from grace was occurring in slow motion and with a galactic-sized audience.

He and Sawyer stared at each other for a few seconds. "This is your last transmit to me," Sawyer finally said, his voice cold.

"Benedict." There was none of the anger in Dr. King's voice that Anissa had heard in other transmits, only pleading.

"The only reason I'm not cutting the transmission right now and severing ties with you forever is that I want an explanation for the utter clusterfuck you've brought on to me, Anissa, and Prime University." Sawyer's voice started to rise. "My entire crew has been forced to hide out on my ship to avoid the media. You willingly partnered with and *offered university funds* to a fucking murderer, never minding that bio-longevity has been discredited for decades." He threw up his hands. "What the *fuck*, you bastard?"

Dr. King flinched but didn't respond.

"This is Anissa," Sawyer said, gesturing to her.

She didn't know if she should acknowledge Dr. King or not. She gave the screen a tiny nod.

"We found Anissa in a pit when we were trawling around looking for the Immortal Spacefarer's treasure," Sawyer said. "She was in stasis for over a hundred years. Crale Mollon murdered her mother and her crew and left Anissa there. Do you happen to know why?"

"I didn't know about the existence of Anissa Alto until a couple of days ago," Dr. King replied. "And I'm not using up my transmit credits to talk about her, Benedict."

"What the hell are you talking about?"

"I've been detained by the authorities," Dr. King said. "Didn't you look at the originating transmit address, or did you stomp in your office too pissed off to check?" There was a mocking tone to his voice, one that clearly came easily to him and irritated Sawyer, judging by the clench of his jaw.

"I'm fucking done here," Sawyer said. "Never contact me again." His hand reached to tap the End tab, but Dr. King spoke before he could.

"I want you to come to the Bliss brig before I'm sent to a prison colony," Dr. King said.

That got Sawyer's attention. "You don't have the scrip to hire a decent lawyer?"

"I'm pleading guilty to all charges, Benedict. And I've tendered my resignation to the university, effective immediately."

Shock blossomed across Sawyer's face. "What?"

"I want to tell you, face-to-face, man-to-man, why I did what I did," Dr. King said. "Right now, my lawyer is negotiating a deal for me. I'll be on a prison colony for at least six years."

"That isn't long enough."

"It is for me." There was an air of finality in Dr. King's voice. "Dr. Polchin wishes to speak to Anissa, as well."

The mention of the man's name sent chills slithering down Anissa's spine and rage clogged her throat. It took a few seconds for her to find her voice. "All I want if I'm to see Dr. *Mollon*," she said, exaggerating the name, "is thirty seconds alone with him and a laser weapon on its kill setting."

"You aren't going to get that. I think he's being extradited to Lareshi space after this." Dr. King had the audacity to smirk at her. "I thought you'd appreciate that, given that they still utilize capital punishment."

"That's too good for him," Anissa shot back. "If the Laresh System has any sense of justice, they'll shoot him in the knee and leave him in the jungles on Brodil. Let nature take its course."

"You really have been asleep for the last hundred years, haven't you? Brodil's prison colony was shut down over fifty years ago for cruel and unusual punishment."

How in the Four Hells had Sawyer been able to tolerate this man for his entire life? Before Anissa could respond, Sawyer said, "Let me check with the dockmaster's office before I see you. We're confined to the *Phantom* thanks to Mollon's and your fuckery."

"Those restrictions will be lifted. My lawyer is working on that, too."

"Of course he is." Sawyer ended the transmit before Dr. King could speak again, then leaned back heavily in his chair.

He reached for Anissa's hands and kneaded them, and she suspected that the motion was just as much for his comfort and reassurance as hers. He traced over the tiny white scars, left over from training mishaps and the civil war. "Do you want to go to the station's brig?"

"Yes, and no."

"Yeah, I get that."

"How long do you think it'll be before Mollon's extradited?"

He shrugged. "Justice doesn't take long in Rodanta. Maybe a couple of days, tops. If you want to speak with him, it might be best to do it now."

"What if I have to testify at his trial?"

"If he's smart, he'll plead guilty to avoid a death sentence, so there won't be a trial." The New Transmit light flashed green, and Sawyer tapped it with a little more force than necessary. "Huh," he said. "It's from a lawyer." He and Anissa quickly skimmed the short message that stated that they could leave the *Phantom* after notifying the dockmaster's office and that Dr. King and Crale Mollon requested their presences at their earliest convenience.

An irritated sigh escaped Sawyer. "Fuck this."

"Is that a yes or no, you'll visit your dad?"

"That's a yes, but I'll be doing it tomorrow morning when I'm not so fucking angry." He turned to Anissa. "What about you?"

"Tomorrow," she said. "I'll see Mollon tomorrow morning, too."

Sawyer typed a message back to the lawyer's address then stood. "Come here," he said.

Anissa melted into his arms; she hadn't realized until that moment how much she needed that. "Thank you," she said.

"What for?"

"For everything," she said. "You've been my friend…"

"Are you implying that I do with my friends everything I've done with you? Because let me assure you, I don't."

That coaxed a smile from her. "No."

He tucked a few strands of hair behind her ear. For a moment, the look on his face erased all the worry and anger from her, and all she could focus on was the warmth in his eyes, and beyond that, something deeper. She tilted her face upward and kissed him, leaning into him and drawing him closer to her.

He broke the kiss with no small amount of reluctance. "We have to go back to the lounge," he said, his voice rough. "If we don't, we're going to get up to unprofessional behavior in the office, and someone will come back here and make things even more awkward."

"Are things awkward?"

"Not between us," said Sawyer. "But they suspect something, and I don't know about you, but I don't feel like explaining things to them just yet."

She understood his rationale.

"We will eventually," he said. "I think they're already figuring things out anyway. I just—I want us to have some time alone together first, if that's even possible right now."

"Should I spend the night in my cabin?" she asked, thinking of everyone else on board.

His eyes darkened, and he sent a look her way that thrilled her to her core. "Absolutely not."

CHAPTER 15

SAWYER AND ANISSA managed to avoid the throng of reporters hovering around the station docks, but the gods only knew how long that would last. As far as Sawyer could tell from the news reports, they'd not yet released Anissa's name or image. The image of Sawyer circulating was a professional shot taken nearly ten years earlier, and he was far more put together in that picture than he was now. He knew the anonymity wouldn't last forever, and he was hopeful that the Rodantan authorities would let him leave the station and escape the impending madness for a while.

He squared his shoulders and held on to Anissa's hand as they walked, undetected, through the station to the brig. "Do you want me to go with you to see Mollon?"

She shook her head. "No. I have to do this alone."

Just as he needed to confront his father alone. "If you change your mind..."

"I won't."

Bliss Station's brig was small, mainly used for holding people on drunk and disorderly charges or other minor crimes that only incurred fines as punishment. They held those who had committed more serious crimes there temporarily before transferring them to a prison colony. Given the ease with which Dr. King had pleaded guilty as soon as he was presented with the evidence against him, Sawyer felt his decision to see him one last time was appropriate.

He and Anissa were separated and escorted in opposite directions. Sawyer was led to a small room and ordered to sit in a chair facing a row of dingy metal bars that stretched from floor to ceiling. No modern force-fields here, he noted. Behind them was his father, still wearing an impeccably cut suit, but the fabric was wrinkled from sleeping in it. His normally perfectly styled silver hair was mussed and the bags under his eyes even more pronounced than in his last transmit.

He dragged a chair as close to the bars as he could. "Benedict. You came."

"I'm here for answers," Sawyer said curtly. "Not excuses."

"Where do you want me to start?"

"Are you fucking serious?"

"Serious as a hole in the head, you ungrateful bastard."

It wasn't the first time that insult had been lobbed at Sawyer, but it would be the last. "You know, you've said variations on that for years, and I could never figure out why I was so ungrateful. Was it because I didn't work at the university the way you wanted me to, or because you've been angry for years that I wouldn't share my mother's inheritance with you?"

Dr. King glowered at him.

"My mother was a far better parent than you ever were. Better person, too."

"She coddled you."

"By coddling, you mean encouraging and loving. She was right to leave you. I always thought that."

"Come now, Benedict," Dr. King said. "We aren't here to talk about your dear departed mother. I asked you to come here so I could tell my side of the story."

"I like how you think saying 'my side of the story' somehow means yours and Mollon's actions were justified."

"I didn't know the exact details of Farel's life and research until very recently."

"But you did know details," Sawyer said. "You could have gone to the authorities with your information. You knew he was a murderer."

"He's a scientist!" Dr. King was vehement in his declaration, and he leaned forward, fists curled in his lap.

"Bio-longevity *isn't* a fucking science, Dad. It was discredited years ago." He clenched his hands into fists in frustration then released them, trying to keep himself from shouting. "Fucking hell, how many times does this need to be said?"

"He extended the lifespan of that girl you've been hiding!"

"No, he didn't," Sawyer said. "He placed her in stasis. Her mother tweaked her genes a little, but nothing that would have affected her lifespan. He killed her mother and her research crew. Did you know that?"

Dr. King flinched. Maybe the old man still had a shred of morality in him after all.

"Farel assured me that was necessary," he said.

Nope, no moral fiber at all.

He continued, "His research was stolen. He took it back. You're a scientist, Benedict. You understand the importance of research."

Stolen research? Not a chance in hell. "I do, but I would never kill someone over it!" Sawyer's voice rose. "Why did you do this, and why the ever-loving fuck are you pleading guilty? You're a walking, talking piece of shit, Dad, but this is low, even for you!"

"Do you feel better?"

"No!"

"Will you feel better after I tell you that I'm dying?"

Sawyer froze, his gaze connecting with his father's. There was no trace of arrogance in his cosmetically enhanced face, no sign of trickery or manipulation. Sawyer's voice was flat. "What?"

"Culfa Syndrome," said Dr. King. "Incurable. I have a year at the most."

Culfa Syndrome, the inevitable result of being bitten by a mosquito from its namesake planet. "When were you on Culfa?"

"Before you were born. I don't even remember being bitten, but here we are. I started blacking out about six months ago. You know what this means, don't you?"

Sawyer did. It was one of the many reasons he'd never visited Culfa, an inhospitable planet not far from the Section Five border that was home to hundreds of varieties of lethal insects. "And you thought Crale Mollon could save you?"

"I heard rumors of treatment options originating from Sector Five. That's how Farel got in touch with me."

"He said he had a cure?"

"No, he said he could extend my lifespan before my organs started shutting down. First, the blackouts start, and then organ failure. There wasn't any point in looking into transplants or cloned organs."

There wasn't enough time to do so. Culfa Syndrome hid in the body's genes, altering them at their most basic level. A vaccine against the disease still didn't exist; the recovery rate after diagnosis was zero. Sawyer thought of the way the Vine virus had spread through the *Spindle*. Both were insidious and deadly. "Farel promised he could give me more time," Dr. King said.

"Why the hell were you on Culfa to begin with?"

"It was in my grad student days," Dr. King said. "Studying dangerous insect species and being a badass, much the way you think looking for the basis of children's fairy tales makes you an academic wunderkind."

Sawyer reached down inside himself, looking for a shred of sympathy for his father, and found nothing.

It had taken thirty-five years for him to admit to himself what he'd always known. *I hate this man.*

No, not quite hate. There wasn't a sense of joy or relief in knowing his father was dying. There was nothing.

I feel completely indifferent to whether he lives or dies. "Is that why you're pleading guilty?"

"I'm a dead man, anyway. My lawyer said he could get me onto a more comfortable prison colony if I agreed to a plea bargain. Medical care and all."

That fact didn't annoy Sawyer as much as it could have as he knew the medical care on prison colonies was bare bones; Dr. King would likely be kept on a steady diet of painkillers once the organ failure set in. "Do you have any idea of the damage and grief Mollon inflicted on Anissa?"

"She lived," Dr. King snapped. "She will continue living, and I'm sure you will continue fucking her. I never thought you were such a shameless opportunist, Benedict."

He flinched, and Dr. King chuckled. "I was guessing at that last part, but I can see I've hit a raw nerve."

Sawyer wanted to tell him he was wrong, that his and Anissa's relationship wasn't like that, but what was the point? Dr. King was a selfish, thoughtless sack of space junk, and Sawyer didn't owe him a thing.

Once again, his eyes met Dr. King's, and Sawyer felt nothing for the dying man in front of him, only an intense urge to leave and never see him again.

He gave in to those feelings and stood up. "I'm done here."

"Of course you are."

"I have nothing more to say, Dad," Sawyer said.

"You aren't going to tell me to enjoy prison or that I deserve it?"

"No." He walked to the door, but before he opened it he turned back to his father, taking one last look at him, burning the image into his memory. The swollen face from lack of sleep, the wrinkled suit, the mussed hair.

"I guess I hope you die peacefully," he finally said. "Goodbye, Dad."

The cell door opened when he pressed his hand to the palm pad, and he walked out without a backward glance.

Anissa's insides were shaking, the need for violence nearly overpowering her. It didn't diminish when she saw Crale Mollon behind a set of bars, the cot behind him rumpled from his sleep the night before.

They stared at each other, a battle of wills. She wished she knew what he was thinking.

He spoke first. "I've been expecting you." He gestured to the chair on the other side of the bars, near the cell door. "Take a seat."

She would not obey a single order he issued. "Go fuck yourself."

"I bet it feels good to say that after so long. And I bet it's killing you that you can't exact your own justice."

"I'm only here to ask one question," Anissa said.

"Only one? I thought in addition to wanting to know why I did it, you'd want to know why I left you in that pit, and why I altered your DNA."

That last statement threw Anissa for a loop. "What?"

"I'm told that you know about the elongation of your telomeres." Anissa froze at the words, a motion he picked up on. "I was asked about that during my interrogation."

"I—yes."

"And did you think it was your mother who did it?"

She crossed her arms over her chest and narrowed her eyes.

"My dear girl, the alterations to your DNA precipitated our breakup."

Breakup?

It took a few seconds for the full import of Mollon's words to reach her.

My mother and Mollon were a couple.

"I can see the gears turning in your head," Mollon said. "In about five more seconds, I imagine you'll figure out our connection."

No...

Her knees went weak, and she had to concentrate on not swaying on her feet.

"I know your mother never talked about your father," Mollon said. "About *me*. She tried to keep me away from you as much as she could, but the scientific community in the Empire was so small, so connected. She wasn't willing to stop her research altogether, and the Rodantan universities weren't quite as renowned as they are now."

By all the gods in all the heavens... Anissa forgot herself, and she had to sit down.

"That got your attention," Mollon said.

Anissa's mouth went dry, and it took a couple of attempts before she could form any coherent words. "Why?"

"Ah, now you want to know why."

"How could you do this to us?"

"You mean, how could I do this to my own daughter? You were the first newborn I had access to, although for all the genetic engineering I did, nothing made a difference to your expected lifespan. Your mother took you away before I could do any more research."

Rage made her vision swim and her words sharp. "You took everything from us!"

"It was *our* research," Mollon said. "Your mother took you and our findings and kept on researching without giving me the credit I was owed."

"They were *her* discoveries," Anissa said, "and *you* stole them."

"She wouldn't have made those breakthroughs without me!" Mollon finally seemed to grow agitated, and he rose from his chair and paced around behind his barricade.

"No," said Anissa. "She did it all well after you were out of the picture. But I'm not here to argue about that since it's a discredited field, anyway." Her voice hardened, and her resolve steeled itself. "I want to know how the fuck you managed to live so long, why you left me in that pit, and what you were doing with Devon King and Prime University."

He dramatically exhaled before rattling off his reply. "Fifty-year stasis with a self-regulated waking schedule on an obscure planet in Section Five, you were supposed to be a demonstration of the success of bio-longevity treatments, and the money and research opportunities that inevitably flow when one discovers the secrets to a potentially infinite lifespan. Does that answer your questions?"

The reasons for his actions were mind-numbingly selfish. "So you murdered my mother and the *Spindle*'s crew and left me half-dead for *money*?"

"I hadn't intended to turn you into a carnival sideshow," Mollon said. "There was no way I could continue my research with the data I'd already collected without alerting everyone to the fact that I was involved in the *Spindle*'s unfortunate accident."

More puzzle pieces began to fit themselves together. "So, you knock yourself out for fifty years and stay hidden in an area that cuts itself off from the rest of space until there's no one left who knows who you are. Then you can pick up your research without anyone being the wiser."

"You're smarter than I expected. For an idiot soldier, anyway."

Anissa didn't respond to that.

She and Mollon stared at each other; she could feel his contempt for her in the marrow of her bones. "Why are you telling me all of this?" she finally asked.

"Because I didn't have a fucking chance in the Four Hells when the authorities found my Lareshi ID implant. And Devon King was only too happy to tell them what he knew in exchange for serving his time on a prison planet that isn't an utter hellhole, for all the good that'll do him." He barked out a short, humorless laugh. "What, did you think I had a change of heart and felt guilty about refusing to give up my research?"

No, she hadn't. But she hadn't expected him to speak so freely to her, either.

"Do you know what the Lareshi courts are going to do to me?" he asked.

She didn't respond. What the Lareshi courts could do to Crale Mollon was nothing compared to what she wanted to do to him.

"They're going to jettison me into open space without an EVA suit and broadcast it for the whole System to see. Their worst punishment, reserved for the people they think are the worst criminals."

"Are you seriously suggesting that you aren't a criminal?"

"I'm a scientist!"

"You're no better than an astrologer." It wasn't the best comeback, but it was the truth.

"Again, you're a soldier with a basic education. I don't expect you to understand, and if you were capable of it, you could see things from my perspective. Besides, wouldn't that mean that your mother was nothing better than an astrologer, too?"

Anissa wanted to slap the smirk off his face. "That was different. That was before they discovered that bio-longevity is impossible. She would have eventually moved on."

"Into cybernetics."

She remembered the scant information she and Sawyer had been able to glean from the university databases. "Like you?"

"Yes, and that brings me to my next point." He gripped the cell's bars with both hands, sticking his face out between them. "I'm not going back to Lareshi space just to get sucked out an airlock."

"It's definitely too good for you."

"This is it for me, daughter." Anissa felt herself blanch at the reminder.

Mollon opened his mouth and poked his fingers in, feeling around his teeth. "What the hell are you doing?" she said.

"I told you," Mollon said, moving his hand away to speak. "I'm not going back to the Laresh System."

He pulled at something, and a small mewl of pain escaped him. When he removed his fingers, he held a bloody tooth between them. He spat a mouthful of blood onto the cell floor.

His face turned pale, and he stumbled away from the cell bars, dropping the tooth to the floor. He lurched backward, hands wildly groping the air for invisible purchase, before clutching at his throat.

Before Anissa could leave to get help, or even consider if she wanted to, Mollon fell on his back, skull cracking against the floor. A whoosh of air escaped him, and his eyes closed.

What in the Four Hells...?

Anissa bolted from her spot and rushed for the door, but

as she opened it, an authority officer rushed in. "We saw it all on the monitors," he said tersely.

A wave of nausea crested over her. "I... I think he's dead."

"I do, too."

"He pulled out his tooth," Anissa said weakly. "I've never seen anything like that before."

The officer unlocked the cell door and quickly examined Dr. Mollon and the tooth with gloved hands. "We'll need to order an autopsy to be sure," he said, "But it looks like it was a suicide." He held up the tooth. "I've never seen this before, either, but I've heard of it. He probably had a cybernetic implant that would trigger instant death if this was removed."

"It wasn't instant."

"Yeah, I know." The officer seemed to realize that Anissa had witnessed it and he softened. "I'm sorry."

"Don't be. I just—I wasn't expecting it."

The officer spoke into a comm badge clipped to his collar. "Jalil here. I'll need a mortuary crew in cell room two ASAP. Thanks." He turned back to Anissa. "I'm sure we could arrange counseling for you, if you like."

She shook her head. "I'm good, but thanks."

Anissa crossed the short distance to the bars, where Officer Jalil continued checking the dead Dr. Mollon. His face was frozen in a silent scream, an expression she'd seen before, during the civil war, but it was still just as horrifying as the first time she saw it.

He didn't even face any real sort of justice.

Of course, he'd had to go and kill himself with some kind of cybernetic suicide switch. He ended up with everything he'd ever wanted, including his own chosen method of execution. He was dead, but that didn't offer any relief to Anissa.

That fucker was my father.

"Can I go now?" she asked the officer.

"We got everything on visual and audio, so no need for a statement. But check with reception."

She bit her lip and nodded, then walked away. As she reached the door, the officer said casually, "I'm sorry for your loss."

"Thank you, but that wasn't a loss to me."

She waited until the door slid shut behind her before bursting into tears.

According to the authorities officer watching over the cells, Sawyer was still with his father. Anissa stuffed some tissues from the box on the officer's desk into her pocket and decided to take a short walk, if there wasn't a big crowd outside.

She didn't know what else to do or where to go. She just needed to get away for a few minutes and try to process what just happened.

There was a small group of people hanging out near the authorities' station entrance, but no one bothered her when she walked out. Anissa had deliberately chosen to dress in nondescript clothes today, and an ordinary-looking woman with shaggy dark hair, wearing black flight pants and a gray sweater, didn't draw any attention. Still, she kept her head down and didn't make eye contact with anyone.

There was a small sit-down cafe close by and she headed there, not knowing where else to go before she went back to the station to find Sawyer.

"What can I get you?"

The voice of the server behind the counter startled her, and she jumped. When she looked closely at the man's face, she saw he wasn't one at all. He was a very well-constructed android, but an android nonetheless. Anissa appreciated that. She didn't want to deal with real people right now.

She reached into her pocket and pulled out the little amount of scrip she had there. "What can I get for two scrip?" She looked behind the android at the menu screen.

The android rattled off a list of cheap drinks as if he didn't care if she read the menu or not. He was an android; he probably didn't.

"The tea is fine," Anissa said, and lay her scrip on the counter.

The android offered her an artificial smile and placed a cup in front of her. "Enjoy your day!"

She thanked him and took a spot at a table near the window. She looked out at the station, at the small group of gawkers, and a watery sigh escaped her.

The speed with which everything had happened back there appalled her.

Despite Sawyer's job offer, she wasn't sure she was needed on board the *Phantom*, either. Now that Crale Mollon was dead, she didn't know what else to do with herself.

What was she going to do about Sawyer?

She was in love with the man. The last thing she wanted was to be a burden on him. Love made things so much more complicated.

"Miss?" The android's voice snapped her out of her funk.

"Yes?"

"There is a ten-minute limit on loitering within this establishment. You have been here seven minutes. This is a courtesy reminder."

Well, at least androids were nicer about kicking patrons out of tiny cafes than real people. "Thanks, I guess."

She saw Sawyer walk out of the authorities' station, his expression unreadable. Evidently, some of the reporters clustered outside the doors recognized him because a few immediately clamored for his attention. Anissa could hear them all the way from her spot in the cafe, a spot she would have to vacate in a couple of minutes.

"Dr. Sawyer! My agency is prepared to offer you a very generous settlement if you give us an exclusive!"

That shouted statement galvanized the rest into action, clustering around him like a gaggle of carrion birds on flesh. They descended on him, peppering questions about his father, the university, whether the bio-longevity rumors were true; converging on him until he was no longer visible. The commotion attracted some passersby, who stood to the side, watching it all unfold.

She couldn't let him be mobbed like that. Setting aside her tea, she stood up from her stool and rushed out of the café and elbowed her way through the crowd until she could grab Sawyer's sweater sleeve.

"Where did you go?" he asked over the din.

"I needed a few minutes to think."

He clasped her hand, and together they forced their way through the small mob that had grown exponentially. Opportunistic carrion, all of them.

At least no one seemed to know who she was; they all kept their questions directed at Sawyer. But Anissa knew that wasn't going to last.

They hurried back to the dock, keeping their eyes away from the people who decided to follow them, neither speaking until they reached the docks. They were quickly admitted, and both breathed sighs of relief when the doors closed behind them.

They were quiet as they walked to the *Phantom*'s dock, not speaking until they were on board the ship. "What happened with Mollon?" Sawyer finally asked.

"What happened with your dad?"

Sawyer's expression was sad and frustrated. Half-moons

ringed under his eyes. "I... that was really fucked up back there. My dad's a fucked-up person."

"So's mine."

It took a few seconds for the meaning of Anissa's words to register for Sawyer. His words were soft but urgent. "Oh. Oh, *no*."

"He's dead now. He killed himself in front of me."

"So that's why there was a stretcher in the foyer."

She nodded.

"Do you want to talk about it?" he asked.

Did she? Yes and no. She had no doubt that he would provide a sympathetic ear, as she would for him, but she wanted to avoid this weird grief that was consuming her for as long as possible.

He was waiting for an answer. "Not yet," she said.

"Okay."

"Let's go to the sim chamber," she said. "I need to not feel anything for a while." She wanted to float in zero-g and pretend the rest of the galaxy didn't exist for as long as she could. She wanted to do something that would keep nightmares at bay, bad dreams where Crale Mollon admitted to murdering Vicora and genetically engineering their infant daughter. Dreams that featured him ripping out a tooth and committing suicide, escaping punishment.

Crale Mollon got everything he wanted in the end, including choosing his own, more merciful, death.

"What else do you need?" he asked. She searched his face, but there wasn't a trace of suggestion there, just concern and affection.

Before she could stop herself, she said, "I need you to love me."

He wrapped his arms around her, holding her in an embrace so tight it nearly crushed the air from her lungs. "Oh, Anissa, I already do."

THE DOCKMASTER'S office was rigid in its refusal to refund Sawyer for unused time in his dock, but he gave up arguing with them faster than either expected. It was irritating that he would be paying for time he wouldn't be docked at Bliss, but according to the dockmaster, he *had* signed a contract. So he gave in, accepted the loss, and assured them the *Phantom* would return in a few months' time. There was no point in further pissing off the people he would be depending on again in the near future.

He and Anissa were looking forward to escaping the zoo that Bliss Station had turned into, and he was sure Bliss was glad to be rid of the commotion the *Phantom*'s presence caused, albeit temporarily. Not just Anissa, he thought. The entire crew, including Tash for at least part of the mission, was looking forward to searching for the Immortal Spacefarer's treasure once again.

If it even exists, Sawyer thought ruefully. He was fairly certain that the origins of the myth would be stumbled upon someday even if it wasn't by his crew. Even though he was excited about being back in open space, wistfulness tugged at him. This was going to be the last archaeological mission he'd be taking for a long time.

In the wake of the bio-longevity scandal at Prime University and the subsequent and unrelenting media exposure, he'd agreed to resign his position in the archaeology department, and in four months' time he would be taking up a new one at Laresh First University on a one-year contract. His days cruising through space at his own pace were numbered, and he would soon be analyzing ancient materials from the lab, but he was okay with that. He wouldn't be teaching or having to deal with a draconian university president. It was time for a change.

He looked over the *Phantom*'s bridge, to where Anissa was planted in the pilot's seat. It would be her first time piloting the ship since she earned her license two weeks' prior, and he could tell by the sparkle in her eyes and the set of her shoulders, that she was excited to do it.

She leaned over the console toward the speaker. "This is the *Phantom*, requesting clearance to depart in five minutes. Have you received our flight plan?"

"Got it. You're cleared for departure in five minutes, *Phantom*."

She had shown remarkable resilience in the face of all the attention she'd ended up receiving once her identity had inevitably been uncovered. She was still raw from grief; healing from the shock of learning Mollon was her father, and his suicide in front of her had left an indelible impression. Sawyer's unremitting rage at his father was ebbing away, two months after the scandal broke, but he knew a part of him would never forgive Dr. King for what he had been and what he had done.

Devon King still hadn't shown a shred of remorse for his part in Mollon's schemes and had even conducted media interviews from his hovel on the prison colony. His justifications revolved around his failing health, but no one in Rodantan or Lareshi space accepted those excuses. He was going to die alone in a filthy hut with only the most rudimentary health care to see him through his remaining months. It was better than he deserved, Sawyer thought.

What rankled him as well was that Dr. King *still* hadn't ceased trying to meddle in Sawyer's life. He continued to send transmits, trying to plead his case, and no matter how often Sawyer blocked his address he'd send missives from different ones. Sawyer had no idea how he managed to keep bribing prison employees to allow such things.

The *Phantom*'s engines roared to life, sending the comforting, familiar vibrations running under their feet for the first time since the scandal broke.

She gave him a smile that made his heart stutter. She was nervous but excited. He knew she would be fine.

Outside the forward viewscreen, the dock's warning lights flashed from green to red as the sensor scanned for life forms. A loud klaxon sounded throughout the bay as the airlock doors yawned open, and the *Phantom* was sucked out into the black vacuum of space.

"How'd I do, Captain?" said Anissa.

"Let's see how you handle her in jumpspace."

Sawyer slid into the copilot's seat and watched Anissa plot a course to the nearest jumpgate. "I have part one handled," she said. "I may need your help when we get to that gate, though."

"No, you won't. You wouldn't have your license if you did."

She gave him a withering look. "It's my first time handling a gate entrance in a converted freighter alone." This time, Enzo wasn't there as backup, and Sawyer had every intention of keeping his hands off the controls.

"And I told you, you've got this."

"What else do I have, Dr. Sawyer?"

He laced his fingers through hers. "It isn't much, but... me."

She laughed and tightened her grip on him. "You're underestimating yourself."

Sawyer kissed her, lust already surging through his veins. He would never stop wanting this woman. "I love you."

Was it too soon to let the ship do what she was programmed to do and take a break in the sim chamber before they reached the jumpgate?

Anissa's eyes never left his face. "I love you, too."

ABOUT THE AUTHOR

Jessica Marting is a sci-fi and paranormal romance author, art enthusiast (not quite an artist, despite all that time in art school), an avid reader, and makeup collector. She lives in Toronto.

Sign up for her newsletter at jessicamarting.com/newsletter for pre-order alerts, sales, freebies, and more.

Magic & Mechanicals

Wolf's Lady

Sea Change

Bound in Blood

Dragon's Keep

Zone Cyborgs

Haven

Paradise

Oasis

Safe Harbor

Sanctuary

Refuge

The Commons

Supernova

Celestial Chaos

Standalone Novels & Novellas

Spindle's End

Trade Secrets

Neon Vice

Dead Ringer

Escape From Europa 10

Castaways

Demon's Favor

9 781989 780190